Praise for Gillian Roberts

"[Gillian Roberts is] the Dorothy Parker of mystery writers . . . giving more wit per page than most writers give per book."
—NANCY PICKARD

A Hole in Juan

"Gillian Roberts has written an exciting mystery that will keep you reading long into the night. Amanda Pepper is such a cool character with great determination to get to the bottom of things. The Amanda Pepper series is also a fun read and at the same time one that will keep you guessing throughout the book."
—*Mysteries Galore*

Till the End of Tom

"Roberts . . . manages time after time, to take the restraints within the traditional mystery structure and stroke them. Her narratives are contemporary, highly readable and, hardest of all, unique. *Till the End of Tom* will amuse and entertain."
—*Crimespree Magazine*

Claire and Present Danger

"Fresh and lively . . . with a hip sensibility . . . it all adds up to fun for the reader."
—Baltimore *Sun*

Helen Hath No Fury

"Roberts's gentle sense of humor enlivens the entire story. . . . Amanda is younger, funnier, and more with-it than most mystery heroines, [with] gemlike insights into modern womanhood."
—*San Jose Mercury News*

Adam and Evil

"Literate and stylish."
—*Pittsburgh Tribune-Review*

The Bluest Blood

"I'm not convinced that anyone offers better one-liners than those delivered by Amanda Pepper."
—*Alfred Hitchcock Mystery Magazine*

The Mummers' Curse

"The comic gift is like a charm: You either have it or you don't. Gillian Roberts has it and uses it to good advantage."
—*The San Diego Union-Tribune*

In the Dead of Summer

"Tart-tongued, warm-hearted Amanda's sixth case is as engaging as her others, and here she gets to do more detection than usual."
—*Kirkus Reviews*

How I Spent My Summer Vacation

"Delightful . . . colorful . . . Roberts plunks her mystery amid the glitter and grime of casino life."
—Los Angeles *Daily News*

With Friends Like These...

"A pleasurable whodunit with real motives, enough clues to allow a skillful reader of mysteries to make some intelligent guesses, and a plethora of suspects."
—*Chicago Tribune*

I'd Rather Be in Philadelphia

"Literate, amusing, and surprising, while at the same time spinning a crack whodunit puzzle."
—*Chicago Sun-Times*

Philly Stakes

"Lively . . . breezy . . . entertaining."
—*San Francisco Chronicle*

Caught Dead in Philadelphia

"A stylish, wittily observant, and highly enjoyable novel."
—*Ellery Queen's Mystery Magazine*

By Gillian Roberts

Caught Dead in Philadelphia
Philly Stakes
I'd Rather Be in Philadelphia
With Friends Like These . . .
How I Spent My Summer Vacation
In the Dead of Summer
The Mummers' Curse
The Bluest Blood
Adam and Evil
Helen Hath No Fury
Claire and Present Danger
Till the End of Tom
A Hole in Juan
All's Well That Ends

Books published by The Random House Publishing Group
are available at quantity discounts on bulk purchases for
premium, educational, fund-raising, and special sales use.
For details, please call 1-800-733-3000.

A HOLE IN
JUAN

AN AMANDA PEPPER MYSTERY

GILLIAN
ROBERTS

BALLANTINE BOOKS • NEW YORK

2007 Ballantine Books Mass Market Edition

Published in the United States by Ballantine Books, an imprint of The Random House Publishing Group, a division of Random House, Inc., New York.

BALLANTINE and colophon are registered trademarks of Random House, Inc.

Originally published in hardcover in the United States by Ballantine Books, an imprint of The Random House Publishing Group, a division of Random House, Inc., in 2006.

This book contains an excerpt from the forthcoming book *All's Well That Ends* by Judith Greber. This excerpt has been set for this edition only and may not reflect the final content of the forthcoming edition.

ISBN 978-0-345-48020-0

Cover design: Carl Galian
Cover illustration: Ben Perrini

Printed in the United States of America

www.ballantinebooks.com

OPM   9   8   7   6   5   4   3   2   1

This is for Henry Aaron Greber.
So is anything else he wants.

Acknowledgments

Many thanks to clever Christine Day for coming up with the title for this book as well as to the crew who helped me fill the holes in my education and put that hole in Juan: Carol Shmurak, Tom Griffith, Karen Tannert, Andi Shechter, and Camille Minichino. Thanks, too, for all the other suggestions from Dorothy L'ers whose generously shared collective knowledge is awe-inspiring.

Still more gratitude to a trio of talented writers whose thoughtful comments and suggestions were, as always, invaluable: Jo Keroes, Louise Ure, and Marilyn Wallace. As Wilbur told Charlotte, "It is not often that someone comes along who is a true friend and a good writer," and here I am, blessed with three such women.

Always, for too many reasons to ever list, besos y abrazos, Roberto, and (decades now!) of amazed appreciation to my allies in these felonious pursuits, Joe Blades and Jean Naggar.

Any "holes" in Juan are mine—but lots more flaws and stumbles are now among the missing thanks to all these wonderful people.

One

TUESDAY. A DAY WITHOUT HONOR OR DISTINCTION. NONE of Monday's dread, none of Wednesday's halfway-through-the-week exhilaration, and nobody says, "T.G.I.T.!"

The week already felt long. I lurched out of bed, not exactly greeting the day. Insanity of sorts is part of any high school, but lately Philly Prep's version seemed more ominous. Something more serious was in the air, a tension, or subliminal rumbling.

I thought of the animals who'd felt the undersea earthquake and anticipated the tsunami, saving themselves by running for the safety of the hills. I'd have done the same if only I could locate the hills.

I had spent too much time lately obsessing about it, as if gnawing at nothingness would somehow reveal a solid center. Mackenzie had just about convinced me I was imagining the problem, or at least exaggerating it. After all, I spent my workweek with adolescents, their mercurial moods, their brains drowned in hormones.

"Let me get this right: You're sayin' teenagers are odd," he'd murmured. "An' your point is?"

I dragged myself to the bathroom and washed and dressed and tried to believe he was correct, and I was inventing a problem. I had to change my standards of what constituted normal and okay.

The phone rang, and I raced to answer it. I had a sleeping visitor on the sofabed and didn't want to wake him.

It was Carol Parillo, a Philly Prep math teacher and friend. She sounded as if she were phoning from a submarine.

"Amanda, I'm sick," she said. Actually, she said "Abadda, I sig," her voice hoarse and congested. "In case—hate to do this—but in case—could you and Mackenzie be at the school party Friday? Just in case?"

Given how I felt about school lately, spending extra time with the students was the last thing I wanted, but she sounded so wretched I couldn't refuse. I simply prayed for a miraculous cure for her.

Mackenzie pulled on a V-neck sweater the color of merlot. It combined with his salt-and-pepper hair and his pale blue eyes to create an interestingly patriotic trio of colors. Once he'd gotten it settled on his shoulders, he looked at me, his expression quizzical. "Somethin' on your mind, isn't there?"

"That phone call . . ." I broke the news as gently as I could. He did not jump up and down in jubilation at the idea of chaperoning a school dance. I should have waited till we'd had our coffee.

"An' I'm to go, too?"

"Remember the 'whither thou goest' part of the marriage vows?" I searched for my shoes.

"Actually not," he said. "I don't think they said that at City Hall."

"It's a tradition."

"The whither-thou-goest thing? If you're followin' that script, I think you're supposed to follow me."

"No—the party itself. It's Mischief Night, and this is the keeping-them-off-the-street party."

"Aren't you glad you're a cat?" C.K. asked Macavity, who lay curled on the duvet, mostly asleep. The part that wasn't asleep looked bemused. "You don't have to chaperone anything, ever."

"Or work," I grumbled.

I suspect that when Macavity finally activates himself, he phones the neighbors' tabbies, Siamese, Manx, and Persians to compare the deadlines, pressures, billable hours, exams, commutes, and alarm clocks their humans endure versus their own self-centered, sensual existence devoted to enjoying the comforts for which their people labor. "And they think they're the smarter species!" one will say, triggering a round of feline hysteria.

"I would like to have the end of October lopped off the calendar," Mackenzie said. "It's not a great time when your mother's a witch."

My mother-in-law declared herself a witch, or Wiccan, but from what I'd seen, her professed magic seemed indistinguishable from common sense and keen observation. But who knows? Maybe that's what magic is. Personally, I thought she was a smart woman who, faced with eight children plus strays taken in for years, decided to be more effective by claiming to be a witch. I'm not sure anybody ever actually believed it—I'm sure Mackenzie does not—but they all tacitly agreed to behave as if they did.

So her strategy worked, which definitely is magic.

"Things always got stirred up around Halloween," he said. "She'd be everywhere, on the radio, on street corners, in letters to the editor, protesting because witches were defamed—and because their outfits were mud-ugly as well."

My mother-in-law's wardrobe has the palette of a psychedelic nightmare, and since she finds few ready-made pieces that please her, she designs and sews her dramatically draped garments. The idea that she'd wear a pointed hat and shapeless black gown—let alone the green makeup—was beyond insulting.

"Even without a witch in the family, I'd hate costume parties," he said.

"You don't have to wear a costume Friday—if we actually do have to go. It's optional."

"Good," he said. "Why disguise yourself unless you're involved in criminal activity?"

A cop's rather narrow worldview, even if he was now a full-time student and not a homicide detective.

He stood in front of the mirror, studying his image. This was part of his morning routine. Part of my morning routine was watching him watching himself. He claimed he was making certain his clothing matched, wasn't ripped or stained, and that buttons were buttoned, zippers zipped.

I knew better. We were both admiring him. Not even under torture would he admit to such vanity, but I wasn't about to torture him because I didn't think he had to justify anything. The man was aesthetically pleasing, and the sight of him brightened my day, so why not his, too? No wonder he didn't like costumes and disguises.

"I'll get our lunches ready." I tiptoed out of our bedroom into the open space of the loft, padding silently past our houseguest.

Our marriage—spur of the moment and informal though it had been, and not yet one month old—had given us a new solidity and status in Mackenzie's enormous family. Translated, this meant that, like other family members, we now qualified as a great place to send anybody causing grief to his assigned unit.

The Mackenzie clan believes the theory that it takes a village to raise a child and, happily, there are so many Mackenzies that they *are* that village. They believe a change of scene is as good as long-term therapy, and it's their habit to separate and rotate family members when necessary.

Nobody had pointed out this small print in the marriage

contract. I knew that while he was growing up, C. K.
Mackenzie's already huge family had often expanded. I
never asked why extra children had landed there, some
staying on for years, but apparently relocation worked as
well as any other plan.

Rotating family was a brilliant idea—in theory. In prac-
tice, it meant we were now saddled with a lovesick sixteen-
year-old Iowa high-school dropout named Pip.

I'd thought his name was literary, cute, Dickensian, but
it turns out he was first a "pipsqueak" and then simply
considered "a pip of a kid." Pip had needed time out from
his mother, C.K.'s sister Lutie, who was between spouses
and didn't feel equipped to continue waging battle with her
son.

His heart had been broken by one Bunny Brookings, and
he could no longer see the point of remaining in a school
so full of Bunny, or, in fact, any other school. Instead, he
wanted to drop out and get involved with crime—on the
side of good, he insisted, the way his idolized uncle, my
new husband, had done.

He'd be a cop, he said. Or maybe a crime scene investigator, a forensic something. Whatever he was destined to
be, he wanted to begin the process of becoming it this instant.

Pip had loved having an uncle who was a homicide detective. Now, he'd grudgingly accepted C.K.'s decision to
leave the force and work on a Ph.D. in criminology, but he
wasn't pleased. He wasn't fond of abstractions and theory,
didn't care about studying the roots of crime or trying to
figure out how to prevent future crimes. He wanted chases
and shoot-outs, but he was settling for recollections of
crimes past. Stories about C.K.'s current moonlighting as a
PI were a decided letdown.

Currently, Ozzie Bright, the owner of Bright Investigations and our landlord-partner, C.K., and I were rotating surveillance on one Berta Polley, who claimed complete disability from a supermarket slip on a lettuce leaf. She was, she said, confined to her bed with excruciating back pain.

The market's produce manager insisted that the woman had staged the fall, and had done it slowly and comfortably. "More like sitting herself down on the floor, if you ask me," he'd said.

We were taking turns waiting for Berta to appear at her door, demonstrating the ability to descend the stairs and to walk, but so far there'd been no sign of her, and it appeared to be possible that the only lying she was doing was, in fact, in bed.

Needless to say, sitting and staring at nothing in a bloodless, eventless investigation did not meet Pip's minimal standards.

I tiptoed past the sofabed in my stockings, not wanting to wake him because his energy blast in the A.M. was too much for me. When he slept, he looked comatose, all skinny six feet of him almost adorable, but the instant he awoke, he was alert and unfortunately back to obsessive interest in blood and guts.

This week, I wished we lived in a normal place with walls, instead of the loft's wide open spaces. Our bedroom and the bathroom were sectioned off, but the rest was free range.

I worried about leaving a teen at loose ends while Mackenzie and I both worked, but Lutie had known the situation and thought it would be all right. Pip was basically a good kid, simply lost at the moment, and Philadelphia was as good a place in which to be lost as anywhere else, she'd said.

We'd spent the weekend showing Pip the city, acquainting him with the SEPTA schedules for buses and trains, giving him the short introductory tour of Independence Mall, standing in line to see the Liberty Bell, walking up and down the Parkway, then giving him guidebooks plus a personalized list of worthwhile things to see while we worked, although I heard him mutter "museums" with less than enthusiasm. But that's what we'd done. Yesterday, before we left for work, we made sure we'd exchanged cell numbers and expressed hope that this would work out to everyone's benefit.

He'd been home when he was supposed to be at the end of his first solo day, which was the good news. The bad news was that he'd been there all day, watching TV. But all right, we'd told each other late at night. He was acclimating. It took time.

I reminded myself that in many societies, Pip would be considered fully grown. Finished and complete. He'd be married and working and on his way to becoming an elder of the tribe. I was silly to worry about him.

But I did. I worried that he'd become too acclimated to us.

I worried about myself, afraid I'd OD on teens. I worked with them all week long and had become comfortable with adults-only evenings and weekends, during which time I could decompress. Having Pip here around the clock was like staying on the thrill ride too long.

I busied my hands and mind with hard-boiled eggs and tuna salad sandwiches and apples. We stretched our pennies every which way while we juggled the financial realities of our current life. C.K.'s tuition at the University of Pennsylvania was high. My school, Philly Prep, paid next to nothing. And now, we'd added Pip to the mix and, truth be told, the boy—lovesick or not—ate like a mastodon. Was it shallow of me to have noticed that?

I wrote him a reminder that there was food in the refrigerator. I added a P.S., asking him to phone me if he wasn't going to be home by the time I returned. I tidied up the pile of brochures and the list of suggestions we'd given him, hoping he'd act on at least one of them today.

By that time, Mackenzie had started the coffee and had a breakfast of cereal and fruit ready for the two of us. The system worked. I handed him his bagged lunch, and sighed.

Mackenzie looked up, a spoonful of cereal and blueberries midway to his mouth. "Worried about that party?"

I shook my head. "You're the one worried about that."

"Then it's that business again?"

Of course. When the beginning of the term was marked by silent anger in a class, in this case the seniors, and when other teachers also complained about minor but unsettling rebellions and disruptions, I'd been sad that this wasn't going to be a banner year with that group. Then, when I'd intercepted a note ("it's too late for that—shut up or else") and of course nobody knew who'd written it—the person whose desk it was on claimed to have found it there and to not know what it meant—I worried, but only a little. But I worried more when one day later, I saw a ripped piece of paper on the floor after class and the remains of it read:

l give in
ll see
panic!
dy knows!!

It was the same time when confusing notices appeared on the student board, which was normally filled with mundane announcements—lost backpacks, texts, bikes, need a ride to . . . and lately, lots of flyers about Friday's party. They featured a jack-o'-lantern with a body attached, on

the gallows. The printed notice said DON'T GET HUNG UP
(AND DON'T HANG US UP!). COME TO THE MISCHIEF NIGHT
PARTY! But someone had been adding comments with a
felt-tipped pen, such as "Guess who'll hang?" and "Wise
up and don't put yourself in this picture!"

Stupid, like the notes. Meaning nothing—except what if
they did? Did schools that later made gory headlines ignore
nothings like this, dismiss tensions and pretend only wee
innocents dwelt within the schoolhouse?

"It'll be better today," Mackenzie said.

I hoped so. Yesterday the tension in the room had been
oatmeal thick.

"Mischief Night," C.K. grumbled. "If it's simply mischief—why the fuss of having a school event so as to keep
the kids off the streets? Mischief's no big thing."

"Some parts of the country call it Cabbage Night. Would
that make it more significant?"

He grinned. "From cabbage crop to coleslaw on lots of
front porches? That's *mischief*. That's my point."

"Some places call it Devil's Night. Lots of arson. How
about that? The idea goes back to the Druids. It was their
new year, when the Celtic elves, fairies, and ghosts walked
the earth."

Mackenzie nuzzled my ear. "I love it when you get all
teachery," he whispered. "Tell me more about Mischief
Night."

Pedagogical seduction.

Intriguing.

Interrupted.

A voice from the sofabed shouted, "Radical! We don't
have Mischief Night at home. I love this city!"

I stared at the lanky boy in pajamas, remembering C.K.'s
mother's big-hearted acceptance of any child who needed a
home. I didn't want to seem cruel. I liked Pip. I like children. I'd like to have children someday—but not have them

arrive as sixteen-year-old high-school dropouts with spiked hair.

"I'm gonna stay here forever!"

Tuesday was not looking good. Not yet eight A.M., and I was ready to crawl back into bed, to try to enjoy the comforts and serenity my cat took for granted.

Two

THE OCTOBER MORNING WAS BRIGHTER THAN I WAS, AND not yet as cold as it would surely be by the weekend. My childhood memories of Halloween are of the miracle of being transformed by a costume. With my homemade ballgown on, I wasn't dressed as Cinderella—I was Cinderella.

Unfortunately, my mother could read the thermometer.

That transformative magic of disguise is endangered in Philadelphia in late October. Would the prince have fallen for Cinderella if she'd had to wear a bulky coat atop her gown or layers of sweaters underneath?

Year after year, I left to trick-or-treat—swaddled, disgruntled, and unhappy—and then I forgot all about it as the other adults, who'd also sent out disappointed, insulated children, pretended to be amazed by my disguise.

In any case, today was brisk and invigorating, and I was glad I'd decided to walk. School is only a few miles away, and city miles are interesting.

This is probably a blot on my English-teacher-as-upholder-of-our-cultural-legacy report card, but I'm not a great fan of Henry David Thoreau's *Walden.* It's enjoyable reading, and it has many wise observations, and the countless times I've taught the book, I've shown proper reverence. But I knew myself to be a hypocrite.

I, too, want to know, as did Thoreau, "what . . . is the chief end of man, and what are the true necessaries and means of life?" But given that desire, why hightail it away from community and variety to hole up in the woods? I'd stay in the city because one of the "true necessaries" of life is other people, and where better to study life than in the thick of it?

My book wouldn't have been called *Walden*. It would have been called *Philadelphia*.

Besides, I'd read that Henry David took one of the "true necessaries" of life—his dirty laundry—home to Mom during his famous time of roughing it. As far as I'm concerned, there goes the integrity of life in the wilderness.

My route to school always involves a taste of history whether I walk through Independence Mall or veer slightly to the north and pass the new Constitution Center, which is a visual pleasure even from the outside. I enjoy its combed and manicured green swath of lawn—my kind of nature—sweeping up to its sleek façade, and I'm proud of the city for creating this deserved and elegant celebration of an amazing piece of writing and thought.

We'd tried making the place part of our communal outings, but Pip never looked excited by the idea, not even when we pointed out that the law was a part of the criminal justice system.

I'm not sure he was happy that civilization had found a way to settle disputes without fists or guns.

I hoped my students would be more enthusiastic when I presented the idea. I wanted to join forces with the social studies teacher, Louis Applegate, for an interdisciplinary unit that hinged on a trip to this center. I made a mental note to speak to him about it today. I knew we taught many of the same students.

And with that thought I was into a teaching mode, and I mentally rehearsed the day. Anxiety about the seniors remained, but I was excited as well about the juniors' poetry reading, and hoped nothing—not stage fright or technical difficulties—would keep it from running smoothly. I was still in mild shock that they'd instigated the idea. I'd originally worried that it was a prank, a Mischief Night prequel, because why would students suddenly want to tape and broadcast their original poems?

But they seemed sincere and appealingly innocent, so now I hoped it would be precisely as they'd envisioned it.

When you walk, you see things you miss completely if you drive by, and not for the first time, I observed how Halloween had mutated from one night to a season. Halloween flags waved on poles, Halloween wreaths filled front doors, pumpkins were painted onto windows, and jack-o'-lanterns, plastic and real, sat in entries and on sills. Half the magazine covers on the newsstand promised recipes or decorating ideas for All Hallow's Eve. That dreadful cobwebby stuff ringed a shoe-repair shop's window, black cats arched against imaginary moons, and scarecrows guarded produce in two groceries I passed.

I peered into the window of a not-yet-open stationery store and considered a long rack of Halloween greeting cards. I really wanted to know what sentiments the holiday engendered.

What were we so determinedly celebrating? Tricks and treats? Ghosts and goblins? Orange and black? Maybe we hadn't come all that far from those Druid creatures who roamed the earth one night a year and needed to be appeased, although probably not with preprinted greeting cards.

Next thing would be demands for a National Day of Haunting.

I was still vaguely amused by the excess of it all when I entered Philly Prep and greeted our newest secretary, Harriet Rummell. The school had been running through office personnel almost on a weekly basis, and I wasn't sure how long Ms. Rummell would be with us, either.

This is not to say she had any of the flaws of the past secretaries. She was neither a hostile antagonist, a hoarder of school supplies, a twittering puzzle-happy incompetent, nor too terrified to function.

Another thing the solitary Thoreau missed knowing about was how many and various are the ways in which co-workers can grate one upon the other.

Harriet Rummell was a happy woman. Her happiness was based on how wonderfully well her life was going. I'm not knocking that, but Harriet also took it for granted that the entire world wanted to share the details of her joy, and nothing short of binding and gagging her would disabuse her of that idea.

That, I'm knocking.

Maybe even that wouldn't be bad—except that it took so little to make Harriet happy, and not necessarily anything even mildly amusing. It simply took an event or idea that had happened to her.

"Good morning, Miss Pepper!" She had sweet, small features. The horn-rimmed glasses that constantly slid down her small nose echoed and underlined the roundness of her face, as did her mop of brown curls. She was something like a child's drawing—all circles and loops, and an almost eternal wide smile.

She giggled. "Or should I call you Mrs. Mackenzie?"

We'd been through this almost every day since I'd told her I had to change my personnel records, adding my student-husband to my medical insurance. Her joke was way beyond stale, but as I said, it took precious little to amuse Harriet, repeatedly. "I'm still keeping my maiden name," I said as quietly as I could. "Just like I was yesterday. Our students already seem confused about most things. I'm trying not to add to their burden."

She giggled and beamed, shaking her curls as if she could not get over my wit. Once she'd regained control, she straightened her face into her all-business expression. "Big day, huh?" she said. "Derek Ludo was in, and he told me. As if I needed a reminder! How often do we tape an actual TV show here?"

I bit my bottom lip. Nobody but Harriet would define videotaping a poetry reading for the school's closed-circuit system as a TV show.

"Bet you're excited," she said. "Mrs. Producer herself."

Nobody was the producer. Derek Ludo was one of the school techies helping the juniors broadcast their poetry to those schoolmates who wanted to see it.

"I hope it's not out of line for me to compliment you, my not being a teacher and all," she said, "but you do come up with such creative ideas, like a TV show!" She nodded emphatically and pushed her horn-rimmed glasses up her nose again.

"It's not really all that—"

"It's a quality I value in people."

The muscles of my back twitched. I knew where she was headed—where all Harriet conversations headed. We were en route to Erroll Davine, her fiancé.

Harriet had been engaged to Erroll Davine since she graduated from high school. By using my sleuthing powers—Pip would be proud of me—and by virtue of her incessant chatter about Erroll, I had figured the engagement to be twelve and a half years old. "Erroll's had a hard time finding himself," she'd said by way of explanation.

Erroll's lost self had once seemed to be hiding in long-distance trucking school, later in a course on how to become a supersalesman, followed by a year's worth of acting lessons, two semesters of computer repair instruction, preparation for a real estate license, and now, in taxidermy school. Harriet had—"Of course!" she said brightly—

assumed the burden of supporting the two of them as Erroll slogged up and down the learning curve.

I was tempted to shake the blinkers off her eyes, but the woman was so happy with her freeloader, it would have been cruel.

"Erroll's like you that way," she was now saying. "Maybe all real achievers are creative visionaries. Just yesterday, he was so concerned about getting a groundhog's tongue right he was in torment. He's such a perfectionist, and tongues are really difficult, you know. All kinds of tongues, not just a groundhog's."

I nodded, smiled, tried not to think about groundhog tongues, and turned to check my mailbox. I found a lighter than usual deposit of detritus. "This all?" I asked.

She nodded sagely. "The headmaster didn't have any messages today." Although she chortled at most everything, she was always solemn about Maurice Havermeyer, who emphatically deserved to be laughed at. Harriet dropped her voice to a reverent hush when she said even his title. Judging by her tone, "the headmaster" was almost in a league with Erroll the would-be taxidermist.

"As I was saying," she went on, "this groundhog caused him so much trouble—"

She was put on hold, and my question of who wanted a stuffed groundhog in the first place remained unasked, when Juan Angel Reyes entered the office.

The new science teacher was a dapper man who looked as if he slept in a clothes press, rigid in dress and deed, from what I'd gathered. He'd been quickly nicknamed "Dr. Jar" by the students, a put-down that made fun both of his obsession with monogramming his clothing and possessions and of what I'd been told were his repeated reminders to his classes that he was about to receive his doctorate and that as soon as he had it, he would have no more to do with this school and its dim students who were unworthy of him. He was here for the money, pathetic as that amount was, and the flexible schedule he'd been offered. But once his monogram becomes J.A.R. Ph.D., he'd be in a high-paying research job in a heartbeat.

I'm sure he never put it that way, but that was the message the students heard, larded with contempt for the lot of us.

"Good morning!" Harriet all but trilled.

Reyes nodded—almost a bow. He didn't seem one for small talk, particularly if it was taxidermy-based, and to Harriet's credit, she understood that. Reyes made the nod-and-bow gesture to me as well as he passed. I smelled cigarettes on him, as I had other mornings. It surprised me once again. He seemed fastidious to a fault, and *eau de* cigarettes didn't go with that. I could envision him carefully changing into a Victorian smoking jacket of an evening and lighting a pipe or a ceremonial cigar, but not requiring the sort of nervously urgent preclass smoke his aroma suggested.

He emptied his mailbox and gave the pickings a cursory glance, then looked back at me. "You teach seniors, too, do you not?" he asked me.

I nodded. "Some of them."

"You teach the class with the tennis boys and their girls? That Steegmuller and Wilson and—"

I nodded again. A goodly portion of the school's tennis team was in one section, but even so, referring to them as "the tennis boys" and to their girlfriends as "their girls" seemed off.

He cleared his throat and turned his back to Harriet. "May I ask you something?"

One more nod.

"Have you noticed—in your room—have the students misbehaved? I mean, more than whatever the norm for this school might be?" He kept his voice low, as if this were an urgent but secret question.

I could have answered him directly. These were the students I'd been worrying about. I could have shared my concerns, but I didn't, because Dr. Jar was so reserved and held back and angry about finding himself here among the peons that it was hard to step closer, to agree, to become a colleague and share the distress. "What do you mean by *misbehave*?" I asked instead. "I've heard about a lot of pranks lately. Halloween-related pranks. Orange and black paint missing from the art room, the mustard packets gone from the lunchroom."

"I mean . . . worrisome behavior," he said. "I do not consider them pranks."

"Like what?"

"Many things. Supplies go missing. Dropping bottles, glass tubing, that sort of thing, and then they reappear—and disappear again! Chemicals, too, acetone, sodium, agar-agar—maybe more. One day last week, all the beakers were gone when class began. And then I find them neat and tidy in the back room, on a high shelf. Then, Friday past, I'd scheduled a retest." He pursed his mouth and shook his head. "They do not study. They do not apply themselves."

Had he read the description of the school before taking the job? Surely there were lots of positions for science teachers, so why pick a school that specialized in students who didn't function well in large, traditional schoolrooms?

"They failed miserably on the first examination."

"All of them?"

"Most. And they behaved as if it were my fault!"

I personally believe that if an entire class does poorly, the teacher should at least consider his own culpability. If a subject falls in the forest and nobody understood it, how can you be sure you taught it? However, this wasn't the time to share my philosophy.

"You'd think I had deliberately cheated them," he said, "with their carrying on about their grades, especially the big sports boys. Whining about how they had a game and couldn't really study. Why should I care? I was destroying their chances at college, they said. I was destroying their lives." He said all this without a smile, with no appreciation of adolescent hyperbole.

"In order to appease them, this one time, I rescheduled the examination, and gave them fair warning that it would of course be a new test, but ultimately, that was not to be because there was a fire drill if you recall."

I did. It had nearly derailed the original poetry-reading session. The kids were sufficiently shy and awkward about performing and the fire drill interrupted them precisely when they'd mustered their courage. It broke the mood and moment, and then, when it was learned that it was a false alarm, that somehow demoralized them. I'd had to become a cheerleader, all but waving pom-poms and leaping into the air to get them back on track.

"Yes, well, then," he continued. "Only when we were all downstairs and outside did I realize that three of the class members had never showed up in class. They joined us, so to speak, on the sidewalk."

"Are you saying those kids pulled the—"

"I have said nothing except what I have said. I am a scientist and I rely on verification before reaching a conclusion, and at this point, I have none. I am merely reporting the facts of the matter, which I find disquieting. James, Nita, and Seth were not in class where they belonged. All three had reasons. One was at the counselor's office and forgot to get a note. The other was feeling ill and had been in the bathroom, and the third . . . I don't remember, but there is no reason not to think they had their excuses at the ready."

I tend to discount students' exaggerated reports on faculty failings. I'm sure they provide equally distorted reports about my classroom to other teachers, but they were right about this man; he was not easy to like.

"The net effect," he said, "was that the alarm and drill diminished the time available to the point where I was unable to administer the retest."

"What will you do?"

"Their original marks stand. I see no other recourse. They're a bad lot, all of them. Infuriating. I regret passing up other job offers."

I felt a moment's pang on behalf of the students who'd had nothing to do with setting off the alarm—if, in fact, anyone had purposely done it. It had been known to go off when the humidity was too high, or the electrical system in the school was overloaded. "I meant about the three students who weren't in class. I know them, and they're good kids."

He raised his eyebrows.

"Nita and Seth are good students as well. I can't imagine they'd have any reason to do something like that." James—Jimmy—less so, but he seemed contented with being a C student, and in fact, he'd told me with some pride that meant he was "the norm," which showed that he'd picked something up in math class. His family was wealthy and he knew they'd find a college that would be a fit for his agility at tennis and his ability to pay full tuition. He didn't have to set off alarms to meet his personal goals.

"These students are a disappointment. Sloppy thinkers, lazy, only interested in their petty lives," he said. "If they're so worried about college, they should have worked harder the first eleven years of school."

I'd heard grumbles about how tough he was and, of course, that translated into how unfair he was. But that was so common as to be generic, and since I was in favor of higher standards, I had tuned the complaints out.

"It doesn't make sense," I said. "Why prevent a retest when you did poorly on the original? Why avoid a chance to do better?"

"Not everyone did poorly on the original, just the majority. As a point in fact, as you suspected, Seth and Nita performed adequately."

"So they wouldn't want a re—"

"You are once again putting words into my mouth. In any case, I don't believe that making sense is one of their priorities. As I said, there has been a series of events, this only the most recent. Pipettes in the wrong drawer, a bell jar missing two days, then back, five thermometers gone— but then there they are, in the sink. I think they do it just to prove they can. A crucible tong, sodium, and an evaporating dish are still missing, and who knows where they will turn up. Somebody thinks this is funny." His eyebrows had pulled close to each other. "They are a spiteful group and they are taunting me for reasons I do not yet comprehend."

"They? Who?"

His lips tightened now. His entire face moved toward its center and he lost more of his good looks with each squinch. For once, he seemed less than absolutely sure of what to say. "Who knows who removes things, then returns them? I thought once Erik Steegmuller was the one, and that girl Nita, or maybe her friend Allie, and then Seth and Jimmy. Others, too, like Wilson. Each time, I think I know who, but then somebody else seems the culprit. It's all of them. They are all after me."

I envisioned the seniors, disorganized except on a court with a coach's guidance. Who among them would bother? Would think of a plan of harassment and carry it out? And why?

"I refuse to bend to adolescent perversity." He spoke softly, but I nonetheless felt he was lecturing me.

"It might help to talk with your class about what's going on," I said.

He pulled back from me. *Recoiled* would be more accurate. "As far as they're concerned," he said, "I have noticed nothing of their shenanigans. I will never honor their actions by acknowledging them."

"Maybe it's a sort of hazing—a good-natured testing of the newcomer."

"Good-natured! It's—it's anything but! It's disruptive, and—"

"No," I interrupted him. "To answer your initial question, no. I haven't had any incidents like the ones you described." I felt hypocritical, giving him only the literal truth. I wasn't missing supplies and I couldn't correlate the fire alarm with any of my students. Plus, I was now feeling less anxiety about that class. It appeared that the sullen agitation in English class might well be the aftermath of the struggle between the students and Mr. Reyes. He was to blame for some of my woes. I didn't like the way he characterized them, even though they were mostly sloppy thinkers, and self-centered, and lazy.

They were Philly Prep's bread and butter. Kids who didn't perform adequately elsewhere, who needed smaller classes, more personal attention. What had he expected? Embryonic rocket scientists filling his classroom's chairs?

"Thank you for your time, then," he said, and he huffed out at top speed.

I stared after him, a good-looking, intelligent, yet unattractive man. While physics might not be his special field, he was a scientist who surely knew that for every action there was an equal reaction. And so forth and so on until, I thought, it was an avalanche of reactions, tumbling into my classroom in the form of hostile seniors.

It was hard to know who'd made the first move, or to tell

whether Juan Reyes was being persecuted or was, in fact, the persecutor himself.

But I could almost see the dangerous pendulum swinging—action, reaction, wider and wider, more and more out of control.

What I couldn't see was a way to stop it.

Three

DR. JAR'S WAR WOULDN'T LEAVE MY MIND. IF HE REFUSED to confront the students about what he considered deliberate attacks on him, how could he even find out if they were real?

If they were real, what did the students have to gain by their pranks, or were they blindly reacting?

If their plots to annoy him were unacknowledged, what would they need to do next to be noticed?

And how did I extricate myself from their loop so that I could have a decent semester with my seniors?

As I climbed the stairs, I saw Nita Kloster and Allie Deroche, who were not only best friends but also the girlfriends of best friends—Donny Wilson and Erik Steegmuller—two of what Juan Reyes had called the "tennis boys."

I couldn't hear what they were saying, but their body language seemed overly animated for early morning. Their heads shook and nodded, agreeing and disagreeing, their fingers pointed down the hallway, they shrugged, frowned, and each in turn took a deep, theatrical breath.

Or maybe, as Mackenzie would have suggested, I was once again overreacting. They were seventeen years old and their engines didn't need a slow start.

Allie spotted me when I was a few steps from the top of

the double staircase, and nodded and smiled—too much of a smile, I thought.

Then she turned back to Nita, leaned close and whispered, all the while leading her friend farther down the hall, away from me and away from my classroom door.

Nita looked my way while she listened to Allie's whisper, then turned back and continued the whispered conversation.

Conspirators. I heard my mind declare this and realized I had been contaminated by Jar. Would I have even noted the ordinary scene of two girls sharing secrets if I hadn't had the encounter with him?

For better or for worse, a school is too filled with on-going life to allow much brooding or pondering. The bell is always about to ring and present you with a new mass of personalities and issues, not to mention learning material, to deal with. You have no choice but to move on.

So even if I wanted to figure out what was going on with Nita and Allie or their classmates in Juan Reyes's class, there was no time to do so. A few minutes were given over to the clerical duties of homeroom, followed quickly by my first period class, my juniors, and, as Harriet would have it, their "TV show."

This class had a spark and enthusiasm for almost anything, most recently poetry, which I need not say isn't always a guaranteed hit.

Today, they were almost visibly thrumming with excitement. Big-time closed-circuit TV.

We'd been dipping into various genres, and I tried to find works that had an element with which they could identify. I try to do this when possible, and, since that's what makes great literature great, it's always possible. With poetry, it's easy to find works that touch on the universal emotions—love, death, grief, and joy. As a plus, poems are short, and brevity is the prime consideration with many of my students.

I also try to correlate—when it makes sense—the history, times, and social problems reflected in the prose and poetry we read. Sometimes it works and they discover the idea that fiction and poetry might be relevant to the larger world.

It doesn't always work. There are whiny questions about why we have to talk about Puritans when we read *The Scarlet Letter*. Didn't that stuff belong in history class? They wanted everything kept circumscribed and too often behaved as if it were rude of me to snatch ideas from another discipline and try to show the connections.

But so far, this class was open for whatever I suggested. If there were a pageant for high school sections, they'd win the Miss Congeniality prize. They'd shown enthusiasm for Whitman, and still more for Ginsberg's "Howl" and for Dylan's lyrics, and had responded emotionally when we read World War I poems by Siegfried Sassoon, Edna St. Vincent Millay, and with actual gasps at the opening lines of Wilfred Owen's "Anthem for Doomed Youth." "What passing-bells for these who die as cattle?"

They were excited that poetry was not always their stereotypical image of a man skipping in a field of daisies and rhapsodizing about it, but that it could be powerful, funny, or revelatory. It could be whatever the poet's talents allowed.

And then a series of students separately confessed to me that they, too, found expression and solace by writing poems and, to my absolute amazement, they were willing to go public with their creations.

That was a fine teaching day as far as my professional ego was concerned, because I felt I'd created a safe enough atmosphere for them to be willing to express themselves—even adolescent boys, which made it something akin to a miracle.

Last week, the day of the false alarm, about a dozen had read their work to their classmates, and it was such an unanticipated treat that the class suggested we bring the "show," as they called it, to the school at large.

Going public with some of the goopy June-moon-swoon cute-puppy verses was beside the point. Their words were as close to their honest emotions as they could get—or, perhaps, afford to get—at this age and in public, and I wanted to encourage them, to endorse verbal creativity as a desirable activity.

The poets, working hard to overcome shyness and terror, agreed, and today was the day. I was delighted. As incomprehensible as it seemed to me, polls had shown a majority of the U.S. populace would choose death rather than speak in public. This event was stealth public speaking and the innocent bards had suggested it themselves.

All went well from start to finish. Alison Brody had a brief attack of stage fright when the camera was brought into the classroom, but she got over it and was able to deliver her surprisingly touching sonnet about her grandmother's death. I was proud and, I admit, astonished at how she'd empathized with the woman, basing each stanza on a name the woman had been called, from baby nicknames to "darling" to Mrs. Brody, Mama, and Grandma. Alison had been able to see her as a woman with a history of her own, and that was no mean feat.

And Joey Myers, despite self-consciousness that dyed his cheeks vermilion, was brave and resolute enough to read his verses about his dog, a sweet but intellectually challenged pooch. His nose reddened as he related the dog's death, and he spoke his final line in a thickened voice:

The good thing was
We never let him know that

Dogs should be smart.
He died feeling clever and wise.

Having said his piece, eyes on the floor, Joey cleared his
throat, then looked up and around and glared, daring anybody to question his manliness just because he'd loved his
dumb doggie.

Nobody did.

Lily's poem "Supposing" was overly reminiscent of John
Lennon's "Imagine," and of course it was about peace and
loving one another. ("Supposing there's no labels, and only
human beings, no boundaries between them . . .") And
even though it so closely followed the rhythms of the original that you could hum its melody as she read, she called it
an "homage"—and who were we to disagree?

Along the same blameless lines, Cheryl Stevens had perhaps absorbed too much Dylan—or perhaps it was Sassoon's
poem "Does It Matter?" that began, "Does it matter?—
losing your legs? For people will always be kind . . ." But
the passionate emotions of her poem "Does It Count?"
were personal. Her adored older cousin had returned from
Iraq blind and it was clear that she, too, had been scarred
by what she saw as the meaninglessness of his loss.

The news tallies casualties and we
Check the numbers dead and sigh.
A wound makes you an also-ran.
You don't count.
They should describe each injury,
Say what the still-breathing have left,
What part is broken, gone or bleeding, how much, how
*   long the pain.*
Make people understand that
Being twenty-one and blind forever counts.

The next stanza began, "They teach us not to kill . . . unless they change their minds," and went on to the contradictions of war and a metaphorical blindness.

Cheryl had something special. I was sure that if she kept at it, borrowing and adapting or not, she would hack through all the other voices and find her own, and when she did, it would be well worth hearing.

The reading went smoothly without a noticeable hitch, and classmates who'd already heard these works were attentive and supportive, applauding each poet with convincing enthusiasm. We ended the hour on a high, having done something innovative and brave—and we were talking about Philly Prep, not your most intellectually stimulating or academically involved school.

Take that, Juan Reyes!

It had been a great morning. "I'm so proud of all of you," I said.

And I was, but a proud English teacher should remember where, chronologically, pride goeth.

THE TENTH GRADERS HAD ENJOYED *A SEPARATE PEACE*, though not as wildly as I'd hoped. At first, they complained about the fictionalized prep school's playing fields, the lunches served, and the exquisite-sounding surrounds versus the urban realities of Philly Prep. Their prep school had concrete sidewalks ringing the building, the gymnasium for basketball, and a tennis court up on the third floor where there'd once been a roof garden.

I pointed out the rigorous academic requirements of the novel's school, and the fact that there were no girls on that campus, and they simmered down and moved on to the issues the book presented.

The 1950s sensibility that wrote it and the 1940s sensibilities that informed it were a stretch for them—but worthwhile when we "translated" some of what the book took for granted—World War II and the home front, rationing, the draft, and the attitudes toward the war and service. Once again, history seeped into the English classroom, but this group didn't seem to find that an intrusion.

This morning, we talked about the pivotal moment in the book when Gene jostles the tree branch and doesn't reach to help Finney, who is also balancing on it, thereby ensuring his friend's plummet to earth.

"Don't forget," Ma'ayan Atias said. "Finney had saved Gene on that branch. And Finney hadn't caused the problem then, the way Gene did now."

"Good point," I said. "Why do you think Gene suddenly jostled the branch?"

"Gene was scared of jumping off that tree," Ben said. "He, like, had to, or—"

"Or what?" Ma'ayan snapped. "Gene was scared of *losing!* Everything was about losing or winning to him."

"But—but it wasn't a contest, really." Ben's cheeks slowly turned color until they looked as if somebody had scraped them. Ma'ayan was a formidable debater made even more so by her self-assurance. And she had the ultimate weapon—she was cute, thereby rendering boys her age, particularly Benjamin, tongue-tied or speechless.

"Yes it was!" she said with great authority.

Ben had the dogged appeal of someone doomed to lose, but determined to stay the course. "Finney was better at sports," he said softly.

"But Gene was better at academics," I said, joining the match.

"Yes," Ben said. "Yes. But . . . sports are more important—not with teachers, but with kids?" His wistfulness was heartbreaking. Ben appeared made completely of Tinkertoys, sticks and spools, with a large—intelligent—head on top. He grew almost visibly day by day, and he didn't look as if all the new inches had been wired yet, so he didn't function as a unit. It was obvious that athletics would have to wait until he got the neurons firing in sync.

"But also, also—because Finney didn't have to follow the rules. That's another reason Gene was angry, even if he didn't say so." Ma'ayan waved her hand in the air while she spoke. Speaking in turn was the rule of the classroom, raising your hand first. Her hand followed the rules, signaling that she wanted to be called on, but the rest of her couldn't contain her idea one second longer.

"What does that mean?" I asked her. "Why might that be so?"

"Because . . . because Finney wasn't worried about what people thought the way Gene was. He wore that pink shirt, except why that was such a big deal, I don't know."

Ben swallowed hard before speaking. "Because it made him look—*pink*. You know, *pink*—"

"*Gay*," a male voice interrupted from the back of the room, and there was a burst of nudge-nudge laughter.

Only a brief burst after a glance from me, but the winks and faces continued on. They always do, and it always depresses me.

"Jeez," Ma'ayan said, her posture and expression of incredulous disdain as regal and remote as Queen Victoria's must have been. "Like wearing a certain color makes you whatever! But anyway, Finney wasn't afraid to wear it."

"It might be worth considering," I said, interrupting her, "that a pink shirt was more outrageous when this book took place. So think of what it meant that Finney didn't mind wearing it. And try to expand your minds a bit and think about this: The boys at this school would all be wearing white shirts, and any colored shirt might suggest something, aside from a sexual preference."

"Unconventional! Not worrying about what people think!" Ella, a diminutive blonde, had gotten a word in and she sat back and smiled at her accomplishment.

"He said it was to honor the bombing of Central Europe," Ben said softly, glancing at Ma'ayan to see whether she'd noticed.

"But it wasn't, really," she replied. "He made that up! Maybe Gene wished he could be that way, that . . ." She wrinkled her brow and actually paused for a breath as she searched for the word. "That free?" she asked.

"You know how you can get angry with somebody because they have—I mean inside, their personality, what you want?" The freckled red-haired boy's name refused to stick in my mind. I knew it wasn't Jack because that's the name my brain insisted was his. Maybe he wouldn't mind being called not-Jack . . . "I mean you *like* that person, but you're jealous," not-Jack added.

"Would you—could you—hate that person if he's your friend?" I felt like a referee, but they were doing the hard lifting, and I was enjoying the back-and-forth.

They thought for a while, then Ben of the elbows spoke again. "Maybe more if he's your friend," he said. "Because they like you, but you're having these secret bad feelings about them, so you'd hate them for making you feel that way, wouldn't you?"

He always looked at Ma'ayan as he spoke, and I could see—even if she refused to—a desperate and heartbreaking lovesickness. He was trying to win the fair maiden's attention through his mental agility, but the fair maiden was in love with her own thoughts, not his, and definitely not with the nonthinking parts of him.

The dramas contained in one single classroom could fill a library.

Somebody mentioned the idea of collateral damage—unintended consequences—about unthinkingly doing something like shaking that limb, and not considering what permanent damage could radiate from that one wobbling tree branch. They liked that idea a great deal, and went off on a track of things they—or hypothetical people—had done that wound up backfiring. Guns bought for protection injuring their owners was a favorite, and an appallingly high percentage of them knew of such examples.

I was surprised at how quickly the minutes passed, how enjoyable the hour had been.

And then the messenger arrived. "Miss Rummell said to give you this. It came in after you left this morning," she said, and I nodded, sure it was another of Havermeyer's inane messages. I was eager for lunch, and I opened the envelope quickly, my mind elsewhere—at least until I read the block letters:

SOMEBODY TOOK THE TEST FOR THE SENIOR'S AND DUPLICATED IT. ALOT OF PEOPLE SAW IT. THOUGHT YOU'D WANT TO KNOW. YOU'RE FRIEND.

I winced at the apostrophe, at *a lot* made into one word, and then at the *you're,* and hoped the writer wasn't one of my students. But that was only a holding action against considering the message, which was both upsetting—and impossible.

Those tests had been locked in my desk drawer since Friday. Because of Pip's arrival, I'd been prepared well in advance for once, and I'd stored the exam there.

I went back to my desk and tried the center drawer. Still locked. I took out my keys and unlocked it, and there were the tests. I counted them. All there.

I'd put them there Friday afternoon, locked the desk, and hadn't unlocked it until now. The key had been with me since I turned it with great satisfaction at the end of last week.

How about that: a locked-drawer mystery.

Maybe Reyes had been right, and something was seriously out of kilter with the seniors. I had been able to tolerate the idea when it was directed at him. He was new, he was rigid, he was unconcerned with their welfare, but now the malevolence was directing itself at me. Did I fit any of those categories? What did this mean? And what do you do to undo something that couldn't have happened in the first place?

Four

I DIDN'T GO DOWNSTAIRS BUT INSTEAD ATE MY HARD-
boiled egg and apple at my desk, working on a revised
exam, obsessed not only with making up new questions for
the seniors but with asking them of myself. Who could
have stolen the exam and how could they have done it, and
who was my semiliterate confidante who ratted?

I came up with no answers, but I did come up with new
questions and I went to the office to see about duplicating
them. Harriet had her faults, but inefficiency wasn't one of
them, nor was an unwillingness to help the staff. "I'm in a
bit of a rush," I said. "I had to change the exam at the last
minute. Could I have the copies for next period?"

Past experience made my stomach quiver after asking a
question like that.

"Of course!" she said. "These things happen." She stood
up and headed toward the copier.

During the reign of Helga the Office Witch, nothing was
ever duplicated in less than three days, and only after begging and pleading one's case for urgency, and then it was
accomplished with a scowl and a clear message that asking
her to push the button on the copy machine—which faculty could not use—was a nearly insupportable outrage.

Harriet's amiability seemed nothing less than miraculous. I watched her place the sheet and press the required
number and set the machine humming—and it was obvi-

ous how a student could get a copy. "Do you do all the duplicating yourself?" I asked. A student aide could simply
print out an extra when he manned the machine.

"Exams? Definitely," she said. "Too tempting to the students otherwise, don't you think?"

That was wise, and a comfort, but I was sad to lose my
easy solution.

"I love your wedding band," she said as the pages piled
up. I looked down at my finger. The ring was still an un-
adorned gold band. I, too, loved it, but couldn't imagine
what was remarkable about it.

"We've been looking, too," she said, and now I knew
that what had appealed to her had little to do with rings.
She felt we had a bond, were soul sisters, both paired with
what she referred to as "scholars" who also moonlighted
in order to stay afloat. Her scholar, however, was often
derailed from his part-time day jobs due to the rigors of
taxidermy and the irrational behavior of his various em-
ployers.

We had so much in common. Both of us were helping
with our guys' tuitions. "They don't give scholarships for
taxidermy," she said, shaking her head at the madness of financial aid distribution. "And the specimens are so expensive. His wolf-rug specimen cost over six hundred dollars!"

I often couldn't bear hearing what was being killed so as
to be stuffed and made to look as if it were still alive. There
was a hideous contradiction in the lifelike dead things con-
cept, but it seemed to have escaped Harriet and Erroll.

"It would be less expensive if he could bring his own
specimens, but road kill isn't any good, and where would
Erroll find a wolf or mountain lion on his own?"

I pictured lion-vendor stands ringing the school of taxidermy. *Run! Mountain lions, run!* I mentally telegraphed,
wherever they'd managed to still be alive. Luckily, Harriet
couldn't hear my thoughts, only the small noises I made in

an attempt to signify amazement and wonder. I thought of them as my Harriet sounds because they satisfied her need for approval without my ever saying I approved.

The test pages had long since popped out of the printer, but it seemed rude to grab them and run.

"I can't wait till he graduates," Harriet said. "You can't imagine how well they do—not that he's in it for the money. He's in it for the art. It's nice that it also affords a comfortable living."

Except, of course, for the poor stuffed animal. Frankly, given his history of delaying marriage while he flirted with careers, Erroll didn't seem in much of a rush to become as one with Harriet. Taxidermy was already taking much longer than anticipated. He'd had to repeat the fur course, she'd told me, because he'd gotten the flu, and prior to the groundhog tongue issues, he had difficulties with the bird course. Turkeys, she'd informed me solemnly, were difficult. "Not the fat kind we have for Thanksgiving. But with the wild ones, the body making isn't easy, and he had problems with it. He has to try again with a new bird, poor man."

Run, turkeys, run! Or better still—you're birds—fly! Could those infamously ineffective brains—I'd heard that when it rains, they look up to check the weather and drown—could those brains anticipate danger?

I did not want to become emotionally involved with the fate of wild turkeys, so I reverted to her other topic: her marriage-in-waiting. "Wedding bands, eh? Does this mean Erroll's about to . . ." I wasn't sure if people graduated from taxidermy school or received any sort of degree. ". . . finish?"

Her tolerant chuckle implied that the idea of completing such a difficult course of study in a matter of mere years was so naive, one could only laugh. "His licensing is away off—but looking can't hurt, can it? Did I tell you about when he won an interschool competition? He stuffed a raccoon with amazing results."

Run, raccoons, run!

"You mark my words—he'll be a master taxidermist soon."

I never knew how to respond to these anecdotes. Taxidermy school was apparently very hands-on, and Harriet had related an unending series of triumphs with everything from a vulture—apparently the body work on vultures was a snap compared to wild turkeys—to a dog. "Euthanized, the poor old thing," Harriet had said. "The owners were quite pleased, and Erroll topped the class once again." The taxidermy school sounded close to a sweatshop, using students to offer cut-rate pet preservation services.

"Will he . . . when he's finished studying—will he be on his own?" I couldn't recall ever passing a taxidermy shop. Where was the vast reservoir of need for such services?

"We simply don't know that yet," she said. "People come recruiting, but we haven't decided."

I envisioned sober-faced men going to interviews, their briefcases filled with small stuffed creatures—the fur of which Erroll would have finally learned to make glossy and natural-looking. I pictured a résumé stuck with hair and bristles.

"Oh look! I so enjoy talking with you I didn't realize they were done, so here they are!" Harriet handed me the stack of revised exams and the master. She was a great school secretary, and for that I'd listen to anything she wanted to say about Erroll's bright future, and the decimation of wildlife everywhere.

En route back to my classroom, I saw Nita Kloster and Allie Deroche once again in a huddle not far from my—locked—classroom door. What was it about that spot? Their heads were close and their hunched shoulders and hand gestures suggested an intense conversation about something less than pleasant. Either a romance was breaking up, which would necessitate endless analysis and conferencing, or they were disagreeing about details of Friday evening's school party. They were the co-chairs of the committee, and maybe there were unresolved issues such as whether Mischief Night had the same orange-and-black color scheme as Halloween.

They saw me and stopped talking. "You're early for class," I said. "Everything okay?"

They glanced at each other. "Sure. It's too noisy in the lunchroom," Allie said.

I agreed, but nobody under thirty had ever thought so before. "Everything going smoothly with the party?" I asked.

They stared at me and then at each other, as if I'd been unintelligible. I wanted to tell them that it wasn't easy making conversation with them, finding topics other than "Hey, did you steal my exam? And if you did, why on earth would you show it to your classmates? Was it all just to get me?"

Nita and Allie were pretty and poised and part of what constituted the A-list, the elite at Philly Prep. But despite being in the ruling clique, they weren't stereotypical mean-spirited queen bees as far as I could tell. They were amazingly energetic on behalf of the school, and lavished creativity on sport and social events.

Before today, whenever I'd had occasion to mention the party with them, they'd been apt to roll their eyes and list all the logistical problems they were having, so my question seemed natural. Their reaction did not.

"I was wondering," I said, "who's welcome and who's not. I mean, I know outsiders will be there—people can bring dates from other schools, right? But can people who don't go here show up on their own? Are there any ground rules?" I wanted to find out if Pip could come, but I didn't want to ask them outright and make them feel obliged to break rules for me.

I expected their usual no-nonsense responses—these are the rules, period. Instead, they looked even more startled, as if now I'd gone from unintelligible to threatening.

Their eyes widened, their brows lowered. "Why are you asking?" Nita finally asked. "Did somebody say something?"

Now I felt as if we were speaking separate languages.

Allie smiled artificially. "Oh, I heard about Ms. Parillo being sick and you're subbing for her. So you must mean your—*husband*! Of *course* you can bring him."

"Well, I actually meant . . . but if there aren't any problems about extra guests, people who don't go to this school, then okay. Thanks."

Nita still looked troubled, unsure of what I meant. Allie seemed to tilt toward me, as if to hear more clearly. Or even, I thought, to hear what I wasn't saying.

"And how's it going?" I asked. "The preparations and everything?"

"You know," Nita said. "Something always goes wrong."

Allie relaxed her posture. "Nita's such a drama queen. Everything's *fine*." She wagged her finger and pursed her mouth in mock-condemnation of her best friend.

Nita smiled and said nothing. "Absolutely."

We were involved in a charade, only they knew what the actual answer was, and I hadn't a clue.

I looked at my watch. "Showtime," I said.

They groaned. They always groaned, and they were among the best students. "Is the test hard?" Allie asked.

"Not if you paid attention in class and did the assignments." We all smiled ferociously. "Actually, you've still got a few minutes left." I unlocked my door and left the smiling, lying duo in the hallway. It was an effort to not turn around again, to see if—or more likely, to verify that—they were again into the agitated conversation I'd interrupted, a conversation I was sure could explain why my innocuous question about the party had upset them.

The test, of course, still nagged at me. I thought back over who'd had my keys. Nita had gone to the book room for me last week, taking along my ring of keys, most recently when I'd been short one copy of *Oedipus*. She could have duplicated the desk drawer key for future use. It was a big city and we were in the heart of it. There'd be a locksmith somewhere nearby, and I so seldom locked my desk that I wouldn't notice the missing key for days. But logically, since I had never locked up a test before this weekend, and nothing else of value was in my desk, why would she—a good student—or anyone, in fact, go to all that trouble?

She'd gone to the book room for me several times, but so had other students in this and other classes. In fact, I was no longer sure she was the one who'd gone for me last week. And if somebody had, in fact, duplicated the key in advance, how long had this idea been building? And why? Panic over grades as college applications approached was real, and parental expectations were always insanely out of touch with reality. I understood the pressures, but how would this help?

Maybe I'd never locked the drawer. Maybe I imagined it. Maybe before I'd locked the drawer I'd left the room between periods, or during lunch, and somebody had spotted the opportunity, in which case it could be anybody.

I wished I'd said something more about the exam to Nita and Allie, just to see their expressions, their reactions, but now it was too late.

As they entered, the seniors had the sideways-glancing, vaguely frowning faces of a class facing a major test. I wanted to study their expressions as they read the questions—wanted to see who looked shocked or dismayed.

Maybe no one would, because the note itself was a hoax.

Then I laughed at myself, thinking back to today's discussion of *A Separate Peace,* in which Finney refuses to believe World War II is really going on. I was pulling a mini-Finney—and he wound up dead. Literature can be so instructive.

I watched them, making mental notes, and I realized I was preparing a dossier on each student to share with Mackenzie, to get his fix on who the culprit might be.

Two of the students, Erik Steegmuller and Donny Wilson, by chance Allie and Nita's boyfriends, had seemed particularly grim and worried lately. Normally, they considered physical, not necessarily mental, attendance sufficient. Their brains were seas of hormones, with a few basketballs and tennis balls afloat in there.

They weren't history-making stars on the courts, just fine athletes, and in any case, this wasn't the sort of school scouts canvassed. And neither Erik nor Wilson, as he was known, came from families that could generously endow or gift a university. That they were going to have to gain admission by their records alone was apparently a thought that hadn't occurred to them until a few weeks ago. I knew they were now working feverishly with independent college advisors to find a school so desperate that it would want them—in essence, the collegiate equivalent of Philly Prep. But even with such a school, they couldn't afford to fail English.

Today, they seemed cocky, overly self-assured, elbows into the other's side and winks as they found their seats. I'd like to think that was the body language of the insufficiently gifted who might well balance the scales by stealing an exam, except that it was also their normal behavior. They were like ill-trained puppies, only not as cute.

"It isn't fair, you know," redheaded Susan Blackburn

told me in a sweet voice that barely masked the steel within it. "I think it's against the rules."

I wondered if someday I'd find out that Susan had become a lawyer. Philly Prep didn't have that many rules, but she could quote each one of them from memory—especially when it suited her side of the argument. "We just had a test with Dr. Ja—I mean Mr. Reyes."

This semester, the headmaster had instituted a master calendar with the objective of having the staff stagger the schedule of major exams. Apparently, parents had been protesting the burdens on their overworked offspring. Given that this was the least academic private school in the Delaware Valley, possibly in the entire Commonwealth of Pennsylvania, possibly in the solar system, the complete fiction of our students being crushed under the weight of assignments verged on the ludicrous. Nonetheless, nonoverlapping exams were the new rule, and bad luck if you and the math teacher both finished units and wanted to test and move on.

Where is the No Teacher Left Behind program?

Our students, consistently underestimating the faculty's intelligence, played us off against one another, behaving like children ferrying back and forth between parents. "Dad said we could do it if you said it was okay," and so forth. "We already had a test with this other teacher, and the rules say . . . !"

This had been going on since the start of the semester, and it was growing old.

I knew they were lying. Of all the faculty, Juan Angel Reyes would be the last person to break a rule, or to suddenly change his mind and give a test he'd told me he was not giving.

"What kind of exam?" I hoped I sounded only mildly interested.

"Chemistry, of course!" Susan's righteous indignation

was over the top. Her zeal and tone of desperation made it obvious she was toying with the truth.

"No, I meant that it was a pop quiz, wasn't it?" Susan's jaw dropped enough to please me. She was bright and did well, and I didn't even know why she'd protest, except for the sport of it. Definitely going to be a lawyer. I wondered if she already knew that.

Seth Fremont, across the aisle from her, raised his eyebrows and looked amused by the entire performance. Clearly, her plan of attack had been announced in advance. His eyebrows and grin clearly said, "I told you it wouldn't work."

Susan grimaced at him.

Nita, who'd been watching carefully, turned her head so that the back of it was to Seth.

I eyed her carefully. Was she the test thief? She seemed hyperattentive, but I knew her writing, and she surely wasn't the semiliterate tattler.

Maybe nobody I taught was actually that poor a writer. Maybe the note's illiteracy was a disguise.

Maybe Nita had taken the test to help out her boyfriend, Erik. She didn't need to steal anything, but love does strange things to people.

Still, it bothered me even more to think that the brightest students in the class were the ones behaving most oddly. "Mr. Reyes wouldn't break the rules," I said, pushing my advantage.

Allie's eyebrows shot up and she rolled her eyeballs up as close to the brows as she could get. She looked like a comic-book drawing of incredulity. "Oh yes he would. *He* breaks the rules a lot." Her words—a challenge, a taunt— were spoken in a stage whisper designed to reach me.

It reached everyone. I heard a snort of laughter from the right side of the room, and saw more eye-rolling.

"In the mornings, he breaks the rules." Wilson sang the

lines as if they were the lyrics to a familiar folk tune, but he sang softly, as if he—almost—didn't want me to hear.

"*They* break the rules. Miss Banks, too."

Of course I wanted to know more. Tisha Banks was a student teacher in art. I'd heard that in September Louis Applegate had tried his luck with her and failed. Was it possible that one month later she was intensely involved with Juan Angel Reyes? Why didn't I know these things— and how did they? And precisely what rules were they breaking in the mornings? *Those* rules?

I wanted to say, "Tell all." But I was the teacher, they were the students, and gossip was neither appropriate— much to my sorrow—nor on the curriculum. So I had to pretend to be as naïve and oblivious as they thought I was and squelch their merriment by giving out the revised exam.

We'd completed a unit on Greek drama, reading the Oedipus cycle: *Oedipus Rex, Oedipus at Colonus,* and *Antigone.* They'd seemed to enjoy and comprehend the plays, and the discussions—until the great sullen freeze set in—were animated and thoughtful, which made any motive behind stealing the exam even murkier.

Now, as I spoke briefly about the test, the clique's members, "the team" as they called themselves, exchanged glances, as if reaffirming that they were all there—Erik and Wilson, Nita and Allie, Seth, Jimmy, Mark, and Susan.

With all their foibles, I loved this group. Even in a school like ours, where the word *academic* was . . . academic and generally irrelevant, our sports leagues were insignificant in the larger scheme of school athletics. We rated the tiniest notices in the newspaper, if we rated at all. Still, these were our stars, and what they lacked in scholastic ambition, they made up for with good nature and humor—or used to. They played off each other, on the courts or off, and the result was a comfortable sense of goodwill.

This was why the suggestion that they'd been maliciously conniving sat so poorly with me, and why the sense of subterranean conflict was so upsetting.

I scanned the room as I spoke. Nobody looked particularly worried or anxious. In fact, at least half a dozen students didn't even look interested. I would have liked to ascribe this to guilt, to having memorized the pilfered test, but in truth, the combination of apathy and senior cool made displays of anxiety almost nonexistent. One might show hostility, but not fear, be angry with a teacher and her exam, be furious about the way the world worked—e.g., college admissions—but that was not the same as worrying about one's performance on any given exam.

They settled down quickly with a final flurry of desk-clearing and pen-retrieving and then sighed and began the exam. I wished I had the leisure to truly study each of the twenty faces in the room as it studied the paper in front of it. Instead, I glanced and scanned.

Perhaps I did it too obviously. Perhaps the guilty party observed my actions, saw the exam, grasped what had happened, and remained expressionless. But it all looked normal: scowls, sighs, head scratches, and nothing incriminating.

Nothing, that is, until Nita gave Seth a look of pure fury. He in turn looked startled, then openly confused. Her eyes glanced back to the examination paper, and then to him. And then, with a final slow head shake, her expression a mix of disgust and surprised betrayal, she settled down to the task at hand.

If I'd been a more Victorian type, I would have swooned. Seth Fremont simply wasn't the type to steal an exam and, like Susan, Nita, and Allie, he'd have no need. Less need than anybody else in his class, in fact. I looked at my grade book, to unnecessarily confirm what I already knew—that he had an A average so far, and I knew this wasn't an aberration. He'd always been an outstanding student. Plus, he was captain of the tennis team, and he'd been the star of the student production of *Our Town* last year. Seth was the real thing, the student you think about on discouraged days. He was here because his parents had recognized that he needed a smaller class size than the public schools afforded, and Philly Prep was an easy walk from his home. So why would he pilfer an exam? To impress his peers? But as far as I could see, he was well liked. He didn't have to curry favor.

Was some substance messing with his synapses? I so did not want to think about that.

I watched as the class concentrated, biting their lips, swallowing hard, looking blankly toward the windows as if asking for divine intervention and, to my painful sorrow and increasing confusion, first Erik, then Jimmy, looked over to Seth, both with expressions that suggested they wanted to strangle him.

For forty-five minutes, I watched young faces grimace and stare into space. I didn't know how many of them found their answers, but I do know that I found none, only growing panic about the need for one.

Five

THE REST OF THE SCHOOL DAY PASSED UNEVENTFULLY, BUT my spirits and energy were low and the minutes seemed made of slowly melting tar. At times, it feels too difficult finding a balance on the periphery of teens' confusing and confused lives. Sometimes it feels like being a long-term uninvited guest; other times, like being a fellow prisoner.

Finally, the bell rang and my room emptied with undue speed. The students were obviously having no more fun than I was.

Juan Reyes's classroom was on the other side of the hall from mine, and he was passing my room as I left it. I greeted him, considering him in a new way, given the snickers about trysts with the young student teacher.

His return nod was brisk and businesslike. "Miss Pepper," he said. I wondered if he'd always been so excessively correct and unbending, or if two months of Philly Prep disappointment had been enough to harden him.

He wasn't one to share in the dark humor of the teaching staff. At the end of a bone-tiring day, what else is there to do but laugh, but Reyes had so far never shown even a trace of humor. I wanted to warn the student teacher that no matter how handsome a man is—and Juan Angel Reyes was quite elegantly crafted—he wasn't going to make a great partner if he had no sense of humor.

Even if we couldn't laugh about it, now that I'd been

subjected to some of the same whatever-it-was by the seniors, I wanted to talk with him, to commiserate, speculate, and maybe together comprehend what neither of us could manage separately. I smiled and paused, but he passed me.

Okay, I'd force sociability on him. "Do you have a minute?" I asked as he reached the top of the staircase. I wasn't certain whether he was a loner—with the rumored exception of the student teacher—if he was shy or awkward, and hadn't found a way to feel a part of the staff, or if, as his demeanor suggested, he simply had no time for the likes of us.

He'd have been a wonderful model or department store mannequin. He looked right, dressed beautifully, and was completely appealing until he spoke. And then his manner of delivery and that startling lack of humor erased the possibilities he had from a distance.

He carried a small stack of textbooks in one arm and held his briefcase with his free hand, but Juan Angel Reyes was nothing if not a gentleman. He struggled to rebalance his load in order to shake my hand. "Please, no," I said. "The books—"

My fears were immediately realized as chemistry workbooks toppled to the floor. We both stooped to gather them up, and he apologized profusely. He was U.S.-born and raised, but he had an Old World and, in fact, old century, set of manners.

"How was today?" I asked when we were reassembled. "Any better?" Selfish of me, but I wanted to know if I'd become part of a spreading malaise, or if the seniors had turned their pranks—I hoped that was all they were—on me, if it was now my turn.

His lips set, he shook his head.

No better. I was ashamed to admit that gave me some relief. "The seniors again?"

"Perhaps it's because I'm new and they feel like the kings of the mountain. Perhaps I don't understand how to keep control the way I would wish and they take advantage. This is not, I realize, a college classroom. Not a place that these people necessarily want to be, and not a subject they necessarily want to learn. Physics, maybe, if I could make them see how it applied to ball games, but other than that, they are too cocky about being important in this tiny fishpond. About being seniors. Nothing is worth taking seriously."

"Did something happen today?"

He sighed. "They talked a lot about Mischief Night," he said. "It felt . . . it seemed some kind of warning."

"Directed at you?"

He stood even taller and looked ready to deny such a ridiculous idea. But then he exhaled sharply, shook his head, and said, "I'm not certain."

"I'm sure the talk was about the party Friday night."

He sighed and shrugged. "Yes, I understand. But they . . . I was thinking of attending, to see what this is all about, and then I heard them deliberately . . ."

"Yes?"

"They said some people weren't welcome."

"To you?" I was astounded.

He shook his head. "No, no. Pretended not to have even heard me. They said it to each other, those tennis girls. The ones in charge of everything. But they said it so others would hear, meaning me, I am certain."

"Did they say any more?"

He looked tired, older than his years. "Nothing specific. And I was still angry about the rotating supplies—about the arrogance of that class's behavior. Today it was pipettes again, but I still don't know how. I keep my supplies in the back, in the prep room, and students go there only with permission."

Or so he had to believe despite all evidence to the contrary.

"I questioned the class, of course, and you know that blank look?"

The same look that had me so depressed. I'm not sure fully matured adults can replicate that look. Perhaps you have to feel unfairly subservient, the student facing the teacher, to passively resist by removing your actual self, leaving only the shell.

"I cannot tolerate this behavior! A chemistry lab has many potential dangers, and ultimately, I'm responsible. No matter what the reason . . ."

He continued to lecture about student responsibility, the need to grow up—about a whole lot of things that didn't apply to me. I knew he felt overwhelmed, but I was a peer. I could only imagine what tone he adopted for the students.

"—discipline needs to be maintained for the good of all and that's why a strict inventory and safety standards are mandatory, not optional. I—"

"Mr. Reyes, I understand."

He seemed to actually notice me then, and he stopped midsentence. And then started up again on another track. "What is the justification for a night devoted to mischief?" he asked without slowing for a response. "There was no such night where I grew up, and I find the idea reprehensible. Teens today have enough bad paths to follow without there being an official date on which to misbehave! What's wrong with this city to have something like that?" He scowled, as if I had created the tradition purely in order to spite him.

"I think—I know—it goes beyond Philadelphia. It has an ancient origin, the way Halloween does, and had to do with ghosts rising from the dead."

"Pshaw!" He waved away my words. "Ancient superstition! Is that an excuse for tormenting fellow human beings?"

"I can see you definitely do feel tormented," I said. Maybe sympathy and a smidge of psychology would get him to ease up.

Wrong. He looked even more furious, albeit in his contained, ready to explode way. "Is it my imagination that there was a so-called accident—acid in my briefcase!"

"That's awful—how? When?"

"While I was in the hallway between classes. Aren't we supposed to be out here? Monitoring the passageways?"

I nodded, feeling guilty because I so seldom made it outside my room between classes. Somebody was always asking a question, or I was busy writing on the board, preparing for the next class.

"Right in this briefcase!"

"Is it—was much harmed?"

He pursed his mouth again and shook his head. "It's still intact and nothing was crucially damaged, but it's the principle. The desecration of property! Who does such things that make no sense?" He cleared his throat and, without moving, seemed to smooth out his clothing and his hair. "Forgive me. It is kind of you to worry about me when you have problems of your own," he said in a softer but still flat tone.

Had he heard about the exam? Or was this simply a bit of conventional speech, part of his ingrained sense of manners? "Not really," I said. "I'm sorry you're having such a bad time."

"The other classes—also sloppy thinkers, but not malicious. But the seniors . . . all I can think of is to punish the entire class. Maybe then they'll be sufficiently upset to turn the guilty party over to me."

There were many things wrong with his proposed course of action. First, it didn't go with his professed desire not to dignify their actions by noticing them. Second, it's pretty much what Stalin and Hitler did to recalcitrant villages, and I've never been eager to use them as mentors. And third, on a personal level, I had a teacher who did that when I was in eighth grade, and her actions stuck with me as an example of what might make me hate a teacher. Whatever the lesson was she had in mind, whatever we were supposed to collectively have learned is long lost, but not my outrage for being punished for something I hadn't done and knew nothing about.

"I don't think it would work," I said. "They're really good friends. I think they'd rather all go down in flames."

"What then? My authority is being undermined. I tried telling the headmaster last week. He was no help and in fact I'm not sure what he actually told me. I couldn't follow him. It was quite strange."

No surprise there. "Unfortunately, the best you could hope for from Havermeyer would be a flurry of meaningless activity resulting in a flyer telling students in semi-academic gobbledygook that it's bad to steal or to torment people, and that chemicals belong in the laboratory because they can be dangerous. Or maybe an assembly in which he pretty much said the same thing, but took an hour to do so."

I'd forgotten again how humor-challenged he was. He solemnly digested my words. "Given those circumstances, what does one do?" he asked gravely.

Time for me to unbend even if he wouldn't, to be honest with him, although being around the man was like snow-shoeing through the Arctic tundra. I told him about my sense that something was going on, and about my stolen examination.

"Ah," he said with great sorrow. Perhaps misery didn't love company, and there was no comfort in numbers, simply greater depression and confusion.

I wondered how a man could stand that straight and tall, holding a briefcase and books, and yet look defeated. "Are you familiar with St. Cassian of Imola?" he suddenly asked.

"I'm afraid saints aren't my area of expertise."

"I'd never heard about him, either," he said. "And saints were part of my expertise. St. Cassian isn't widely known. But I got this in my mailbox at noon. I would like to think of it as another prank, although I am sick of that word." He put his books down on the floor, opened his briefcase and pulled out a sheet of plain paper, a computer print-out with the saint's name in large letters that had a slash through them, and beneath them, as a sort of correction, THE SPANISH INQUISITOR.

"I know that's what they call me, because I gave them a hard test," he said. "They think they are sly and devious, but I know." He shook his head. "They also call me Dr. Jar because of my initials. They apparently find that very funny. But The Spanish Inquisitor at least shows some intelligence, a comprehension of history, even though I am not Spanish. I was born in Massachusetts."

"Maybe you should continue to ignore all of it and hope it really does have to do with Mischief Night."

I knew that what I said was unlikely. The tradition was dying out and it was Mischief Night, not Mischief Week, and surely not a two-month torment for a teacher.

"I went online and looked him up," Reyes said.

"Who?"

"St. Cassian."

I'd forgotten about him.

"He was martyred."

"Weren't all the saints martyred?"

"He was a martyred teacher."

Not good.

"His students hacked him to death."

Really not good. As was the idea that our unscholarly pupils had done research and had ferreted out this martyred teacher so as to torture their chemistry teacher.

"It's even worse than that. Nobody was allowed to actually kill him, only to cut. They had to keep their hackings minor, so that death would take longer and be more painful."

"That's . . ."

"I will tell you what that is. That is what this job feels like to me. Little cuts—more and more little cuts until you bleed to death if you stay long enough. As if it isn't bad enough trying to teach people who don't give a damn about learning. Then this—the death of a thousand cuts—that's what the whole thing feels like. Hack, hack, hack! The lying, the stealing, the false alarms, the covering up for each other—and this threat!" Again, he waved the sheet of paper.

"I'm sure it wasn't meant to be taken literally."

He seemed ready to protest; then he sighed and nodded. "Maybe not, but it was meant as another nonlethal cut. All I tried to do is teach them." He shoved the paper back into his briefcase, nodded to me, and walked toward the staircase, but paused again. "Are you sure you are all right yourself?"

"Me?" I thought about that misspelled note, about the locked-drawer puzzle. "I'm upset, of course."

"I would be, too," he said. "If something like that happened to me."

I did a double take. Hadn't something precisely like that happened to him? "I don't understand. You told me this morning, and then now—things like the stolen test *have* been happening to you."

"Stolen test?"

"Isn't that what we're talking about?"

His eyes opened wider than they'd been, but his lips now

held tightly closed for too long a pause, as if he were thinking something through. "I apologize," he finally said. "It's
obvious I misspoke."

"About what?"

"No, no. I should not have . . . Undoubtedly, it means it
was a tempest in a teapot and it is now all over and it is
only my inexperience that made me think it was anything
more than that." He looked at his watch and *tsk*ed. "And
now I must leave. I have a meeting with my dissertation ad-
visor quite soon."

"Wait! What's over? What tempest in what teapot?"

He walked down several steps, then he turned halfway.
"If you haven't heard, then it's nothing, and it was never
anything, and I am not a bearer of tales." He paused for a
second, his mouth pursed once more, and I was almost
convinced he was preparing a lecture for me about how a
chemistry teacher must never tell tales. Instead, he shook
his head, turned back, and made his deliberate way down
the marble staircase. He walked with his customary dignity, or rigidity, and with no excess speed, but I nevertheless had the distinct feeling he was running away from me
as quickly as he could.

I watched his silhouette as he reached the door, one arm
cradling the stack of books, the briefcase in the other.

His poor acid-burned briefcase. What was wrong with
those kids? As if it needed reassurance, I patted my own
briefcase with my free hand, promising it that I wouldn't
allow a drop of anything foreign to touch it.

Except that I was patting my pocketbook. I looked to
verify that there was no other strap on my right or left
shoulder.

With a surge of relief, I remembered that I had given up
on a briefcase per se and was experimenting with a backpack, especially on days I walked to school. I had obvi-

ously left the classroom too quickly in order to speak with Jar.

Good thing I'd noticed before I'd walked all the way home.

I went back into my room and saw the backpack on the floor beside my desk. Given Reyes's story of acid in his briefcase, I felt compelled to peer inside, double-checking that everything was there, unharmed.

I had been holding the green plastic envelope with the seniors' exams the entire time, so that was no problem. I saw folders for various classes, and all looked in place.

Except for my attendance book. I looked at my desk, where it sits most periods. I looked at the green plastic folder I'd been carrying.

I checked the entire room, the insides of each desk, which was foolish, since I would never have left it there, and disheartening because I found some objects I'd be happier not having seen.

I checked under my desk, in each of the drawers, then went back into the hallway to see if I'd dropped it out there.

It was nowhere. Whatever was going on now included me, and nothing had slowed or played itself out. Instead, whatever it was had escalated.

We'd gone from bad to much worse.

Six

THE WALK HOME DID NOTHING TO CLEAR MY HEAD DE-
spite the delicious autumn snap in the air. I was tired, worried, and feeling put-upon.

Apparently, Pip's travels hadn't energized him, either. I
was surprised to find him already home, worried to note
that his normally alarming energy level seemed to have flat-
lined, annoyed, finally, to realize that once again he'd spent
the day slouched on the sofa, watching TV.

Macavity sat atop the set, watching Pip and keeping his
opinions to himself. There was, I suppose, a sort of cama-
raderie in their mutual staring.

"How was your day?" I asked as I settled myself back
into home.

"Fine, I guess."

He was not having a great time, then, but maybe that
was good. Maybe being unmoored was becoming less appealing. "What did you do?"

"Not much."

"See anything interesting?"

"Not really."

I picked up the list of sights and outings I'd so carefully
crafted for him, wondering how pathetic or onerous he
found it. "So . . . did you go out today at all?" I asked.

He nodded, his eyes still on the screen where a golden-haired boy on a skateboard defied the laws of physics. "For lunch," he said. "The burger place up the street."

I kept silent because what else was there to say but that an expensive trek from Iowa to Philadelphia for the sake of comparative burger-tasting did not make sense. Why run away—even if sanctioned—and not explore the place you ran to? Was simply not being home enough?

"How was the burger?" I finally managed. "We haven't tried that place yet." To be honest, aside from our need to pinch every penny, the place was so unimpressive-looking that I thought its sign should say, "Go home and enjoy a decent meal."

He shrugged, his eyes on the TV. "Okay, I guess."

Was he depressed? He hadn't seemed that way till now. Dramatically heartbroken, yes, because of Bunny Brookings, but still . . . I was formulating diplomatic questions that would help me know whether we had to get help when he pointed at the TV. "See that?" he asked me.

I looked at the screen, saw that the skateboarder had been replaced by a bungee jumper, and looked back at Pip.

"His tail," he said. "The cat's tail. Macavity's. He's doing it on purpose. Not just putting it on the screen, but I think he's watching where my eyes are and he puts his tail right there."

What a smart cat to do that during high-speed athletic feats. What great eye-tail coordination. But anybody who was ever owned by a cat knows they feel obliged to cover up the object of your attention if it is anything besides the cat itself.

"I got up twice and moved his tail and he waited till I was sitting back down and put it right there—right in the middle of the screen. And then he flicked it and left it dangling." Pip smiled and gave the cat a thumbs-up.

He wasn't depressed. Relief.

"He's doing it because he can," he said. "Just because he can."

I agreed, and with skateboarders, bungee jumpers, and my cat continuing to display Annoying Sports Tricks, I started dinner. Meals were different with Pip in the house. I found myself reviewing each part of the menu against a "healthy enough for a growing teenaged boy" list. And that clashed with the "is this enough like a burger to appeal to that boy?" I knew he'd find the roast chicken, salad, and rice sadly lacking.

Too bad, then. You leave home, you're supposed to be ready to suffer for your freedom. And with the chicken roasting and the rest of dinner ready for final prep, I had an hour, so I settled in with the seniors' exams.

This was possibly the fastest I'd ever marked tests—reading with furious urgency, then entering the grades on a sheet of notepaper, feeling a hot wash of anger and misery with each reminder that somebody else had my roll book, which meant as well the grades for all my classes and therefore, a goodly portion of my brain. I'd write down a grade, then try to gauge how closely it might have resembled the student's existing record. Of course, with school in session a mere two months, I didn't have a profound knowledge of any given student's margin of error, of how they might do on a bad day or a particularly good one. Or on one when they'd thought they knew every question on the exam beforehand.

Nonetheless, my first reaction was surprise, and then a conviction that I must have misgraded the papers. But even when double-checked, even without any accurate listing of prior marks, the seniors' test results looked absolutely normal.

I'd made the retest as difficult and as different from the original as I could, but within minor variations, the bell-shaped curve was so perfect, you could almost hear it

chime. The twelfth graders who'd scraped by in the past—
Donny Wilson among them—still barely squeaked into the
passing zone, the handful of A students retained their places
of honor, and the people in the middle were still there.

And Seth, at whom so many fierce and furious glances
had been aimed, was precisely where I'd expect him to
be—on the small incline of those receiving A's, along with
Susan and Nita.

I couldn't decide how to interpret this, if it was proof of
his guilt—somebody else's guilt—or precisely the opposite,
and I finally had to declare a hung jury, proof of nothing. I
emotionally shuffled back to square one and tried to lose
my churning thoughts by chopping vegetables for the salad.

Several inane shows later, when the TV was blessedly
silent and Mackenzie was home, the oak table no longer
held senior exams but instead our dinner. Pip, not surprisingly, didn't have much to offer in the way of conversation.
I didn't want to ask for a critique of the greasy hamburger
place down the block or whose TV whirly or slide or leap
was best, or which *Happy Days* rerun was most engaging.

Mackenzie's day of detection wasn't much more engaging, and he had nothing to satisfy Pip's yearning for tales of
blood and gore. He'd done his moonlighting in the morning, staring at a patio, and his biggest problem had been
trying to stay awake.

That meant I'd be staring at that patio tomorrow after
school. Soon, the money the insurance company was willing to pay for the unproductive staring would dry up. Berta
Polley would be given her disability payments.

Mackenzie sliced off a piece of chicken, complimented
the chef, and paused with it speared on his fork. "It is actually possible that she's disabled." He slowly shook his
head. Somebody telling the truth, his expression seemed to
say. Wonders would never cease.

I in turn told them about the tenth grade's poetry performance. Pip listened politely, but it was obvious that the word *poetry* was a hot-button reminder of reasons to never return to school.

"How was that other class?" Mackenzie took a second helping of salad. Pip stared at the silent TV. "The one making you antsy. Better today?"

"Worse. Somebody stole—"

"Hey!" Pip said, interested again.

Another thing that takes getting used to is that extra set of ears—human, not cat—processing whatever you said in what you used to consider the privacy of your own home.

"Don't they know not to steal from a PI?" Pip said. "Are they that stupid?"

I enjoyed the return of his animation, and I was flattered, but I am not a licensed PI yet, and I once again tried to explain my apprentice status, that I not only worked with Mackenzie, but for him. "Your uncle was able to be licensed immediately because of having been a cop, but I actually—"

"What did they steal?" Mackenzie asked.

"An exam," I said. "And then my roll book. But I don't know if it was the same person."

Pip slumped down again. A test! No masked men scaling buildings, disarming alarm systems, taking hostages . . .

"Sorry," I said. "It isn't exciting, I know, but it's upsetting."

He looked embarrassed to be caught out so easily. Then he got himself back on topic. "The thief—what did you do to him?"

"That is not good detecting," C.K. said. "You've leaped to the conclusion it's a 'him.' Don't make assumptions. Keep an open mind."

Pip nodded solemnly, as if he'd just heard word from on high.

"In any case, I didn't do a thing," I said, "because I don't know who took it. I heard in time and I made up a new exam."

I told them about the anonymous note, and I told them about the new test version and the reaction it produced.

"Grade them," Pip said. I thought he was trying to reinstate himself as a sleuth. "The one who does poorly is the thief."

"If past history's any indication, there's likely to be more than one doin' poorly," Mackenzie said with a wink.

"But a good theory all the same," I added. "Nonetheless, I've already marked them, while you were watching TV, and . . ." I shook my head. "The grades fell out the way they always do. Or I think so. As I said, my grade book's missing."

Pip showed increased interest. "You know who did it, don't you?" His words sounded more a hope than a question.

I shook my head. "I don't know anything for sure."

"Not for sure? That's what people say when they have a strong suspicion," Mackenzie said, and again Pip nodded. If he'd had a notebook with him, he'd have written the words down. "You have a theory, then?" Mackenzie asked.

I didn't want to give credence to the looks of outraged betrayal his classmates had shot at Seth when they saw what was written on the exam. That wasn't proof of anything.

"Why would somebody show a stolen exam to the entire class? I mean, if he wanted to do better, why give everybody the same advantage?" Pip asked.

"I don't understand that, either. The whole thing is confusing, and apparently I'm not the only one confusing things are happening to." I told them Juan Reyes's story.

Pip folded in his bottom lip and concentrated. "Anybody maybe angry with somebody else? A feud going on?"

Mackenzie raised an eyebrow, but said nothing.

"Because . . . since it doesn't make sense, maybe it—like it doesn't have to do with itself. Like there's another whole reason, like revenge."

"Against teachers?"

"Maybe. Maybe not. Maybe against each other."

"Interestin'." I could see Mackenzie seriously consider his nephew's smarts for the first time.

"Why are you shaking your head?" Pip asked me.

I hadn't realized I was. "I was thinking about feuds," I said, "but a lot of the people in that class, boys and girls, are buddies, on the same team, cheerleaders, girlfriends, boyfriends. The chemistry teacher talks about them as a group: the tennis boys and their girls."

"People jealous of them, maybe?" Pip asked.

I could only shrug. "I haven't heard . . . the thing I'm afraid of is that . . . well, since the test and the grade book . . . that they're angry with me." It pained me to say that, suggested failure on some enormous scale.

"And the chemistry teacher," Mackenzie reminded me.

I shrugged, thinking of that laced-up man and the grumbles I'd heard, the evidence I'd seen of his rigidity. They well might be angry with him. But wonderful, terrific me?

"No disrespect meant," Pip said, "but you're a teacher, and teachers don't know half of what's actually going on."

Not half of it? I didn't know any of it. I didn't even know what *it* was.

I didn't even try to tackle whatever problem I had to which Reyes had so cryptically alluded. I couldn't stand it that I was troubled by so many unknowns I couldn't even discuss them coherently.

We were pushing back from the table, the meal over. Pip and Mackenzie carried plates to the sink. I heard a soft plop and looked up to see Macavity resettled atop the TV, hoping, perhaps, that the end-of-dinner sounds meant someone would turn the tube on and once again provide him with his heating pad. Nobody was looking his way except me. I noticed that this time his tail was curled around himself and not dangling over the blank screen.

Pip's observation returned to me. The cat dangled his tail when he wanted to simply because he could. A test and chemicals and pipettes and a roll book could be missing to present the same message: I can do this if I want to.

Maybe it was all about demonstrating power.

Pip turned from the sink. "I've got the best idea," he said, his eyebrows raised. That plus his hair, spiked unnaturally, made him look as if he'd been electrocuted.

We waited.

"Let me work undercover at your school, and I'll find out who's doing what. They won't suspect me. I'm a kid like them."

We looked at him in silence. Aside from the legal ramifications, I envisioned Pip wiggling into school, thinking he'd be unnoticed. The skinny country boy from Iowa who, despite trying overly hard to look citified, all but still had hayseeds in his hair spikes. "Interesting idea," I finally said. "But I thought you said you hated school."

"Not if I was working it."

"Wouldn't you have to do schoolwork? Don't you think people would get suspicious of a newbie slinking around the halls, peeping and listening?"

"I wouldn't do that! I'd be cool—inconspicuous."

"You're a junior—or would be, if you'd stayed in school," Mackenzie said softly. "We're talkin' seniors. You'd be in a different class, a whole year behind. You know how it is, don't you? They'd barely speak to you."

He looked stricken.

Good. Let him realize he was too young and unequipped to be loose in the world or to qualify for any of his fantasized professions. Let him mull the ramifications of deciding to go out on his own at age sixteen. Meanwhile,

I changed the topic. "You know that party on Friday? I asked about it today." I suddenly remembered the confusion my question produced in Nita and Allie, and Reyes's overheard comment that "some people aren't welcome." They couldn't mean Pip. "If you want to spy then, pick up on whatever you can, that'd be fine."

His brow furrowed, trying to decide whether this would be a worthy or humiliating opportunity.

"Your uncle and I might be there," I added.

His frown deepened. "Do I need a costume?"

"It's optional."

"We're going disguised as chaperones," Mackenzie said. "Amanda's wearing a drab suit with a long drab skirt—brown, I think it has to be—and funny shoes and her hair pulled back in a knot, and I—"

"A suit. Kind of Clark Kent, right?" Pip said. "No offense—I think your idea . . . it isn't good. You'll both just look . . . well, as if you aren't in costume, you're just—"

"Stupid chaperones," Mackenzie said. "Out-of-it old people. Yes, that is the point."

The phone rang. I was already standing, so I answered it. Silence.

"Hello?" I said again. "Hello?"

A throat clearing.

"I'm hanging up," I said.

"Miss . . . Pepper? I . . ." The voice, thin and squeaky, grew ever more attenuated until I couldn't tell whether he—she?—was still trying to speak or not.

"Are you there? I can't hear you. What is it? Who is it?"

"I . . . Please, I'm sorry, I . . ." And in the background, somebody shouting something like "Do it!" and then another voice, lower, more adult, but unintelligible.

And then click and silence.

"Who was that?" Mackenzie asked.

"I have no idea. We should have gotten caller ID. No,

that's wrong—it was a student. Somebody who would call me Miss Pepper. And who was upset—and apologetic. Sorry about something. But then they hung up. Somebody else was in the room, and then, I think, somebody else again."

"Maybe they got scared," Mackenzie said.

"Or they didn't want whoever came in to hear what they would say," Pip said.

I looked at him with new respect. That made sense. Nothing was to be said in front of the adult. The witness.

But nothing said about what? I was so tired of having unending questions and no answers.

Seven

I BEGAN THE NEXT DAY WITH GREAT RESOLVE AND A MAJOR attitude readjustment.

I'd talked with Mackenzie late into the night, in the privacy of our room, and he'd helped me understand that I had lost objectivity and was seeing ghosts and goblins even before Halloween. I was working much too hard to force random and unexceptional happenings—a look, a prank, girlfriends disagreeing with each other, another teacher's power struggle with a class, a pilfered exam, stupid jokes—all fit together into one negative picture.

No more making myself crazy that way, I decided. I was going to step back, observe, and refrain from leaping to conclusions until I saw what in fact was going on.

If anything was.

I hoped Pip would go out and do something today—despite the rain—but if he wanted to stare at the TV, so be it. That, too, was depressingly ordinary and not something to worry over.

Right now, normal reigned—and rained—and began with the fact that I couldn't find a parking space. There's the semblance of a faculty lot behind the school, but we're in the city where real estate's dear and free parking rare; so the space barely holds half the faculty's cars. There's no provision for the overflow except messages from Maurice

Havermeyer urging carpooling, public transit, or the healthful benefits of hoofing it.

His suggestions are valid for both ecology and health, but they are less than appealing when you don't live close to anyone else on the faculty and you have to go on surveillance after school and more so when it's raining.

And when one spot is always reserved for him.

Early as I was, there were no more spaces behind the school. I circled the block, then made wider circles until finally, in despair, I parked three blocks away. Only then did I realize I'd left my umbrella home.

I speed-walked through the downpour, nostalgic for yesterday's brilliant autumn colors and weather. Today, the sky was gunmetal and rain flailed the trees, ripping off red and yellow leaves which, on the sidewalk, became slippery traps.

I broke into a careful trot, one hand holding my backpack over my head. My hair dripped down my neck inside the raincoat as I crossed the street—jaywalking or, more accurately, jayrunning—and headed into the narrow driveway that ran behind the school, resenting every one of the car owners who'd made it to safe harbor.

I stopped when I stepped on glass.

Juan Reyes's Toyota was old but lovingly—one might even say obsessively—maintained, but now its left headlight was smashed.

It had obviously happened here, while the car was parked. Despite the rain—I was too drenched to care—I paused and looked back over his car, as if I'd find clues to who'd smashed the headlight. I found none, of course, but saw jagged marks near his door handle. He'd been keyed.

J A R had been cut into the waxed paint. A crude and ugly monogram.

It was difficult squelching the return of the anxiety. Actually, impossible. It didn't matter if I liked the man. I felt sorry for him. I wasn't overreacting. This was too much.

Once inside, I walked through clusters of students, all hiding from the rain, into the office, shaking myself out like a puppy.

Harriet's eyes were wide behind the horn rims. "Oooooh," she said, "somebody got caught in the storm! Remember—it's just liquid sunshine!"

I understood that hostile expression about wiping a grin off somebody's face and I clenched my fists to keep from doing so.

She smiled. "Have a good day, anyway!" She sounded as if she really meant it, as if each day were a completely new start wherein anything good was not only possible, but probable. That was undoubtedly how she'd endured a dozen years of Erroll.

"You don't happen to have a towel around, do you?"

"There are paper towels in the—"

I imagined my head plastered with them—instant papier-mâché. "Thanks, but never mind. Meanwhile, did anybody turn in a roll book?"

"Are teachers supposed to turn in—"

"I mean, did anybody find one? And then bring it to you?"

"Yours?"

I nodded. Rainwater dribbled down my face.

"Oh, my. That's bad. That's really bad, but no. Nothing. I'll keep my eyes peeled for it." I pulled off my raincoat. The damp had wormed its way through to my bone marrow.

I waited for Harriet, Havermeyer's emissary, to broach the amorphous "thing" to which Reyes had alluded but refused to describe. But Harriet didn't look about to spring bad news on me. She didn't even have the grieving and pitying expression I was sure she'd wear if she were keeping an unpleasant secret from me.

Harriet didn't know about it. I'd have to ask him myself, as soon as I collected whatever lurked in my mailbox, starting with the inevitable bulletin from Maurice Havermeyer, who believed these daily wastes of paper fulfilled his administrative duties.

"Today," his message said, "as the calendar indicates the autumnal proximity of the traditional trick-or-treat ambience of Halloween and the appropriately named Mischief Night, it behooves us all to be on the watchout for those who are apt to pervert the spirit of the season and it would not be amiss in addition to so instruct your students as well, both for observation of their surrounds and for considerations of their own behavior."

What the devil did he mean? Havermeyer's verbosity always tempts me to find a red pencil and give him a failing grade.

English teachers are probably to blame for the Havermeyers of the world. "Write a five-hundred-word essay," we have been known to say, without adding: make each word necessary to clearly express your meaning. In essence, we ask for bulk, not content, so padding and redundancy get built into the system.

I wondered what he meant by being on the *watchout*. Should we carry binoculars? Arm ourselves? Consider anybody in a mask—even on Halloween—a risk? And couldn't he call it a *lookout* the way anybody else would—or did he choose *watch* because it had five letters to *look*'s four? For all the sense of what his message meant, he might as well have declared the school on orange alert. It was the color of the season in any case.

I scooped up the rest of the contents of my mailbox, tossed the meaningless directive, and was about to leave when Harriet issued a loud "Ta-*da!*" and I wheeled around.

She'd placed an enormous pumpkin on the divider-counter. It had a have-a-nice-day face painted on it and a black pointed hat atop a black wig.

My mother-in-law would not have liked that effigy of witchdom one bit. Bad hairdo, orange face, ugly hat.

"What do you think?" Harriet said. "Seasonal and jolly enough? I wanted to get all of us into the spirit."

"Are you going to the party? Bringing Erroll?" It would be fun to see the taxidermist in person. In my mind, he'd become one of his specimens, stuffed and mounted on a simulated lawn.

"Wish I could," she said, with a shake of her hair, "but what with Erroll making up for when he had the flu, and his groundhog due any minute now . . ."

"A real pity," I said. "Some other time, then." I turned to leave, but then I remembered the half dozen letters of recommendation I had to write, and that starting those letters was item number four on today's list of chores, tonight's after-dinner activity. I was going to try once again to avoid the December letter-writing crunch. "Could I have a dozen sheets of letterhead?"

College application time had officially begun when the school year did, but Philly Prep students weren't the most forward-thinking young people. A month from now, they'd be rushing in to ask for recommendations, and by winter break, they'd be in a state of crazed delirium asking not only for the letters but for help with their essays.

And if they weren't panicked by then, their parents definitely would be. Many sacrificed New Year's Eve plans, watching the clock count down to a midnight deadline while they all but guided the hand of a young person who professed to want college, but not if it involved writing an essay.

I try not to take their aversion to expressing themselves on paper personally. I do, however, find it amusing that those same writing-averse seniors are apt to ask me, their English teacher, for a recommendation.

But a handful of students had somehow known to play it smart and endearingly early, and had given me a decent lead time along with envelopes addressed to each of the colleges on their lists. I had every hope of being as organized and efficient as they were.

"No problem," Harriet said, and I once more felt the thrill of obtaining supplies without begging. In years and secretaries past, I'd gotten really good at wheedling, but I was not sorry to give up that acquired talent.

Harriet opened a drawer. "It must be hard writing all those letters. I remember when Erroll was applying . . ."

I found it difficult to believe that taxidermy school required academic letters of recommendation, but what did I know?

Harriet held up a single sheet of paper. "That's odd. I would have sworn I had a good-sized pile of letterhead right where it belongs in that top drawer. But there was only this one. I'm having a senior moment!"

She looked worried. "Well, never mind," she said. "No use crying over spilled paper, or something like that. I'll get you some—and some for me, too—out of the supply closet."

I watched her unlock the walk-in closet door, and tried not to overreact, to instead remain objective, as planned. *Not* to think that if Harriet thought she'd had a stack of letterhead there, she had. Now it was gone. She hadn't had a senior moment. The seniors were having one of their moments. Again.

That's what I tried not to think.

Louis Applegate, who taught history and government, and Edie Friedman, who taught gym, walked in simultaneously but not together. Of all the women I've known who were actively hunting for a man, and by now, in my thirties, I've known my share, Edie Friedman wins the prize as most desperate. But two years ago, when he started teaching here, Louis had asked her out. She'd crossed him off the eligibility list during that first coffee date.

This was amazing to anyone who knew Edie. Her standards were almost nonexistent, and here was a decent-looking and interested bachelor, but she described him as "not there" and left it at that. Tisha Banks, the student teacher, must have felt the same lack of vibes this year.

"Morning," I said to them while I waited for Harriet.

"And to you!" Edie said with a grin. Louis, however, waited before returning the greeting, with a stance that made it clear that maybe this was a good morning and maybe it wasn't, and how would I know what constituted *good,* anyway? He knew more than I did, his posture indicated, and it was quite possible this morning had its flaws.

Behind him, Edie rolled her eyes. I decided that I would figure out the Constitutional Hall project on my own and spare myself the company of Louis Applegate. A dull jerk for a few minutes in the morning is infinitely preferable to a dull jerk for hours on a class outing.

"Must be gremlins underfoot." Harriet carried a ream of paper. "After all, 'tis the season." She tilted her head toward the pumpkin, and Edie complimented her decorating skills.

When it comes to gremlins, I'm pretty much an agnostic. Ditto for ghosties and goblins, though I like the sound of all of them. I wish I could ascribe life's oddments to them. Instead, I believed in humans who wanted to be sure of good recommendations, even if they had to write them themselves, who were smart enough to plan ahead. Letterhead missing now wouldn't be nearly as suspect as letterhead missing in two months.

Of course, that was precisely the sort of thinking I'd decided not to do anymore.

I told myself that stealing letterhead was bad, forging letters of recommendation worse, but that even if I couldn't recall hearing about it here before, it had probably happened and wasn't indicative of anything specifically happening right now.

I glanced at my watch, thanked Harriet, and left the office. Lots of time before school started. Rainy days were deceptive. On clear days, the students lounged around on the street and in the Square across from us, and the school remained in a pleasantly anticipatory hush until the bell rang. But on rainy days, the students treated the school hallways as if they were the pavement, and the din of young voices was already close to deafening. They were supposed to wait in the lunchroom at such times, but they'd perfected a delaying tactic, glancing at their watches and waiting until specifically, individually, asked to move on, then moving two feet, or simply exchanging positions and pausing again, so that it wasn't worth the effort to try to herd them.

I plowed through clumps and clusters of damp young people, and made my way up the marble stairs, which, after a fatal fall on them, had been outfitted with a broad runner in the school colors, maroon and gold. It was a great and overdue help on rainy and snowy days. Before this, large signs had been posted, the ones used when restrooms are being cleaned out. CAUTION: WET FLOOR.

Typical Havermeyer way of handling a problem, albeit abnormally terse for him, but need I say such signs were not a great help? Only luck and teenage agility had saved the students' bodies to date.

I had time for two necessary preclass stops, and the first person I wanted to see wasn't hard to find. Ms. Liddy Moffatt, the school custodian, would have found my grade book if it had spent any time overnight anywhere in the school.

"Yes, ma'am!" she said. "How can I help you today?

You the one left the perfectly usable ballpoint in your room? I think that was all we found, oh, except for some notes. Did you know that somebody named Annabel is hopelessly in love with Chuck?" Liddy, the world's number one recycler, was not above studying the scraps and detritus she collected.

"I—no. I didn't know, and I wish them well, but that pen wasn't—"

"Didn't think it would be you. You're a good conservationist. People like you aren't the ones messing this planet up. But I did find something—a poem—on your floor and I know your kids did that poetry show." She reached into one of the dozen pockets on the oversized apron she wore. "Here it is! Don't want one of your young poets all worried about losing his homework."

I glanced at the sheet she handed me. It had no name or section on it. I looked at the poem:

> *Dim candles burn*
> *Incense on the air*
> *Evening has come*
> *Far in the mist*
> *Against all fear—*

I stopped reading. I didn't remember it from class, and I was not sad about that. It felt like precisely the sort of overly precious and meaningless mood piece that my students had feared all poetry was. I glanced further, and it looked just as bad:

> *Greatness arose*
> *Limited nowhere*
> *Intent fulfilled*
> *Armor and Shield*
> *Resist the night*

I wondered whose work it was as I put it into my back-pack. "Thanks," I said, "but I had a question about my roll book. I must have misplaced it."

She raised an eyebrow.

"I was wondering if you saw it anywhere. You're so thorough, you and your crew . . ." But of course, had she found it, she'd have galloped in with her trophy the way she had with the wretched poem.

She shook her head and said only, "Nope. Would have found it, too, if it was here."

Nothing left, then, but to move on. I headed across the hall to Juan Reyes's closed classroom door wondering whether I should tell him about his car before or after I asked for clarification of my "troubles." I could see advantages and disadvantages to both placements.

Again, students milled about, exchanging gossip, awaiting the bell. Heaven forbid they should actually, willingly enter a classroom before it was compulsory. I made my way around them, greeting some, eavesdropping when I could, trying not to react to the lovesick tenth grade couple staring into each other's faces with stunned and daft-looking adulation, and not to interrogate Seth, who stood in the middle of the crowd in his raingear, the hood still up.

I had to convince Juan Reyes that I understood his reserve, his need to preserve confidences, not to confuse opinion with fact—but despite all that, I needed to know at least this portion of what was going on in my life, because it could be important. It might even help me find my missing roll book.

"Excuse me," I said to the clump of students near Reyes's closed door, a clump that included the usual suspects: Wilson, Susan, Erik, Nita, and Allie. Slowly, they acknowledged me and moved back, still talking to one another. I put my hand on the doorknob, mentally rehearsing how I would circumvent his scruples and get to the truth.

Why did he so intimidate me that I was searching for my words?

The door was locked. I couldn't blame him. I seldom locked mine, since there was nothing much worth taking, but he had every reason to lock up.

However, did that apply when he was inside? Light came from below the door, and I knew his car was outside. Was he hiding from us?

The question shredded under the impact of a sound so all-enveloping my brain rattled and I felt the detonation in my fillings.

Screams filled every bit of airspace the boom had left. Everyone pushed at once, trying to move to wherever they were not, shoving us all near to riot, to trampling and stampeding.

"Don't panic!" I shouted to them—and myself. Enough people near me heard and a small center calmed.

What had happened? My mind refused to comprehend it, but my mouth apparently knew what to do. "Move quietly toward the stairs," I shouted, pushing through the mass of bodies, dividing them up. "Front and back. This part to the back. You"—I waved—"the front."

They had to get away—anywhere away—for fear it, whatever it had been, would happen again.

"Did the furnace explode?" The terrified-looking questioner was Moira deLong, the Romance languages teacher, her voice piercingly high and trembling.

But she at least remembered language. Explode. That was the word for that sound.

"I don't think so—I think—in there—" I pointed at the closed chemistry lab. I turned to the two students nearest to me. "Find Ms. Moffatt. She has keys to all the rooms." I turned to a third student. "Go to the office and tell them there's been an explosion in the chemistry lab, and Mr. Reyes is in there."

"I'll call nine one one. I've got a cell," the student said, and only then did I remember that so did I.

I reached for it, but the screams that had died down resumed and then stopped, as if all breath had been inhaled as the chemistry room door opened, and Juan Angel Reyes stood there, one hand on the knob, so much blood pouring from his face I couldn't tell what was injured. He put his other hand up to his chest, looked as if he might speak, then his eyes rolled up and slowly, slowly, mouth still open in a silent plea, he fell, knees crumpling, the rest of him toppling straight forward to the floor.

Eight

BEDLAM. SOBS. GIRLS IN TEARS, BOYS BACKING UP, AWAY, silently expressing horror.

And blind, rote action, clearing away the wave of students who pushed toward the lab, stemming the tide so that it came no closer to Juan Reyes, the room, and possibly more explosions, and away from each other to clear a path for the paramedics.

All around me, sobbing, and when I took a swift look, I was surprised to see Allie, Susan, and Nita among the distraught.

The paramedics scooped Reyes up, did a quick scan of the lab, while the accompanying police asked if anyone knew anything.

"Chemistry labs," one said wearily. "Every single year one goes up. But it's not usually the teacher who gets hurt." They asked more questions and, one by one, the students shook their heads. Nobody knew much beyond what we'd all felt, heard, and seen.

"He just got there," one young man said. I didn't know him, but he looked ashen and close to being sick. "He *just* walked in. I know because I was leaning on his door. He asked me to move. I could have . . . if I hadn't moved . . . I could have . . ." He put his hand over his mouth and rushed off.

"The door was closed and locked," I said when it was my turn. "People out here couldn't see anything."

"Cigarette filter in the sink. He smoke?" the officer asked me.

I nodded, remembering those morning whiffs.

"Well," the officer said, shaking his head. "My chemistry teacher would have flunked him. Stupid to light up in a lab."

But only if something gaseous was in the air, I thought. And wouldn't we have smelled it? Wouldn't there be a big fire?

The police officer made note of my questions, and then agreed that we both wished we'd been more attentive chemistry students.

Only after they had removed Reyes, taken photographs, and tried to find out whatever they could, which was almost nothing, and only when the gurney was leaving the building, did Maurice Havermeyer emerge.

"What is it?" he asked, as if any of us had an answer. He looked irritated, his morning routine disrupted. Hardly an appropriate response.

He knew as much as any of us did. He'd spoken to the paramedics and police officers. Why question us? "Why aren't these students in class?" he demanded.

I could only gape. "There was a . . . The explosion! Mr. Reyes was seriously hurt—his face—the paramedics—you saw—"

"Students are supposed to be in the auditorium or lunchroom before class on rainy days."

"I know, but they weren't."

"Students need consistency, order, and routine." Havermeyer clapped his hands twice. "Students," he said in a fake singsong nobody could hear. "Students!"

"Maybe we could ring the bell?"

"It has already rung," he said, frowning.

I hadn't heard it over the decibel level. "Again, then?"

He frowned and pursed his lips. "It's on an automatic . . ." He looked around, squinted. "What happened, precisely?"

"Something exploded. In there." I nodded toward the open chemistry lab which now seemed peaceful enough. If there had been a fire, it had been put out.

All around us, students who'd been mute with the police were now free with supposed information.

"Accident."

"I heard he smoked."

"He did! I saw—one day right after school, in there."

"Probably lit a cigarette and *boom*!"

"Probably experimenting with gunpowder. Or a bomb!"

"The door was locked," I told the headmaster, "so nobody could get in quickly right after it—"

"Locked?" he shouted. "At this hour?"

Trust him to fixate on the least significant aspect. Judging by Havermeyer's expression, there was a rule that said you were not to lock yourself in your classroom prior to having something explode on you.

I continued. "Then Mr. Reyes opened the door, covered in blood, and collapsed."

The voices around us continued telling more than I hoped Havermeyer was hearing.

"I heard Mr. Reyes and that girl from art upstairs . . ."

"His head was blown off, did you see?"

"I heard they—like, three times a week in the morning—did she say the door was locked?"

"I heard it was a suicide pact, like Romeo and Juliet."

"Romeo and Juliet took poison!"

"Not both!"

"Okay, but they didn't blow each other up!"

"That was then. This is now. He's secretly married and she—"

"Besides, where is she? You made that up!"

Words reached me in idea fragments and layers, speculation, gossip, and illogical "facts" about what had just happened. But "where is she" registered clearly.

The students were still standing back from the door, so the headmaster and I seemed to be on a small island, surrounded by agitated natives.

"Did the police say what caused the explosion?" he asked me.

Why hadn't he asked them? "They didn't say to me. One did say it seemed accidental, which I'd assume, too." I shrugged. "Horrible, but these things happen in chemistry labs."

"Not in my school," he said emphatically. I remembered at least two other explosions, though nobody had been hurt in them.

"Is he going to *die*?" a sobbing tenth grader asked the headmaster.

Havermeyer had no choice but to actually interact with a student. He turned his back to me, and blustered about probabilities and possibilities and waiting and seeing, and I was no longer the center of his attention.

I didn't know if the paramedics or police searched the room, or the back room, the place Reyes thought nobody entered without his permission. They weren't looking for a second person, after all, unless it was another casualty, who would be near to the explosion site. How thoroughly had they searched?

My mind leapfrogged across a dozen horrifying scenarios about what might be behind the half-open door.

"Students," Havermeyer said, "we can but pray for Mr. Reyes's welfare. In the interim, it's time to return to your—"

Feeling guilty although I couldn't see what rules I was breaking—there was no crime scene tape, no warnings, no posted signs—I ducked into the lab, glass crunching under my shoes. I stepped to the side, and twisted my ankle on what turned out to be Juan Reyes's briefcase. It, too, was sprinkled with glass, as if he'd inadvertently flung it away when the explosion startled him. I lifted it up and shook it to clean it off.

The abandoned, scuffed briefcase, its leather cut where pulled out a particularly large shard, its insides scarred by yesterday's acid attack, brought me close to tears. It was so unlike that fastidious man's painstaking care of his possessions and appearance that it underlined the severity of what had happened.

Shards and fragments seemed everywhere; under my feet and beside me, on the white counter next to a sink. couldn't see what had exploded or where it had been. I also saw dark stains I did not want to think about, and when turned, I saw Tisha Banks, the student teacher. She huddled in the corner, her face down on her knees, trying to become invisible, and now she looked up with fear and shock on her tear-stained face.

"We weren't doing *anything*," she wailed as soon as she saw me. "And then boom! His head—his face! Blood all—" She seemed on the brink of losing all control. "I can't . . I don't . . . I didn't do anything!"

I knelt beside her. Her raincoat, buttoned up to her neck was bloodstained. She had socks on, no shoes, and I noticed flecks of blood on their white surfaces. "Nobody thinks you did. Nobody even knows you're in here. I was worried about you, about whether you were hurt."

"If nobody knows I'm here, how did you?" she whispered.

Honesty seemed the only relief for the awkwardness of the situation. "Tisha, some people are apparently aware of your romantic involvement with Mr. Reyes."

She whimpered, wiped her nose on her raincoat sleeve.

"I wasn't—we didn't—it wasn't like everybody thinks. It wasn't wrong! We were in love."

"You don't have to use the past tense."

She looked at me blankly. I must have sounded as if I were correcting her grammar. "He isn't dead." I hoped that was still true. "You don't have to talk about him in the past."

She shook her head. "I saw his face—his eyes—I heard him scream—"

"He's in bad shape, yes. He's been hurt, but he's unconscious, not dead. And nobody blames you for anything."

"He smoked. A lot. Whenever he could. I didn't think it was right, especially in the lab, but he said he knew precisely where everything was, and that nothing was dangerous if you knew what you were doing and took precautions, and he was angry that there wasn't a single place in this school to smoke. He thought the faculty, at least, should have a place. He said a lot of high schools even had places like that for the students. He said—"

I held her hand and listened, trying to hear more than she seemed able to say.

"—besides, he put it out—he put out his cigarette and that's when—he shouted 'Oh, no!' and all of a sudden, flames and glass and blood and—"

"He shouted before the explosion?"

She started sobbing again, hiccupping out words. "I think so, but—I don't know— It was so fast—loud—"

"Shhh. What shattered?" I thought about those flying shards and couldn't help but think of St. Cassian of Imola and death by a thousand cuts.

"I don't know! Nothing was out, like beakers or bottles, I swear. No gas was on—I would have smelled it. And I didn't touch a thing!"

I made shushing noises and spoke softly, asking if she was all right, if she had been hurt anywhere. She calmed down, and then words erupted out of her again. "We were—we are in love and we're both adults."

"Nobody said anything was wrong." Of course, I didn't know what anybody had said. I gave Pip still more points for knowing that teachers didn't have a clue about what was really going on. I didn't even know what was going on with other teachers, let alone the students.

"I think," I said softly and slowly, "you need to go someplace where you can rest. Home, probably. Take the day off. You are quite understandably shaken and upset. You probably should make a statement."

"About what? To whom?"

Indeed. Who was there? Surely not Maurice Havermeyer. I could hear him still booming orders to move on, move on, and report to your assigned homerooms. He was maintaining his longtime record of being completely ineffective.

"Never mind," I said. "I didn't think that through. This isn't a crime scene and there's no evidence of foul play. I hope you don't mind if I ask you a question, however. Where were you when they checked out the lab? They obviously didn't see you."

She wailed again.

"Tisha? It doesn't matter. You weren't hurt and you were frightened. I can understand why you'd hide; I just can't imagine where."

"In the prep room in back. That's where we—it's private there. Pretty cramped, though. I hid behind his desk in there. They only looked around for a second. I think they were looking for bodies. Out-in-the-open bodies. Or more fire or something. They came near, but they didn't pull out the chair and look underneath. Everything was peaceful, so they went away."

"Had you been waiting for him in the prep room?"

"At first, yes. I wanted to surprise him. Usually, we

don't—I don't get in this early on Wednesday, so we can't . . .
But my dad had an early appointment in Delaware today,
and he said he'd drop me off on the way."

"Did you see any students when you came in here?"

"A few, and I didn't want them noticing me, so I came in
fast." She looked down at her feet. "I have a key," she
whispered.

I let that pass. "You know who the students you saw
were?" She shook her head.

"Did you wait a long time?"

She shrugged. "Not that long." She tilted her head and
reconsidered. "Maybe a little long."

"And he had no way of knowing you were here, am I
correct?"

"Well . . . I left the door unlocked, kind of as a warning.
But otherwise, right. I was in back and I swear I didn't
touch any chemicals. I never, ever do. I'm scared to death
of them!"

"How long do you think you waited for Mr. Reyes?" It
felt ludicrous using his surname with his lover, but the man
had such a wall of propriety around him that it felt overly
intimate on my part to call him Juan.

"Don't know." She was probably a visual whiz, but she
left a lot to be desired verbally. "A while. Just . . . a while.
Is this going to . . . am I going to flunk now? Not get my degree?" Her nose reddened dangerously again.

"I doubt it. Nobody's going to know, anyway. Let's get
you out of here, all right?"

She looked at me appraisingly before she whispered, "I
need my clothes."

I looked down at her buttoned-up raincoat.

She swallowed hard. I nodded, and she stood up and tiptoed carefully. The telltale red marks on her socks meant
she'd already had enough contact with the broken glass.

While she put her jeans and sweater back on, I crunched

around. The room was dim. The police or paramedics must have turned the switch back off. I wondered if turning the switch had set off the explosion. I tried to remember Reyes as he staggered out of the room. He'd still been in his rain-coat.

I couldn't have said what I was looking for, but I found only glass and stains. Blood, I thought, and something else. On the floor, on the counter, in the sink where the skeletal remains of Reyes's umbrella also rested.

Tisha re-entered the lab as Havermeyer poked his head in. "What is going on here?"

"Ms. Banks and I realized that Mr. Reyes's briefcase was still in the room." I raised my arm, showing it to him. "She's taking it to him. We're sure it will be a comfort to him to know it's safe."

Tisha timidly nodded at the headmaster.

He peered at the lab, his bottom lip jutting out in per-turbation. "What are we going to do about the classes scheduled—"

"Ms. Moffat and her crew can have it back to normal in a jiffy," I said. "It's only glass and . . . whatever. Then we need a substitute teacher."

"I'm aware of that. I meant . . ." I don't know what he meant. He inhaled, seemed about to present an oration, but instead looked at the pocket watch he wore on a fob right next to his faux Phi Beta Kappa key. "I believe your homeroom is already in session, Miss Pepper," he said sternly, and then he turned and lumbered off toward the staircase.

Tisha watched his retreat, then looked at me. "Thanks," she said. "I don't think he knew who I was."

"He wouldn't."

"But I've met him three times and—"

"Trust me. It's nothing personal."

"I don't think he realized I was in there and—"

"He didn't. You're safe. And I'm sure Miss Jouilliat—" I rushed through the art teacher's name because nobody I knew of was sure of its pronunciation. I, for one, was willing to swear that she herself pronounced it differently each time, as a sort of performance art of her own. "Want me to go upstairs with you to talk with her?" I was hoping she'd say yes. Getting to the light and air of the third floor art room—which was half glass and always reminded me of a Parisian studio, or Hollywood's version of the same—would be a relief.

She considered, then shook her head. "Thanks, but she'll know what happened. Do you really want me to take his briefcase to the hospital?"

"If you change your clothing first. I don't think the sight of his blood all over your coat will make for an easy visit or help him. Besides"—I glanced out the window—"you don't need it. Looks like it's clearing."

She was a few steps away when I realized I still had questions. "One second more, please," I called out.

She looked at me apprehensively.

"Was Louis Applegate angry about your dating Mr. Reyes?"

"Louis!" She looked disoriented, furrowing her brow. "No. I mean, who would ever know? Louis is so . . ." She shook her head. "He never said anything, if that's what you mean."

I didn't know if that's what I meant, or what Louis Applegate might have felt or done.

And one more question, please. "While you were waiting for Mr. Reyes, were you wearing—"

She blushed, and said, "You know already. I told you, I—"

"—headphones?"

She swallowed and cleared her throat and her skin regained its normal peachy tone. She was a pretty girl, fair, with Titian red-gold curls, and she and Juan Angel must have been a lovely-looking couple. "Oh. That. Sure. I was listening to music."

Headphones, earplugs, loud music. She wouldn't have heard a marching band enter that laboratory. "How did you hear Juan Angel enter the lab?"

"I didn't!" She smiled briefly. "I *smelled* him. It. He must have closed the door behind him, locked it, and lit a cigarette. I smelled it and went in and he was standing there, looking around the lab. He looked surprised, but glad, and I said . . . I made a joke about smoking, said that was for . . ." Her voice dropped to near inaudibility. ". . . after. I . . . I was there, near the prep room, and I . . . I was kind of dancing and I . . . you know." She grabbed imaginary lapels of the raincoat and opened and closed it, flashing the memory of Juan Reyes.

How varied and surprising were the preschool activities at Philly Prep.

"He laughed. He was soaking wet, and he put his umbrella in the sink and turned on the water so he could put his cigarette under it while he watched me dance—and—he shouted 'oh, no!' and there was this flash, and noise, and glass and blood—" Her voice rose again, up toward ranges only dogs could hear. "I was dancing, he was laughing—and then, and then—"

"It's all right." I hoped I spoke the truth.

She shook her head. "He was *laughing*!"

The image of that solemn man laughing touched me, and I couldn't bear to think of what had happened then.

"I don't understand," she whimpered.

That made two of us.

Nine

MY ROOM SWARMED WITH STUDENTS, NOT ONE OF WHOM seemed able to settle down.

I couldn't blame them. If they were like me, their pulses and blood pressures were still circling the stratosphere.

The image of Juan Reyes ripped, bloody, and falling was unshakable, as were worries about how he was and when we could find out and what had happened. I shushed my homeroom into their seats while I fielded questions.

"Will he live?"

"We all hope so," I said. "He looked seriously injured."

"Will he be . . . you know, all scarred and—"

"The Phantom of the Opera!"

"We don't have any information yet," I said. "I promise to keep you informed with anything we find out, but you have to give it time."

"Did a student do it?" a freckle-faced girl asked.

"Do what?"

"It. We were all around there," she said. "I just guess . . . why did it happen if nobody . . . ?"

I tried to think of who "all" I'd seen near the chemistry lab and I could remember some of my tenth graders, and a few seniors—the "tennis boys and their girls," I thought, but was it relevant?

"Some people didn't like him," a normally silent girl whispered.

"It had to be on purpose," another ninth grader said. "I heard—" He grimaced as if squeezing his brain to recall what he'd heard.

"What?"

"People talking funny."

"Meaning what?" I heard the rumblings of protest from the rest of the class.

"Like . . . somebody saying, 'Did you do it?' "

"When was this?"

"I don't know when, but before the explosion."

"Who said it?"

"Cut it out, Hatch," somebody called from the back of the room.

"Hatch always says he knows stuff," another voice said.

"Makes him feel big."

"Whatever he says—he's lying."

This produced laughter, and I didn't know whether to take the remark seriously or not. Instead, I tried to ignore their voices and focus on Hatch, who was also ignoring them. He stared straight ahead, biting his lower lip, his eyes focused on nothing except, I hoped, his memory. He tilted his head to the side, and said, "I'm not lying. I don't know them. They're older and aren't in my classes."

"See? That's what he always does!"

"Grow up, Hatch!"

"Boy or girl?" I asked.

He looked defeated and shook his head. "It was like a whisper. But loud enough for me to hear."

"See? See?"

"It coulda meant anything."

"If he heard it in the first place."

"Thank you for trying," I said, quieting the rest of them down. "And if you remember anything more—any of you—feel free to tell me, or Dr. Havermeyer, or any of the faculty. But you should know that the police consider it an accident. Sometimes we want terrible events to have a reason, somebody to blame, but that isn't always the case."

Warring camps blasted each other inside my brain. Accident! one side screamed while it fired away. The room was locked by the time I and most of the students were up there; the student teacher hadn't smelled gas, and she would have had to, given the long time she waited for Reyes. And she had no reason to blow up her lover.

The other side of the battlefield was filled with logicians who pointed out that the police had no reason to suspect anything but an accident, and may have ignored signs pointing otherwise. They thought Juan Reyes had been in there alone, and had himself created the explosion. And he was unconscious and unable to tell them otherwise. So the fact that it wasn't declared a crime scene didn't mean there had not been a crime.

"I heard it was terrorists." That was George, a pudgy ninth grader whose voice was in the process of changing, quite publicly, and who was normally taciturn, presumably waiting until his vocal cords found their range and stayed there. This sentence had cost him. *Heard* broke in the middle and *terrorists* ended on a brittle high note.

"Because he's an alien."

"From space?"

"From *Spain.* Probably a spy."

"Okay," I said. "Enough. We've reached the ridiculous. Terrorists have nothing to do with this or us, and Mr. Reyes is a native-born citizen and certainly not a spy." The bell was going to ring any minute. "I need to take roll, but as my roll book is missing, I'm going to pass a paper around the room and—"

"What's that behind you?"

I turned. The roll book sat primly atop my desk.

I whirled back around and scanned the class, looking

for an expression that suggested involvement in this. Glee, amusement, interest even.

Twenty-two ninth grade faces looked back at me; twenty-two faces I saw briefly once a day for homeroom, twenty-two people who had no reason to care what grades I gave my classes. None of the voices and none of the expressions hinted at anything out of the ordinary.

When the bell rang again for the end of homeroom, I examined the roll book, flipping its pages. I saw no sign of tampering. No white-out, no funny-looking grades, nothing.

I seriously considered whether I was going stark, raving mad.

MY FIRST-PERIOD CLASS, THE POETS, ARRIVED ARMED TO the teeth with questions about the explosion. I couldn't blame them. And yet I had no answers, so the questions seemed pointless. Therefore I didn't so much guide the discussion back to the poetry unit as haul and shove and drag it back there.

But once there, they seemed to accept the idea and, in fact, to decide that reveling in yesterday's performance and accomplishments was almost as interesting as analyzing the explosion.

"My friend Annie? She thought it was really cool, and so did her whole class! I think they want to do one." Alison Brody's eyes were wide, and she smiled as she spoke, making her difficult to understand for a moment. I realized again how brave it had been for some of them to go public that way, and I was delighted anew by how the process had worked out. Nothing validates a teenager more than approval from a peer—and who would have anticipated getting it through poetry?

The approval was not, apparently, universal. Carl, a wiry boy who always seemed worried about being too small to be noticed, shouted out. "Yeah, well, Derek, you know, the kid who did the tech part? He got in trouble from it. He's got detention."

"Why? He did a terrific job."

"His teacher didn't like Derek working for you."

"He wasn't working for me!" That made it sound as if I'd acquired an indentured servant. "He was getting experience with sound and—"

"Right, but he ran over into the next period—putting the equipment away and all, so he was like five minutes late to class and his teacher gave him detention."

"Which teacher?" I asked, but I guessed the answer before Carl said, "Mr. Applegate."

"I'll write him a note. Derek shouldn't be penalized. It was all set up in advance, and he had permission."

"From the other teacher, the first-period one. That's what Mr. Applegate said. Not from him." Carl's interest had wandered to the girl across the aisle who was brushing her long hair with a vacant expression on her face.

"Alicia?" I asked, and she looked as startled awake as Sleeping Beauty must have been when the prince made it through the hedge and planted one on her. She blinked, then put the brush away in her purse.

"Let's hear what you collected," I said after a quick check of who was in class.

Because only a small portion of the class had shared original poetry, I'd asked the rest of the students to find poems that mattered to them, and to share those with the class. In other words, they, too, in their ego-protected way, had become participants in my stealth public speaking and poetry program. They read, blushing, protesting, explaining why they'd picked this or that poem: "I like the way it rhymes and sounds when the raven says 'Nevermore.' " "Because Elizabeth Barrett Browning and Robert Browning loved each other so much," said with scarlet ears and zero eye contact. "Because I guess it made me see people long ago had the same feelings I did and, no offense, Miss Pepper, but because this isn't a girl poem. It's about war."

And so forth and so on.

I stood in the hall between periods, staring at the closed door of the chemistry classroom as if it would reveal something—the *why*, at least, of what had happened. And the *who*, if there was one, would be kind of great.

I was so absorbed in trying to see the invisible that it took me a moment to realize there was pressure on my forearm. "Pepper, is it?" I finally heard.

I stared into the gray eyes of a stranger.

"It is Amanda Pepper, isn't it?" he asked, removing his hand from my arm.

I nodded, though I disliked being referred to as an *it*.

"Detective Norton. If I could have a few minutes of your time?"

"I have a class in four minutes," I said. "You can have those." This had to be about hiding Tisha Banks, my only current crime.

"Won't take long," he said, visibly unimpressed by my pedagogical responsibilities. "You knew the injured teacher, Juan Angel Reyes?"

I nodded and pointed. "His room was—is—right across there, so of course."

"You were friends, confidantes, perhaps?"

Students slowed down as they passed us, their ears revolving in my direction like satellite dishes. "Colleagues," I said.

"He said—"

"He's conscious?" I felt a wave of relief and smiled. "Thank heavens!"

Detective Norton seemed overly interested in my response and slow to offer up his. "He was," he said after too long a pause, during which he watched me as if he thought I might bolt. "Briefly. Kind of in and out, but his throat's seriously hurt so he can't talk much at all even when awake. He said your name."

"Mine? Why?"

"That's my question." With no subtlety, he led me away from the door and the students filing in as slowly as they could. When we were nearly across the landing, he spoke again. "Were you and Mr. Reyes perhaps more than colleagues?"

My jaw dropped comic-book fashion. Perhaps faces do that when the mouth part disengages from the brain part. I didn't know whether to laugh, cry, shout, or turn my back. Instead, I took several deep breaths, hoped that not a single student had heard his suggestion, and finally said that I'd barely known him. "I know nothing personal about him. I'd see him when we left our classrooms at the same time. I'd be very interested in what prompted that question."

He raised his eyebrows, making it quite clear he didn't believe me. "He said your name. He had around two minutes of full consciousness. We asked him what happened and he said your name."

"Are you suggesting that I had something to do with the explosion?"

He shook his head.

"Then why would he say my name?"

"We were hoping you'd answer that."

"I wish I could."

"Why do you *think* he said your name?"

I'm sure Detective Norton considered himself thorough, focused, and determined, and it's possible he was all those things and that they were good traits for a detective. But I found his one-note persistence obnoxious and stupid. "Why does it even matter?" I asked. "It was an accident."

"Apparently. But still, when he came to and we asked what happened, he said your name."

I felt an unpleasant thrum in the pit of my stomach, a sense that I was the crack brain, and that I was lying in some way.

If Reyes had said my name because he thought—or knew—I knew something, that would mean the explosion wasn't an accident. But the only things I "knew" were rumors, fears, gossip, whispers, and Juan Reyes's sense that the seniors were out to get him.

I knew I'd be a half-wit if I shared my thoughts or those amorphous fears and speculations with this dull man whose only talent was hanging on to his pre-existing ideas even when they made no sense. If I breathed suspicion on the seniors this man would haunt and hound them forever, and their futures would be jeopardized for no real reason.

"He was new. Never taught before, and he was having a rough time adjusting," I said instead. "He complained to me. Maybe that's why he said my name."

The detective frowned. "Doesn't make sense to me."

I could have helped it make sense if he'd seemed at all interested, but he wasn't. I could have described Reyes's complaints, or clarified what the "rough time" meant if he'd asked me what I'd meant, but he didn't.

"I really must go to class," I said.

He pursed his lips and exhaled in a manner designed to make me realize how much I had displeased him.

"May I?" I asked. Maybe we were playing Simon Says and I'd forgotten the secret passwords.

"If this is all you're going to say—that you don't know . . . you might as well."

I nodded agreement. "If I think of anything—any reason he'd have said my name—I promise I'll get in touch."

This time, his expression made it clear that my promises weren't worth a response.

                              *   *   *

"WAS MISS BANKS OKAY?" MA'AYAN ASKED ALMOST AS
soon as I was in the room.

"Excuse me?"

"Miss Banks—the new art teacher," she said in her
bright, clear voice. "Is she okay?"

How did she know Tisha Banks had been in there? We'd
been discreet about getting her out, waiting till the halls
were clear. Even Detective Norton hadn't mentioned her
existence.

Interesting if Juan Reyes said my name because he
thought I knew something, but he didn't think Tisha, who
was there, knew. Or perhaps he was simply protecting her.

Ma'ayan continued blissfully, her face innocent and
mildly amused. "My brother phone-texted me. He has art
first period. She came in and then left—and he said there
was blood on her coat!"

"She's fine." I left it at that, and thought instead about
the less than obvious web of connections between students.
Phones that transmitted messages. Brothers and friends
of siblings. Classmates of brothers and sisters. I hadn't
ever thought about how information must be everywhere,
instantly now that in addition to merely passing in the
hallways and spreading the word, they could check their
phones between (or, unhappily, during) classes and find out
the news from other floors. From, in fact, everywhere. The
possibilities were awesome.

In a relatively short while, after the class had a few minutes to whisper and pass notes about the hapless student
teacher, and I to try, unsuccessfully, to decide whether I
should have told Detective Norton about Tisha, we seemed
ready to return to the discussion of *A Separate Peace*.

I think it went well and smoothly, but most of my mind
was still in the chemistry lab and with Detective Norton. I
had to remind myself that the police had accepted it as a

sad but not surprising accident, so why wouldn't I? I was second-guessing them because Juan Reyes had apparently said my name.

Why?

The tenth graders' homework assignment was up on the board and I went over it with them to the accompaniment of moans and groans. "Write out why you think this is called *A Separate Peace*. That's it."

I thought of my headmaster's messages and my obligation to the next generation. "I'm not going to say write five hundred words or any amount. I don't want you to pad it. In fact, I want you to say as much as you can with as few words as you can, but that doesn't mean it might not be long. Write in full sentences and paragraphs and think the question through." More moans, grimaces, and groans. "Tomorrow, we'll read a few at random"—more groans—"and discuss your ideas, then I'll collect them." A final, futile round of heavy sighing.

I smiled. "You've been positively brilliant so far," I said. "Why pretend that writing your thoughts down is so much harder than saying them?"

Next period was a necessarily dry lesson about suffixes and prefixes, but in a way, the unemotional and mechanical nature of that lesson helped push the morning's events into the background. Also, this class barely asked for updates or clarification about the morning. Juan Reyes had had his fifteen minutes of fame and he was no longer a front-page story.

Class ended, lunch was here, and I felt as if I'd accomplished something major, but happily, I did not try to define what it was.

I looked up to see Lucas, one of the second-period tenth graders, back in my room, standing next to my desk, impossibly small for his age. He was a quiet boy who often looked as if he wanted to be part of the discussion, but was shy and fearful. I'd been giving him time, hoping he'd feel sufficiently secure to speak up soon.

Now he stood there swallowing hard. I smiled, tilted my head and said nothing, hoping he'd feel pressured to fill the silence.

"I!" He gulped, looked down at his feet and took a few breaths. "I have to confess," he said in a rush. His skin was scarlet, as if he'd been in the sun too long.

"Confess? To what?"

What else was there? I saw the blood again, felt the impact of the explosion—and looked at tiny Lucas and could only think no-no-no-no!

His shoulders hunched. "I was dared."

"Oh, Lucas." Oh, what a world of things to say about dares and macho games, all too late.

"It was supposed to be a prank. Only a prank."

"A prank," I repeated. I tried to keep my voice soft, but I wasn't sure I succeeded.

He nodded and without turning, waved to the vagueness behind him. "Nicky dared me, but I'm the one who did it. Only me. Then he said he was only joking, but that was later, after I did it."

I looked behind him and indeed saw Nicky, a tenth grader twice Lucas's size, standing in my doorway, his eyes fixed on the floor. "Lucas," I said. "Please—what exactly did he dare you to do?" I tried to envision this undersized boy as a mad scientist, arranging a mysterious concoction to avenge a teacher he couldn't know well. Tenth graders did not take chemistry. Why a grudge against a teacher you didn't know?

"Take the grade book."

"What? The—" Of course. Not the explosion at all. Nothing malicious. Not part of whatever teasing, taunting, threatening bloody war was being waged against Reyes. I knew it was selfish and self-centered and narrow-minded of me—but I felt a ridiculously powerful wave of relief.

They didn't hate me! It had been nothing more than a boy trying to prove himself.

"I meant to put it right back—five minutes, that was all I was going to keep it. I wanted to put it back right after you started looking for it—it was a joke!" He looked as if he was fighting back tears. "To scare you. But then you went into the hallway and blocked the door while you talked to Mr. Reyes and I couldn't, and everybody else left the school, and if I'd come back in with it, you'd have seen me, and I didn't know what to do. I was afraid to just leave it out after you left. Somebody could really take it. I'm really sorry. Am I in big trouble now?"

At this, his co-conspirator Nicky looked up, his features an exaggerated cartoon depiction of woe.

I remembered now—a glimpse of Lucas at the end of the day, the thought he wanted to ask me something—and then no Lucas in sight. And I'd thought, just as I did almost daily in class, that he'd changed his mind and that I needed to protect his painful shyness by not going after him.

"It wasn't much of a joke," I said, making sure I looked at Nicky as well as Lucas. "Did you think I'd find it funny?"

He looked at his toes and shook his head.

Of course he hadn't. It was a dare, an initiation rite, a route into the world of the bigger, stronger, less awkwardly shy boys.

"I didn't touch it, I swear," Lucas said. "I mean I touched it, sure, I had to take it home, but I didn't change anything. I didn't even—I barely even looked inside it." He looked directly at me, and I was startled by the color of his eyes—a dark jade green. "I'm really sorry."

"Are we going to be suspended or . . ." Nicky let the word *expelled* float off, unsaid.

I was torn. Angry about the hours of having a missing roll book, aware of the potential seriousness of the prank. "Do you realize this is a legal document?" I asked, holding the roll book out. Why that should impress them more than its being the holding pen for their academic futures, I don't know, but perhaps the hint that the force of the law was concerned with my records would matter to them.

I was angry, but I was also sorry for Lucas, and aware that Nicky, who'd only instigated the prank and hadn't actually done anything, had included himself among the guilty, asking if both of them would be expelled. That meant that Lucas had passed the test, pulled the sword from the stone, and had a friend and ally, and a relatively ethical one at that. And Lucas's shamefaced confession suggested he wasn't swapping being an outcast for being an outlaw.

"I appreciate your coming to tell me about it," I said. "That must have been a hard thing to do."

"It . . ." His sigh was Herculean. "Yes."

He triggered a memory. I put my hand atop Lucas's. "Did you phone me last night as well?"

His skin, if possible, went from scarlet to vermilion, and he nodded. "I tried . . . I thought . . . I couldn't . . ."

I took my hand away. "Okay, then. I understand." I kept my expression solemn, my message serious, and felt obliged to talk about learning a lesson from this about accepting dares—or making them.

"And for the next month, you'll be on Anserine Probation." I had wanted to use that word for a long time, but it isn't easy to work in something meaning "of or resembling a goose, as in behaving stupidly." "You understand?" I asked.

Of course they didn't, but they looked quite solemn as they nodded.

"No further violations, or . . ." I sighed. That seemed enough of a threat.

They were excessively grateful, and when they went off, the tall and husky and the runt, walking together as if they shared shackles, I felt I'd played my part well.

So aside from that bit of trouble in the morning, Mrs. Lincoln, I thought the day was clipping along rather well.

Ten

I STOPPED IN THE OFFICE BEFORE GOING TO THE LUNCH-room. I was hungry, and the real or imagined aroma of my sandwich nearly made me salivate, but I had to find out about Juan Reyes. I grabbed the junk that had accumulated in my mailbox since morning and greeted Harriet.

"Oh!" she said with real surprise in her voice. "I was just coming to find you. What a day!"

"Thanks, but he found me."

"He? Who?"

"The policeman. He must have gotten my whereabouts from you."

She inhaled raggedly, then nodded. "Yes. He wouldn't tell me why. Is everything okay?"

I shrugged. "I guess they routinely talk to people who were at the scene of an accident."

"And you were, weren't you? He already talked to you—or somebody did?"

I shrugged again. "Anyway, I wanted to find out whether you've heard from the hospital."

She looked completely confused. I realized she hadn't been in search of me about either the policeman or a medical update. I sincerely hoped she hadn't been en route with a hot news flash about stuffed wildlife. "Mr. Reyes," I said. "Have you heard from the hospital?"

"Well, that wasn't—but yes. It's not good news, I'm

afraid. He is in critical condition, in intensive care. Apparently, the glass cut an artery—or was it a vein?—and he lost a lot of blood, and his throat's injured, and possibly an eye, and so he's . . . and there are the other cuts as well and the big problem—if he regains consciousness and lives, of course. The glass . . ." She averted her own glance, as if to soften the message. "They aren't sure about his sight. That jar!"

I did a double take, thinking she was using the chemistry teacher's nickname, but she simply meant the glass that had so mysteriously and profoundly exploded.

Still, I spent a moment pondering whether a jar had so injured Dr. Jar.

"But Miss Pepper—"

"Amanda."

"Amanda. That wasn't why I was coming to see you."

I tensed, waiting to hear about Erroll's latest taxidermical triumph or tragedy.

"I had to tell you that the headmaster wants to see you as soon as possible."

That was never good news. Even Erroll and groundhog tongues were preferable. I glanced over at his office door, thought about my egg salad sandwich. "Is it really urgent?"

She leaned close. "I don't know what it's about, of course, but yes, he said as soon as possible. He said it should be during your lunch hour. Those were his words. He said it was"—she lowered her voice to a reverent near-whisper—" 'a matter of some gravity.' "

I glanced at his closed door again. He'd never once called me in to congratulate me or praise something I'd done, only to enumerate my perceived failings, but I couldn't for the life of me think of what I'd done wrong lately.

Maybe he wanted to commiserate about Juan Reyes.

Or, more likely, he knew about Tisha Banks. Maybe an

observant student had told him about her. I started planning my defense of not telling him about the high jinks in the chemistry lab.

"He's waiting for you now," Harriet said.

It seemed best to get it over with. He periodically grew annoyed with me and I guessed it was time once more. There seemed a cyclical order I hadn't yet deciphered, but in general I knew my crimes before I was summoned.

Had I annoyed any families by giving a low grade or suggesting any area that could use improvement? I couldn't think of any looming disputes, not that I ever knew I was overstepping my bounds—by their lights—before one of those confrontations. On the other hand, Havermeyer had once been apoplectic because my window shades weren't perfectly aligned.

I was fairly certain that window shades were not the problem today, and I was right about that much. Harriet ushered me in to Maurice Havermeyer as if I were an invalid, and as if I couldn't make the trip myself.

His splendid office always made me feel as if I were about to receive a detention rather than what I should have felt like—a colleague, a peer here for a discussion or consultation. But that would have implied that the honest exchange of ideas or working through of problems had a chance of happening inside its paneled splendor.

As always, I wished I could creep closer to the framed diplomas on the wall. Their writing was illegible, the language in which they were written strange—neither Latin nor Greek, and certainly not English, and the degree-granting institutions' names unintelligible—purposely, I thought. But as usual, my headmaster blocked access to his academic credentials.

He waved me into the chair facing his desk while he sat behind its empty expanse, his hands folded above his chest, as if he'd been praying and had grown weary, so he rested his chin—one of his chins—on his fingertips. "I'm afraid we have a serious conflagration," he said gravely.

No. First of all, he wasn't afraid about anything. He was quietly gloating. And second, we'd *had* our conflagration before school even began. If there was another fire in the building, was this the way to handle it?

He sighed, lowered his hands, raised his head, and looked at me directly. "This is a matter that needed your attention," he added. "Your immediate attention, which it did not get. Now we are forced to close the barn door after the chickens flew the coop."

It wasn't the moment to correct him. Or maybe he meant this wasn't an enormous problem, chicken- rather than horse-sized.

"I believe in creativity and the arts as much as the next man," he said.

I nodded, because that seemed the response he wanted, although I would have wanted to know who, precisely, that next man might be and what creativity had to do with my failure to mention Juan Reyes's inamorata.

"I am, after all, an educator."

Again, I did not feel it was the time or my place to correct him.

"And being an educator, I am committed to encouraging the creativity of our young people." He paused. "Would you not say that was so?"

"Excuse me?" My mind was still preparing my defense, sure that Tisha Banks was the missing subject line in his message. She was, after all, art and creativity incarnate—even without her early-morning striptease. "Yes, of course," I said. I wasn't sure what I'd agreed to, but I was close to sure his words had gone full circle. He believed in creativity because he was an educator and therefore believed in creativity.

And most of all—so what? I wished he'd cut to the chase.

"I'm glad we're on the same page with this," he said solemnly.

I was now worried that he'd already cut to and been dwelling in the chase, but whatever our game, he'd forgotten to tell me its name, let alone its rules.

"You must agree that there are limits," he said, his voice low and grave. "Call them boundaries if you like, of good taste, of discretion, of common sense."

He said I must agree. Must I? "Perhaps."

"Societal mores, Miss Pepper. Or should I now call you Mrs. . . . ?"

I shook my head. "Miss Pepper is fine."

He nodded and cleared his throat. "A culture establishes spoken or unspoken agreements so that its people can live in harmony."

If this was his idea of clarification, I had news for him. I knew about societal mores. I'd had sociology. So what?

"We live in difficult times." He had swiveled his desk chair halfway, and was apparently speaking to the window that faced the street, now rain-free. Across the way, in the Square, students enjoyed their lunch hour. I envied them.

"Children to all intents and purposes just like those," he said, waving at the panorama of adolescent life. "Children in fact precisely like our students pick up machine guns and decimate their schoolmates. People drive planes through buildings on purpose, murdering thousands. These are not our parents' times, and neither, therefore, do we live with the same sense of security as they did." He paused, expectantly, swiveling back to face me more directly. "Don't you agree?"

I gave him the minimal nod possible, my neck muscles so tight movement was difficult. Of course those horrific things had happened. How could I or anyone disagree? But

I was suspicious of arguments that began with those ideas, that asked for agreement on simple, verifiable facts. They felt like traps: You agree to the facts because they are facts, and they happened, and then you were supposed to agree with whatever followed, with specious logic apt to leap miles into a foggy void. I wanted to agree to a point, and to that point only, so I kept my nods barely perceptible.

"Given that many of our worst nightmares have in recent years become actuality, when you have a student advocating violence," he said, "you must agree that it is imperative that one should put a stop to it."

Tisha? Advocating violence?

In fact—anybody I knew advocating violence?

Havermeyer waited. He'd told me I must agree, and he was waiting for me to do so. "Of course," I stammered, "I suppose, if in fact—"

"And you must agree that it is your responsibility as an educator and a citizen in these perilous days to report it to me."

I felt as if I had stumbled into a political rally, one whose politics terrified me. What was I was supposed to report? What did "advocating violence" mean? Somebody saying, "drop dead" to another student? A kid with an automatic rifle? "I suppose if it ever—"

"Then why haven't you?"

If he'd taken a large mallet and pounded my head, I couldn't have been more surprised or disoriented. "Dr. Havermeyer," I said in as calm a voice as I could muster, "I thought we were speaking theoretically. In theory, of course, I agree, I think, but in reality, I haven't reported anything to you because happily, I haven't had a single encounter with a student who advocates—"

"Indeed? That is not consistent with the facts. Not only did you not report it to me, as the administrator and proper authority, but you opted to broadcast it to every student in this school."

And finally I got it that Tisha Banks was not the topic, and Havermeyer was not speaking in metaphors, but literally. Our innocuous, terrific poetry reading. The one thing I'd done here lately that had met with everyone's approval had somehow become a wrong thing. Now that I knew what he meant, I could sit up straighter and speak more directly. "I can't imagine what you've heard, but the fact is, none of my students advocate violence."

"That is not what I was told."

"By whom? Because it is what I *am* telling you. In fact, we taped it, so I could show—"

"I have had the opportunity already to view your production."

"And? Surely, you saw—you didn't see anything frightening." Nobody had read a Columbine-type work, not even close. Nobody had even opted for the violence of a typical rap poem, not that I would have censored it had they. Could he be offended by the dumb-dog poem? Was that suddenly anti-American? And then there was the one about the dead grandma. Was there too much death and dying in that? This was ludicrous, except for Havermeyer's expression, which was solemn and annoyed.

"Cheryl Stevens." He spoke her name with the gravity of one sharing the secret of existence.

"Cheryl? Cheryl's *against* violence. That's the entire point of her poem. It's an antiwar poem."

He nodded and looked satisfied, as if I'd just made his point for him. "Precisely."

I gripped the seat of the chair and tried to think of this as a humorous situation. As Alice in the Havermeyer hole where nothing made sense because it was all a game. Things turned topsy-turvy, antiwar equaling pro-violence, failure to report same a dereliction.

Only it wasn't a game. His face was puffed with anger. "Let us be more specific and on target than saying the poem is antiwar. It's an anti*government* poem. Antigovernmental policy and effort."

I took a deep breath. "It's about her cousin, her closest and favorite cousin, who was blinded. It's about the pain war creates. It's about the idea of killing—and the horror of killing. It's part of a great poetic tradition in Western literature."

"You may interpret it as you like, but I saw the tape, and heard the words, and they are inflammatory and most definitely suggest civil disobedience. Revolution, one might say. Insurrection. This is a call for action against the government, or how else would one interpret it?"

I wondered what other job I'd be able to find once I was officially fired. I was not a good salesperson, didn't know fashions, wasn't particularly skilled on the computer. Could we make ends meet if I waited tables? Was the salary with tips any less than I made here? Did I even *care* at this point if I lost the job?

"This is not a personal vendetta or my own idiosyncratic rush to judgment." He laughed with some derision, as if the idea that he could behave weirdly was beyond the pale. "I had a complaint almost immediately," he added with heat in his voice.

I had been mentally opening the help wanted pages and going online to job sites, and it took a real effort to will myself back into the moment.

He looked delighted by the fact that somebody had complained to him. There was joy in having an equally stupid person out there, and he was dumb enough to believe that if two people agreed on something, it was the truth, no matter its actual merit.

I waited to hear the name of the student or parent who'd been that narrow-minded and outraged.

"Louis Applegate was understandably uncomfortable about having you spread seditious propaganda through the student body."

Not a parent being overprotective and not a student unable to think things through. A faculty member. A history teacher. How ludicrous could we get?

I knew Louis was a dry, sexless, sour work of a man, but still and all, he'd surely heard of the Constitution, the Bill of Rights. How could he object to a tenth grader's unpolished but heartfelt poem? I tried to put my incredulity and anger to the side, and think about what I could rationally do about this situation. "I'll talk with him," I said, though I really wanted to shout at him, to shake some sense into him.

Havermeyer looked startled, as if I'd introduced an entirely new subject. "Why would you do that? Louis Applegate is not the problem. Your student is."

"Cheryl? How can you or Louis Applegate think that?" I knew I shouldn't have asked for more information the moment the words escaped my lips.

He sighed and shook his head, playing out his frustration to an imaginary far balcony. "I think the situation has already been sufficiently clarified, but . . . to repeat, if I'm not mistaken, and I am not, I have already stressed that these are not normal times. There are things, ideas—incentives to violence, to noncooperation—that cannot be tolerated, and I would think every citizen with eyes and ears would be well aware of that by this point."

Ideas that cannot be tolerated. Did he hear how that sounded? Ideas, not acts.

"I understand there is a plan to print the poem in the *Inkwire* as well," he said.

I nodded. "All of the poems that were read. The staff suggested it, and since we don't have a literary magazine, I—"

"You agreed? Wouldn't it have sufficed—more than sufficed—for those ideas to have reached every student in the school one time? I'm afraid I do not consider an inflammatory, anti-American poem justifiable under any lights at this time in our history. And surely not disseminated under the banner of this school."

"You're saying we can't print them?"

"Not Cheryl's, and the rest are to be reviewed prior to publication. In any case, by the time the next issue comes out, Cheryl Stevens will no longer be a student at this school, so there is absolutely no justification for printing her work in a newspaper written solely by the student body."

This was unthinkable. I tried to recall anyone else who'd been asked to leave in the years I'd been there. We're a school catering to kids who can't or don't make it elsewhere for a variety of reasons, some potentially serious, most not. We'd struggled along with learning difficulties, personality aberrations, and psychological disturbances— and now were we actually going to throw out a student for writing a poem?

"Before you leap to any wrong conclusions, understand that Cheryl's withdrawal is her decision and precluded any need on my part to suggest it. I have merely had a preliminary discussion with Cheryl's parents this morning, and they themselves suggested finding another more . . . philosophically comfortable, perhaps more suitable place for her."

I had the distinct impression that if asked, Havermeyer would consider the place most suitable and comfortable for Cheryl Stevens to be the Prison of Bad Thoughts, where people's minds get bound and gagged.

"I hope they change their minds," I said. "Upsetting Mr. Applegate over an issue of free speech hardly seems a reason to leave a school."

"This has nothing to do with Mr. Applegate. He merely gave me an early heads-up. Furthermore, he indicated that the rest of the faculty is in sympathy with his views."

I shook my head, still in shock. "How—when did—nobody said—"

And then I remembered Juan Reyes expressing amazement that I'd cared about his problems when I had problems of my own, then refusing to explain himself. I'd been heading for his room this morning determined to extract that refused explanation.

This had to be what it was about. I hadn't made it to the lunchroom yesterday. I'd been preoccupied redoing the seniors' examination. People must have talked about the poetry program, but it hurt to think they'd all thought it was a bad thing.

Then I remembered the brief exchange more clearly. Juan Reyes had seemed sympathetic, not accusatory. He'd said I had problems, not that I'd created problems.

Not everyone condemned me. Maurice Havermeyer was rearranging the truth to suit his thesis. I looked at him. His fleshy face revealed almost nothing, but then there was precious little inside the man to be revealed. Few original thoughts crossed his mind, and those that did were never complex, and always hinged on whether or not a given idea or event was good for the bottom line.

"We stand for certain values here," he said, "and I will not have our good name tarnished. I do not want to give the impression that the staff at this school—that we stand for—that we are in any way defiant of the values and beliefs that make this country great."

"Like freedom of speech? I agree. I'd hate to give the impression we don't stand for it."

He cleared his throat. "This is not censorship. This is common sense for uncommon times."

I wondered where he'd found that phrase.

"This is being cautious in the same way we look for hidden weapons at the airports." He paused to listen to what he'd said, found it good, and nodded. I could see him regain his confidence—his arrogance—and steam ahead. "An educator is the guardian of young souls, so I am therefore personally bothered by the fact that you did nothing to stop this seditious performance and, in fact, aided and abetted it."

Language fit for a spy, an enemy of the country. And all I thought I'd been doing was demonstrating that the arts could be used to express emotions. In short, my job.

"And that you were, furthermore, deliberately planning to assist students in further disseminating words that can only foment unrest."

I didn't know what I disliked most intensely: his language or the impulses behind it. I decided to avoid the blather that would preface what he had in mind. Instead, I'd fall on my sword, force him to say what he wanted. Temp work couldn't be that bad, could it? I looked at him directly. "Are you asking for my resignation?"

That was too straightforward for my headmaster. "Well . . ." he said. "Well . . ."

"Because I don't agree about this. In fact, I think it's a violation of all we teach here, no matter what Louis Applegate says. I think it's a disgrace that somebody who suggests tossing out a student for expressing her sorrow and confusion about a loved one's war injuries should pretend to teach our children social studies. I respect his constitutionally protected right to think it and say it, but surely, not to do it. Actions matter. Thoughts and words are protected, and I think he needs a remedial course in our basic rights, starting with the First Amendment that guarantees freedom of speech."

"He didn't precisely say—nobody said—the Stevens family made this decision on their own."

"Well, if they were given the same twisted interpretation of what Cheryl wrote, I can't blame them. But aside from them, you're upset that I supposedly allowed this to happen, and I'm not upset about it at all, so do you want my resignation?" I itched and yearned for him to tell me he did. I wanted out. I couldn't, wouldn't, surely didn't want to work in this environment.

My entire relationship with Philly Prep's one-man administration had been fraught with tension and dispute and, I suspected, mutual dislike, but this was the nadir. This was disgusting. Despite my fury, I did give a moment or two's thought to the students and work I loved—and to the perilous state of our checkbook—but I nevertheless couldn't see any alternative. I was sure I could find another underpaid job where at least the Bill of Rights was upheld.

"You must learn to not rush headlong into decisions that way, but to think issues through, to reconsider, in these trying times—"

I knew these times were trying. I didn't need re-education from Maurice Havermeyer. "Putting it bluntly," I said, "I cannot understand why we should take away our basic rights—our students' constitutionally guaranteed rights—while we're fighting others who would take them away. And fighting in order that other people should have those rights."

He looked as if I'd whirled him around until his eyes spun. Nothing had gotten through to him. Instead, when he opened his mouth to speak, he'd pushed the PLAY button again after being on hold. "—and reconfigure, perhaps, establish new parameters concerning incendiary material and perhaps consider more discretion, although of course I am not suggesting anything like censorship, but still, we all self-censor, do we not? We don't cry 'fire!' in a crowded theater, and we don't question the right of the man at the airport to have us take off our shoes or examine our handbags. You could explain that to your students, make it clear."

I didn't see why I had to endure any more of his meaningless blather. "I understand," I lied. It shortened the time he'd have to spend saying lots of words and meaning nothing. And to my horror, I did understand.

Having said that, while Havermeyer stammered and backtracked and tried to articulate what he wanted without actually saying anything concrete, I stood up and left the room, powered by the smoke and fumes coming out of my ears.

Eleven

I'D LOST MY APPETITE AND WAS LEFT WITH ROILING EN-
ergy and no place to put it, so I stormed out of the building, ignoring the sporadic sprinkles that were all that remained of the morning's rainstorm, and stomped about till
I found a homeless person leaning against a wall, holding
an umbrella and a damp cardboard sign that said HUNGRY.

I handed him my pristine lunch.

His expression suggested that I'd handed him vermin,
not victuals. "How about money, lady? A man's got to
live."

"Change your sign, then," I snapped. *"Words matter!"*

I stormed on, thoughts circling in on themselves, getting
nowhere. I had long since debated leaving teaching for
more pay or ease, but the problem was, I loved it, so I
stayed. But that was then and this was now, and every muscle and bone of my body wanted only to stomp away.

I looked back at the disgruntled homeless man who was
now too intent on eating my sandwich to notice I was
watching him. The sight was a strong reminder of my own
fragile financial stability. If I left this job in a huff, I might
soon have to find a begging corner of my own.

I wondered how much the man took in in a day.

As frightening as that idea was, this latest impasse felt
like the proverbial *it,* as in "this is!"

Or the final straw.

The one that broke the camel's back.

Or whatever cliché that meant too much, I've had it, can't take it anymore. Those were shopworn because countless brethren had understood how simultaneously furious and bereft a person can feel.

It wasn't as if I was being royally—or even adequately—compensated for a job that deserved hazard pay.

But I did not want to go gently, either. I yearned to express my reasons as loudly as possible, then flounce right out, but that seemed a breach of ethics. I might leave students cheering for my principles, but I'd also be leaving them in the lurch, which negated the worth of any high-minded dramatic exit.

I fumed and huffed and rehearsed speeches I knew I'd never give and circled the block half a dozen times. On one pass, I realized that Juan Reyes's car was still parked behind the school. I didn't know the protocol. Who removed a car in such a case? And should I feel guilty that I failed to remember the monogram and the broken headlight with either the paramedics or the obnoxious detective?

Changing my route, I studied the groups in the Square while I walked around it. As the weather cleared, more and more students had emerged from wherever they'd been waiting. I wanted to watch and feel heartbroken that I would soon sever my ties with them. I soon found myself observing their comings and goings, as if they were animals on the veldt and I was preparing a *National Geographic* documentary.

The subphylums kept to themselves, grade by grade, most often, girls and boys in separate clumps, but emissaries crossed the lines—scouts, spies, messengers, siblings, girlfriends, and boyfriends. I saw Ma'ayan hobnobbing with three girls in the junior class, Ben watching her and trying to keep his surveillance under her radar; a senior boy bear-hugging a sophomore girl who giggled the entire time;

and two junior girls flirting so outrageously with class-mates I could read their body language from across the street where I paced.

Visually eavesdropping distracted me from thoughts of hateful Havermeyer. I'd read that 65 percent of communi-cation is nonverbal, done through posture, gestures, and facial expression; that seemed on the mark across the street.

The body language of the seniors who'd been giving me grief was languid, self-assured, and the occasional pokes and pushes were light and clearly meant as jests. They weren't tightly grouped, but were placed so that they'd be aware of where everyone was, and of what was going on. And somehow, each seemed the prince of his fiefdom, each owned his share of the park.

When my eyes wandered from the boys, I saw the party mavens, Nita and Allie, interacting intensely once again. I wasn't sure when I'd seen what, but I knew I'd seen tension between them lately.

This looked more acute. If I hadn't known better, I'd have thought I was watching the prelude to a catfight. Allie leaned close to say something and Nita turned away while Allie's mouth was still going. Allie grabbed Nita's arm. Nita whirled, shrugging off the hand as she said something, her forehead wrinkling, her chin pushed out pugnaciously.

Allie's hands flew up to her head, as if to contain the pain inside of it. Her shoulders rose, her mouth opened, and she looked to be shouting, although I couldn't hear over the din of traffic and people. Her hair shook a *no-no-no-no* and she was the very picture of barely controlled rage.

Jimmy Manasco—he who was so proudly "the norm"—strolled over to them. He wasn't the easiest-to-love student. He'd been kicked out of parochial school for vague reasons I never knew. He passed his classes, but did little more, and he was a fine athlete. That, plus his parents' wealth, would get him where he wanted to be.

His normal expression was petulant, and he spread a fog of vague unhappiness as he moved through life. He seldom participated in class, preferring to slouch in his seat, a mocking expression on his face, as if those who did speak up and contribute were his inferiors by virtue of their attempts.

But he was attractive and he'd scored the winning basket the week before, and that kept his virtual crown on his head.

Now, his stride toward the two girls perfectly expressed his arrogance, and though nobody had asked him to, and most likely, nobody wanted him to, I knew he was going over to referee. Nita put one hand up, signaling *stop,* but he continued, and then both girls spoke at once, waving their arms. At one point, Allie simply turned her back to him and covered her ears.

Fascinating. Who needed words? No wonder the homeless man had been upset. His body language had been saying "give me money" and I got stuck on the words of the printed sign.

The rest of the tennis boys now openly watched the two girls and Jimmy. Wilson and Erik had shifted so that they were within easy talking distance of each other, and I saw them exchange glances and an occasional word. Mike Novak stood apart from them, talking to an eleventh grade girl, but keeping his body turned so that he could watch as well. And Drew and Mark, the lesser dignitaries of the team, also stood silently watching.

As melodramatic as high school students tended to be, as overblown as every life crisis became, this had the look of something larger, something that applied to and affected the entire group of them.

I corrected myself because the entire group wasn't engaged. It had taken me a minute to realize that Seth, an integral part of that ruling clique, was not part of his home team. He, like the cheese, stood alone. I'm not sure I would have noticed it if I'd only glanced over, because he was near enough to a cluster of other seniors, and he'd angled himself so that he could quietly observe. But out of all the boys with their casual stances, their heads cocked to one side, their hands in their letter jackets, Seth alone looked as if he was studying each word, lip-reading if that was possible.

Nita spun around and marched off, and Allie ran after her with Jimmy waving his hands and shouting something.

Did any of this have to do with the events of the day— the injury to the teacher they'd been harassing? Or the expulsion of Cheryl Stevens?

Probably not. Too much of a stretch, and too much animation and division of opinion over there. It was, in all likelihood, domestic and boring if seen up close, another of their operatic performances when somebody's boyfriend misbehaved, or somebody wanted to wear the wrong thing to the party. However petty the topic, they'd made it a group issue in the past.

Better off not knowing what it was this time, I decided. I stood there, feeling foolish—and hungry now as well. I put my hands into my raincoat pockets, hoping for a long-forgotten protein bar or mints, but instead, my hand touched paper. No surprise. Too often, my pockets were the handiest wastepaper receptacles, and emptying them took on the look of an archaeological dig unearthing my life through receipts, to-do lists, and junk mail.

This was none of those. I looked at the folded orange sheet of paper and had no memory of seeing it before, of putting it into the pocket of my raincoat.

Orange paper meant another notice about Friday's dance, and I was ready to trash it until a quick glance made it clear this was not a routine announcement.

The words in thick black felt-tip marker felt like a slap:

IT WAS NOT AN ACCIDENT!!!!!
WORSE IS GOING TO HAPPEN
SOMEBODY HAS TO STOP IT!!!!

I stood still, the paper in my hand, the letters dark scars
across the orange surface, the words like muffled, semi-
intelligible shouts.

Somebody had put this in my pocket today. Somebody
who knew what Juan Reyes thought I knew, or could find
out.

THE SENIORS ENTERING MY ROOM SHOWED NO SIGN OF
the passions that had raged in the Square. I wish I could believe I'd hallucinated the whole thing, including the note.

Before they were in their seats, they asked if there was
news about Mr. Reyes, and I was surprised by how quiet
they became, so intently waiting for a response that the air
seemed charged. "I called the hospital," Seth said. "All
they'd say was his condition was critical. Is that true?"

I told them what Harriet had told me, though it added
little. "Anybody have any idea what happened in that
room?"

The silence that followed my question was nothing like
the hush before I'd answered them. This was heavy, like the
air before an electrical storm.

It was finally broken by a half-growled "Why would we
know?"

I didn't like the way Wilson had asked, but I tried not to
read anything into it.

"The cops said it was an accident," Erik added.

"I'm sure it was," I said, now sure it wasn't. The warning note I'd gotten felt confirmed because of the speed and
manner of their replies.

"So how are we supposed to know about it, then?" Erik
demanded.

"I meant what might have caused the accident. You're learning chemistry and you know the lab and Mr. Reyes. Any theories?"

They reverted to a third variation on silence, this one the silence of those who have emotionally left the room. They offered nothing beyond shrugs and head shakes. It wasn't the response I'd anticipate from people who truly knew nothing about the explosion. Why weren't they speculating? Gossiping? Wondering?

Why were so many of them reacting the same way?

"Oh, no!" Juan Reyes had said just as his world exploded. He'd known something. And he'd told the police my name. He thought I knew something as well—but what? I looked at the stone-faced seniors, wishing for X-ray vision.

I put the lab explosion on hold for the moment. The day's repeated adrenaline floods were exhausting me, so I tried instead to focus on the more manageable mystery of who had stolen my exam.

I complimented them on how they'd done, while scanning the room to see if anyone reacted oddly. They looked their normal selves, which is to say, anxiously belligerent when about to receive test results.

I handed the exams back and watched relief, disappointment, and stolid acceptance shape their features, but nothing that I could interpret as suspicious.

But of course, that's how it would be. They'd known since yesterday that I'd replaced the stolen exam. Of course they wouldn't show surprise now. My after-the-fact sleuthing was ridiculous and the bottom line was that I'd never know who'd taken the exam or why.

We went over the questions. "I was particularly interested in that last question," I said. "The one about the relevance of the Oedipus cycle. Your responses were varied, and you picked different aspects—commercial, psychological, and political."

Though I didn't say so out loud, some of the aspects picked were too creative, e.g., the one connecting Oedipus to Japanese anime and one to golf, and one gem that consistently discussed the "ancient Geeks."

"I'm pointing that out because we've talked about how many levels and meanings great works of art contain, and I think your responses demonstrated that. Works written thousands of years ago can still touch us, and ethical or psychological issues that troubled the Greeks continue to trouble us today."

I couldn't completely disengage from a depressed, anxious awareness of what had happened today, and I felt as if my words to the class were partially rote.

"Yeah, right," I heard. "Like we're going to marry our mothers!" Two boys in the back of the room slapped hands, ducked, and laughed. I let it go. Even crude and stupid jokes about Oedipus were literary efforts and in the case of those two boys, a definite step forward, especially since one of them was the author of the paper about those ancient Geeks.

No matter how I felt—no matter how they felt—we seemed back on a fairly good classroom footing as long as we weren't talking about Juan Reyes. Somebody brought up Antigone and the issue of civil rights and of the individual versus the state.

And while that may have taken my mind off Juan Reyes a bit, it bumped me smack into my noontime encounter with Maurice Havermeyer, which still burned and rankled.

I saw the headmaster's bloated, angry face, and heard his twisted view of what freedom of speech meant. But given that I was about to quit because of his asinine behavior, what did I have to lose if I used the episode to teach them a final, bonus lesson, bringing the point home?

"If Antigone lived today, what do you think she'd be like?" I asked.

I knew they'd be happy to answer the question and entertain me, to delay moving on to the next unit, which involved long reading assignments. All kids love it when I veer off course and seem to have forgotten what we should be doing. They think it's the result of their devious manipulation, when, in fact, most times, it's something I'd planned all along.

This particular instance was spur of the moment, but it didn't feel like a detour. It felt like a live demonstration of the ideas in the play they'd just read. We'd talked about Antigone's civil disobedience, about her probable immaturity and rashness, about Creon's intractability, about morality versus the law, the state versus the individual, fathers versus sons, Ismene as the "good girl" and what that meant, about assigned gender roles then and now, about fear of breaking those roles. To me, that made my confrontation with Havermeyer right on topic.

They seemed bemused by my question. "If nobody messed with her, she'd be an ordinary housewife," Drew said. And when he was hissed at, he defended himself. "I mean that's where she was headed, only her brother was killed and not allowed to be buried."

"Her personality would be the same, so somebody would have made her irate, especially today," Patti Burton said. "More so today because women are allowed more freedoms."

"She'd belong to Greenpeace," Susan Blackburn offered. "Not just as a member, but as one of the people who ride on the ship saving whales. She wouldn't only talk about it or send money—she'd do it."

"She'd march for civil rights."

"She'd have a political blog. A famous one because she's the king's daughter and all."

Thoughts of the blind king pulled me back to Juan Reyes with his life in the balance and blindness a definite possibility. There was no escaping thoughts of him, and I would no longer try to.

"*Former* king," somebody added. "*Disgraced* king."

"Yeah, like scandal means you can't still be famous. It'd make more people read her than ever!"

I wanted to push them further, but my inner censor squeaked a protest. Shouldn't do this, it squealed, but my censor was a diminutive creature, and I ignored it. "Do you think, on that blog, she could say whatever she wanted?"

"She's Antigone, so of course!"

"It's *imaginary*," Susan Blackburn reminded me. "We're *speculating*. She's mythical."

"I know," I said. "But what if."

"Yes," Nita said. "Of course she can say whatever she wants. This isn't Greece."

"Freedom of speech." Drew nodded and folded his arms across his chest, making it clear that what he'd said was correct and that the topic was now closed for discussion.

"No limits?"

Allie's eyebrows pulled together. "Why would there be?" She seemed angry about something—Antigone?

"What if Antigone's advocating the overthrow of the government?" I asked. "In the play, she was, in essence, doing just that. Saying the king was wrong, that she wouldn't live by his decision."

"Freedom. Of. Speech." Drew repeated his words slowly, to help the cognitively impaired teacher.

I nodded. He smiled.

"I guess," Nita said, "if it's violent overthrow, then maybe the government would be watching the blog."

People called out. They weren't supposed to, but I wasn't about to squelch the discussion.

"Maybe," Susan said. "But they couldn't stop it. You can think stuff and say stuff even if you can't do stuff."

"Sticks and stones can break my bones, but names can never hurt me," Drew added. "My mother taught me to say that."

"Here's another thought," I said. The tiny censor jumped up and down now, screaming, but luckily, he was still tiny. Plus, he had a lifetime of being ignored. He'd handle this. "What if Antigone wrote a play like the one about her? Say she puts a play on her blog about disobeying the king, the law of the land. Or at least disagreeing with him, with it. Could it be produced? If it was produced, would she be in trouble?"

They grew more sure of themselves, and more sure that I wasn't getting it. *"Freedom of speech,"* I heard repeated with a touch of exasperation.

"Long as she's not lying—or libeling the king."

I nodded. "Would freedom of speech apply to other art forms? What if she tried to draw it, to express her feelings visually? Drew an ugly, a foul portrait of the king?"

They weren't as sure at first, but then they nodded. "It's the way artists express themselves," Davida said. "I'd consider that their form of speech, then. And how about political cartoonists? So yes."

"If it was a play? A poem?"

Even though some of the class continued to look at me as if I had lost more than a few of my buttons, as soon as I'd said the word "poem," I saw the glint of recognition in Susan Blackburn's eyes. She leaned to her right and whispered to her neighbor, who then turned to the boy behind her.

"I think I know what this is about," Susan said. "I mean it's about Antigone, yes, but my sister's in eleventh grade. She doesn't go here, but she's good friends with Cheryl Stevens."

"What are you talking about?" a boy said, and then I saw someone lean toward him and whisper, and then the buzz traversed the room at warp speed.

"We're talking about *Antigone*, the ideas in the play. And also," I admitted, "about the Bill of Rights."

"It isn't fair—it isn't legal!" Allie said.

I was once again impressed by the subterranean communication in our tiny high school village. I knew the class's collective knowledge—not academic, but practical, street smarts—would amaze me.

"Which poem was it?"

We weren't even pretending this was about Antigone anymore.

"We heard all of them—which was it?" the boy continued.

When told, the response was immediate.

"That wasn't even bad!"

"She was sad—is that a crime?"

"The guy's blind! Why can't she be angry for what happened to him?"

The air crackled with their electricity. There are few things teens enjoy more than a sense of outrage and unfairness.

I imagined Maurice Havermeyer happening upon this scene. I would so have loved to see him try to defend himself against these righteous twelfth graders and all they'd been taught.

My attention returned to the room where, within seconds, everyone had learned that the author of the antiwar poem was leaving the school. It was possible they knew more than I did about it, since I'd only gotten Havermeyer's version of the story. Their sense of violation seemed even greater than mine.

"We have to do something," Susan said. Many voices agreed.

We had a dissident. Mike Novak, generally interested in nothing outside the basketball court except for his hair, was at least consistent. He shook his head. Yawned. "I'm sure we don't know the whole story," he said. "The school must have good reasons."

His classmates glared at him. He shrugged. The conversation bored him. "If you knew about her since yesterday," he said, "why didn't you already do something? Why now?"

Susan was silent for a moment. "Because I didn't think about it until we were talking about Antigone."

It was a bad day, a terrible day, but I suddenly thought I might cry with happiness. Look at what had been given me, like a gift, a sense of being a genuine, certified *educator*. I had tapped into their unused reservoir of brains, at least a bit, at least for some of them.

Okay, at least for one of them.

Mike Novak was in the minority, though I saw him recruiting Jimmy, who, in his perpetual state of discontent, was ready to disagree with anyone, even to disagree with disagreeing. But the conversation rolled over them, and grew ever more heated and determined.

"We have rights in this country!"

"The law's the law for everybody!"

"Yeah, what are we? Second-class citizens?"

"Slaves?"

I was amazed. Of course, their sudden passion was not abstract. In the eternal war of faculty versus students, their ranks had been attacked, and unfairly, so this was about their personal rights, and this was about them. We were talking about perceived self-interest, but it didn't matter.

"Let's sign a petition."

"Let's boycott school!"

I knew somebody would come up with that one. Normally, I would discourage such an idea, but today, I didn't think it was the worst way of expressing their disgust. It was, in fact, close to my own plans.

They were delighted by each other's suggestions, and I saw a succession of high fives, and more quietly, nods and thumbs-ups.

I watched their animation, listened to the happy whine of mental gears in motion, and tried to superimpose this excited, exciting reaction onto the stolen exam, the threats against Reyes, his keyed car, the harassment, and the idea that they—or at least somebody in this group—had something to do with his accident.

The pictures didn't fit.

I kept hoping Seth would join in, become engaged, but he looked abstracted, as though viewing his classmates from a high and distant peak. Lately, he'd behaved as if he were behind a barricade, one I couldn't see, but was nonetheless impermeable.

This afternoon, he again was the remote observer. Now and then he nodded if he agreed with comments, but he added nothing. In fact, he looked nervous, flicking quick glances at people, then looking away.

Susan stood up, arms crossed over her chest, legs in a firm, wide stance. She looked like the can-do! World War II posters of women in the factories. "We could call ourselves the Antigone Brigade," she said.

I watched her gather support until even Mike and Jimmy grudgingly listened to a wild series of civil protest plans.

I did nothing to stop any of it. It was their right. Right?

And having fomented dissent, or at least given it a try, I felt ready to bid adieu. I didn't need to stay to watch the revolution.

I was on emotional overload, worried about Juan Reyes's future, if he had one, and about what had happened to him, about the series of minor and major pranks and attacks, about the dramatic changes in Seth—but also filled with a rush of love, admiration, and a sense of profound connection to this class for what was happening right now.

Their activism and excitement meant I'd done enough. It was time for me to say good-bye and find a new place where the First Amendment was still in effect.

Twelve

And that was that. The rest of the day went quietly and smoothly. My teaching life had apparently ended not with a bang but a fizzle and no matter what had happened, obligations continued, so I jumped into a phone booth—if only there were still phone booths, changed into my cape—if only I had one—and became PI Girl for the thrill of watching the blank façade of Bertha Polley's house.

I tried to pass the time by imagining how Pip pictured this. Surveillance—what an exciting lie of a word. For Pip's sake, I pretended to be dictating a memo of what I observed. "Subject's patio is three steps up from sidewalk. Furnishings consist of two aluminum-tubing chairs with threadbare red-and-yellow-striped seats and backs and one small round table holding a terra-cotta pot and dead plant. Blue aluminum siding on house façade, and wrought-iron railing around patio. Front yard contains one scraggly bush and packed dirt. Ms. Polley apparently not an avid gardener even before her accident."

I couldn't make it interesting, even for Pip. And I couldn't make Berta Polley appear.

I checked the time, took one last look at the nondescript house, and wished I could jazz up my detective work for Pip, or maybe, being honest, for me.

When I got home, I was the loft's only occupant. Pip was still out. He'd said he had a big day of sightseeing ahead, and I was so happy he wasn't going to spend another day watching TV that I'd forgotten to ask what sights he planned to see.

I felt at loose ends and ethically challenged. If I was going to quit my job, did I still have to mark the accumulated quizzes and essays in my backpack? Probably. I would retain my dignity and not saddle my successor with loose ends. I marked the eleventh grade poetry units and felt another rush of sorrow and anger and disbelief when I came to Cheryl Stevens's. I wondered how this entire episode would affect her. I hoped the same passionate emotions that had led to the poem would continue, and that she'd hold on to her sense of right and wrong. As soon as I was officially a free agent, I would get in touch with her and tell her all of that.

There was an extra poem in the packet. It lacked a name or title, as had the one Liddy Moffatt had found. Maybe one of my students was taking the idea of poems being written by "Anon." too literally?

It was wretched. No wonder it wasn't signed.

Mischief Night and are we scared
For big trouble we're prepared
But what's a prank and what's a crime
And is the only difference time?
Friday till midnight is all right
That's the meaning of that night.
But if it's done another day,
Then somebody's gonna pay
Ghosts and goblins say they will
When they have some time to kill.

Doggerel. I bet it was—wisely—rejected by its author, but just in case not, I put it in the backpack.

Pip walked in as I had my head deep into the freezer,

searching for something spaghetti-compatible. I had garlic, olive oil, and basil, so I felt 90 percent of the way there. "Did you have a good day?" I asked as I found a small package of ground turkey.

"Way good," he said, surprising me with his enthusiasm.

"Did you go to Constitution Hall?"

He shook his head, then saw my expression. "I will, I guess." Then, more emphatically, "I will. Soon, maybe."

"Normally, I'd say do whatever you like. Today I feel as if that trip should be a universal requirement."

"Excuse me?"

"I'll explain later. Where did you go?"

He tossed his rain jacket onto the floor, then reconsidered and hung it on the bright yellow coatrack that, prior to cohabiting with Pip, I would have said nobody could miss. "Kind of related," he said, "at least about the law. Or breaking it. I went to Eastern State."

The old penitentiary—the first one in the world, now a crumbling historic site.

"Really something," he said. "Creepy."

"You know, it was innovative in its time. That idea that prisoners could be—"

"Penitent. The audio said that. They could change, they thought, if they kept them in solitary."

I remembered my trip there and how, walking through its claustrophobic dimness, I found it hard to believe this once represented the most progressive thinking about crime and punishment. "Solitary confinement was thought to keep them away from bad company."

Pip glanced at me quickly, then away. His mother blamed some of his sudden desire to drop out on unsavory new friends. "Better, I guess, than being left to molder in a dungeon," I added.

"Capone's cell had fancy furniture, and rugs, and everything."

"Envious?"

He shook his head. "It's so creepy in there. Even his place. It looks good compared to the plain cells, but they're all little and they don't have windows." He made a dramatic shudder. "And they made the guys wear these thick masks so that they looked like the Mummy—so if they were near anybody, they still couldn't talk to them. And they got fed through these wooden openings into their cells. Creeped me out."

"Did they tell you that one of the prisoners was a dog?"

We both turned, though the voice was unmistakable. Mackenzie had come in quietly, except for the crackling of the paper wrapped around a large square object he carried.

He leaned the package against the wall near the door. "Macavity, cover your ears. Pep the dog was imprisoned for murdering a cat."

Macavity blinked. If only a cat's face had movable muscles, his would have illustrated the disdain he felt for Mackenzie's stab at what might be feline humor. Instead, he flicked his tail, and proved that body language could sometimes be 100 percent of all communication. His message was clear.

Mackenzie sat with us at the table.

"How do you know about the prison and the dog and all?" Pip asked.

Mackenzie raised one eyebrow.

"Oh, yeah. You're studying that kind of thing. But why would you need to know what happened back then?"

"You know the sayin' that those who don't know history are doomed to repeat it?"

Pip was silent for a moment before speaking in a flat, strained voice. "Is everything you guys are saying secretly— no, not so secretly—code? Is it all a way of saying I should go back to school? 'Cause that's what I'm hearing."

Mackenzie cocked his head. "We were talkin' about my education. But if you were to ask me about going back to school, I'd answer honestly. Are you asking my opinion?"

Pip's chin moved forward. "Guess not."

I was watching a patient angler play a prize fish. Interesting.

The microwave defrost cycle signaled it was finished, so I relocated at the range and browned chopped garlic and the ground turkey.

"On my way home, I went to the Pretzel Museum," Pip said.

"And how many samples did you have?" I asked, like any hausfrau preparing dinner would.

"I'll be able to eat."

"Listen, guys," I said. "Today was . . . my day was something I . . ." I turned the ground meat, separating it, and sighed.

Nobody asked what I meant.

"Got a present for us." Mackenzie gestured toward the large square he'd brought in.

"Us?" Pip and I both said.

"The bride and groom," Mackenzie said. "Sorry. You have time to open it? It's from a bunch of guys I used to work with."

I unwrapped it carefully.

"They said it's an original," he said. "A daybill poster— except I don't know what a daybill poster is."

It was a bright yellow-and-red ad for *The Thin Man Goes Home*.

I laughed.

"I don't get it," Pip said. "Why an ad for an old-looking movie?"

"Your uncle's buddies think of us—are laughing at us a little bit—as Nick and Nora, the couple in this film. What a great gift for our home, and they even had it framed."

"You're the thin man?" Pip asked Mackenzie. "You're not that thin. I mean, you're like normal."

"So was he. The thin man was actually the victim in the first movie, but somehow the name stuck. They were sophisticated sleuths. A married couple who liked each other a whole lot, and solved crimes, too. No wonder the guys saw the similarities."

"And they drank and drank and drank," I murmured, wishing life were more like art here. "It's us to a T—stinking rich and stinking drunk. I love it!"

We spent time figuring out precisely where we'd hang it, and finally decided that near the doorway, near, in fact, the yellow coatrack, would be a perfect welcoming spot for my not-abnormally-Thin Man when he came home.

And then it was time for our decidedly un–Nick and Nora dinner. "We forgot the champagne," I murmured, looking over at the poster.

"And the martinis. And the scotch. And whatever else," Mackenzie said. "I don't think William Powell had to study after dinner."

"And Myrna Loy definitely didn't have to do the dishes."

As we ate, the table talk wandered around the Thin Man movies, and I had to admit that it was not an easy job trying to describe their appeal to Pip. We'd have to rent one while he was here. We moved back to the penitentiary and Al Capone, to pretzel making, and a book Mackenzie was reading about the causes of and prognosis for families with high proportions of law-breakers in them.

The talk was flowing too well, the two males completely engaged in their storehouses of knowledge, but one second before I was going to have to force myself and my day into the conversation, and one half second before I was going to have to get annoyed by that need, Mackenzie turned to me. "Were you saying something about your day when I so rudely interrupted?"

I do love that man. "How could a gift be a rude interruption?" I said. "But yes. It was a rough one and . . . I have something important to say."

"Want me to get out of the way?" Pip asked.

We lived in a loft. There wasn't anyplace to send him except the street, our bedroom, or the bathroom. Besides, this wasn't anything personal between Mackenzie and me, and it wasn't a secret. "Not at all. This is a family discussion, and you're part of the family now. I've had a horrible day, but the science teacher had an even worse one. I'll do the rotten events in chronological sequence."

I summarized everything I could remember about this morning: the rain, the scratched car, the explosion, the injuries. I skipped the Tisha Banks part, saving his affair and the striptease and details for later, when alone with Mackenzie.

They looked upset and sympathetic. "Any clue what caused it?"

I shook my head. "He's still in critical condition," I said. "Even if he lives and recuperates, he may be blind."

"I wonder how many chemistry lab accidents there are every year," Mackenzie murmured. "Thousands, I bet."

"I—I'm not sure it was an accident."

Pip sat up straighter.

"How's that?" Mackenzie asked. "How's that possible?"

"I don't know. A feeling, is all. Too many bits and pieces—"

"That bad feelin' you've had all week?" He said it politely, without much inflection, but I knew he was verifying that it was a feeling, not even a theory, and surely nothing with facts to back it up.

"Could somebody plant something with a long fuse? Or a time delay mechanism on it? Did they find anything at all like that?"

"I don't think so. They think it was an accident." I

sounded like a fool. I wanted to lay my head down on the table and give up. I didn't know enough to know what I meant. "I got this, though. Somebody put it in my raincoat pocket this morning." Easy enough to have done. I didn't have a locker, the way the students did. I had a peg on the wall, or the back of a chair, and I didn't monitor whatever I tossed on either one. I stood up and retrieved the wrinkled orange piece of paper and handed it to C.K.

Pip half stood, and leaned over to read it, then looked over at me, wide-eyed.

Mackenzie bit at his bottom lip.

"I know!" I said more sharply than intended. "I know it could be a prank—but why? I don't know what to believe or what to do." I looked over at the framed poster. If Nora had shown this note to Nick, they'd be off and running in pursuit of the truth. My not-overly-Thin Man sighed again instead.

"You should tell the police," he finally said.

"What do I tell them? What do I actually know? They'd laugh at that note—you want to laugh at it, don't you?"

"Maybe not laugh, but . . ."

"Ignore it?"

"That's closer to the mark."

"And if it isn't true—I really don't want to get these kids in trouble. Not that I'd know what kid or which kids it is. But not this close to their college applications going in. By the time an investigation would clear them, it would be too late for them."

"You can't ignore it! I thought you two were crime fighters." Pip gestured toward the entry, toward the poster again. "You have to solve it!"

Mackenzie and I looked at each other, and then at our nephew. "Okay," I said. "But somebody has to write me a script first."

"And put lots of martinis in it, too," C.K. said.

"But you're there," Pip said. "And look—somebody's trying to tell you something. It'd be easy for you to—"

"That's what I wanted to say. I won't be there. I'm quitting."

"Quitting what?" the males asked in unison.

"My job. Teaching." I am ashamed to say that I enjoyed their matching horror.

"Can you just quit like that? Isn't it wrong?" Pip looked like he had a lot more to say, but then he belatedly realized that he was in no position to take a stand against the idea of quitting school. I felt embarrassed to be setting such a bad example for him, but I wasn't doing this gratuitously.

"Because of the explosion?" Mackenzie asked me quietly.

I shook my head. "Because of the poetry reading."

Pip pushed himself away from the table. "Listen, you don't want me for this. Poetry is not my thing."

"That's exactly how I hoped you'd react," I said. That startled him enough to wait to hear me out. "Because that's how almost everybody in my tenth grade class reacted—especially the boys—when I said we were going to have a unit on poetry."

"I'd better declare myself right now," Mackenzie said, looking at his nephew. "I like the stuff."

Pip checked to make sure his uncle wasn't poking fun at him, that he really did have feet of clay.

"Anyway, it turned out that most of them liked the poems I'd picked, and some of them even said they wrote poems themselves."

"Guys?" Pip flashed a quick look at the resident guy, worried now that his uncle had entire legs made of clay.

"Wish I could, but I'm not sufficiently talented," Mackenzie said, shaking his head.

"Okay, mostly girls wrote them," I admitted, "but not all." I explained how the idea had grown and been a success and how we'd performed it—on TV—for the entire school.

While I spoke, Mackenzie stood and cleared the table. I had noticed how intently Pip watched whenever the man of the house did anything vaguely domestic. His mother had been married twice, and from what I gathered, had endured several unformalized but equally unhappy unions. Without knowing a single one of those men, I could almost envision each one by watching Pip's amazement. Dishwashing, poetry loving, and who knew what else? We were either traumatizing the teen or helping him redefine—by lurches and jolts—what it meant to be a male.

"Want me to help, Unc?" he asked. Another small victory.

I plowed on while Pip picked up a dish towel and dried plates, and to feel part of the group, I cleared the place mats and condiments while I spoke. "Not the poetry, but because a *social studies teacher* objected to one of the poems. Said it was un-American, that it might foment violence."

Mackenzie had stopped washing dishes. "What did it say?"

"I'll get it for you, but does it matter? It wasn't pornographic, it wasn't a call to do anything—it was an antiwar lament. This girl's cousin came home blind and she's horrified by what that means to his life. So the poem's her feelings about killing or being sent to war."

"And?" When he wanted to, Mackenzie had the ability to pay attention so fiercely, I felt as if I had a klieg light aimed at me.

"She's been asked to leave the school—not that Havermeyer admitted that. But she's leaving. And I've been advised to stop spreading dissent, and not to publish the poem in the school paper. I mentioned freedom of speech, the Constitution, the Bill of Rights—and all I got back was that these were special times."

He'd turned off the water and dried his hands.

I walked back to the table and slumped down in the chair, and first Mackenzie and then Pip also pulled out chairs and sat back down.

"What are you going to do about it?" Mackenzie asked.

"Honestly?"

"Not dishonestly."

"I don't feel I can continue working there, and I'm going to resign immediately. I'll be able to pick up some other work while I look for another—"

Both Mackenzie and Pip shook their heads, as if they'd rehearsed. I could see a resemblance between them for the first time. "What?" I said. "I'll find something. Maybe I can work for Ozzie more, or for some other—"

Pip put one of his big hands on my arm. "You can't quit."

"With all due respect, Pip, you're a fine one to talk about quitting."

His eyes widened. "I'm a kid! I'm allowed to do stupid things. I'm stupid! Haven't you noticed? I'm sixteen! It's not the same thing at all." He had a cute dimple when he wasn't sulking.

"That's the most ridiculous argument I've ever heard." But it had made me smile, and to once again revise my opinion of the young man's intelligence. "Why can't I quit? Aside from your somehow believing that I'm too old to be stupid."

"Because they're the ones doing the wrong thing, not you." He smacked the table for emphasis. "Let *them* leave!"

"Because it's your job," C.K. added. "An' the girl who wrote the poem—she shouldn't leave, either."

"But she is. Her parents are taking her out, and I can't blame them. I'd do the same. She deserves a better environment for learning and experimenting."

"So do you."

"Not going to have it there. I'm too angry, and there's no fighting him. It's Havermeyer's school and he's got no spine."

My words seemed to float on the air currents in the loft, and to hang up against the high ceiling and the dark skylight, and I realized the two males were watching me, as if I were a specimen. Of what, I couldn't say, but with their every silent inhale and exhale, the air thickened.

"Okay," I finally said. "What is it?"

"You're letting him win," Pip said.

"This isn't some macho game. This is my life. Even so, I admit it—he wins. Everybody else loses."

"Not making anything better by walkin' away." My husband looked sad, perhaps disappointed in me.

"I can't make it better," I said. "I have no super powers."

Mackenzie looked grim. "Of course, you should do whatever seems right to you."

This was not how I'd wanted this to go. Not at all. Instead of murmurs of sympathy and a chorus of "Of course you should get out of that loathsome place! You'll find something better, something more worthy of you!" they were behaving as if I'd suggested treason.

Mackenzie stood up and busied himself at the counter. In a minute, the grinder was pulverizing coffee beans, and he hummed softly as he measured them into the French press. I couldn't make my thoughts settle into any coherent pattern, so I sat where I was, trying to organize them.

I should do what I thought was right, he'd said. What seemed right to me was quitting. Therefore, the end was in sight.

So why didn't I feel relieved?

Mackenzie poured the boiling water into the press, took out two mugs—Pip had not yet developed the habit of coffee—and returned to the table, bearing all the makings. "Why not make the most of the situation?" he asked quietly.

Pip watched his uncle, as if expecting a miraculous fairy-tale sort of ending.

Mackenzie shrugged. "I'd vote for civil disobedience instead." He put his elbow on the table and rested his chin on the palm of his hand and looked as if he'd given me an actual plan, or solution. "It'd be an appropriate response."

He put down his arm and leaned toward me. "Pip's right. You can't simply quit. If you do, do you think Havermeyer's going to go to the kids and explain why you've left? Do you think anybody's going to debate those ideas, learn something from this, do something about this?"

"Of course not. I only—"

Pip beamed. He'd been right, whether or not he knew why.

"Correct. Instead, there will be some mumbled cover-up of a reason, and you'll be out in the cold with nothing gained. You lose, the kids lose."

"And there's no chance you'll find out what happened to the chemistry guy, either," Pip said.

"You are therefore suggesting what?"

"Like I said, civil disobedience. Another right of ours. Protest and keep on keeping on, and spread the word, and print that poem and find out about Reyes and I'll help if I can."

"Me, too," Pip said.

"That's no solution," I said. "Know what'll happen? I'll get fired."

"*Exactly!*"

And slowly the tension drained out of me, and the unease was replaced by energy, and I laughed. "And I'll be no worse off."

"*Precisely!*"

I love how his Louisiana accent makes the word have absolutely no precision. And I loved the idea.

Pip looked at his uncle with renewed hero worship. And to tell the truth, I looked at Mackenzie with just about the same expression.

Of course, there was a downside: This meant I definitely had to mark the rest of those quizzes and essays, after all.

Thirteen

THE NEXT MORNING, THE CHIP ON MY SHOULDER WAS SO large, I had to enter the school building sideways. Worse, I liked wearing it and felt it was the perfect accessory. Coming to school with the express purpose of doing whatever I wanted until I was tossed out had a delicious, seditious feel.

But before insurrection, I needed an update on Juan Reyes.

Harriet's normally happy expression grew solemn. "Very upsetting," she said. "The hospital is so vague! They said they were cautiously optimistic. He wasn't out of danger yet, but he . . . well, I think what they were saying was that it was a good sign because he hadn't died, but really—that isn't enough information!"

I agreed, and I collected the contents of my mailbox. Harriet continued talking.

"It's been a difficult time, if I say so myself. Because on top of poor Mr. Reyes, Erroll was beside himself last night, and I can't really blame him! Imagine somebody *cheating* by using an outside fur-shine expert's help!"

I looked at the mail. Another warning to read to our classes about the Friday night party. Costumes were to be "respectful," behavior was to be "circumspect," and alcoholic beverages and controlled substances were to be altogether absent. That last warning was pretty clear, but the others confused even me.

There was a solicitation from an insurance company and a notice about a new English text that I might be able to review, and a While You Were Out slip, signed by Harriet. Apparently, Mrs. Wilson "needs to speak to you" about "a matter of some importance." However, she would be away from the phone and her home for most of the day.

I pondered the meaning of a message saying that I had to talk with someone who wouldn't be available to do so. What was I to do with this information?

Harriet dusted her smiling jack-o'-lantern, fluffed its black wig and straightened the witch's hat. "Poor Erroll's got an artist's soul, you know. You can't destroy their sensitivities that way and expect them to perform. He didn't do well at all in the competition."

I couldn't see the cause and effect in that, since Erroll would have had to prepare beforehand without knowing about the cheat, but it was not my place to question life in the taxidermy jungle.

"This may mean he'll have to take extra classes." She followed her words with an enormous sigh. "His confidence is shaken." Grief and compassion choked her. "Low self-esteem is *terrible* for a taxidermist. They can't be timid! They can't make a wrong cut! I don't know how to help him, except to stand by my man and cheer him on."

"I'm sure that's precisely what he needs. And by the way—Mrs. Wilson phoned me?" I waved the little pink square as a reminder.

She blinked, then nodded. "Yesterday. An hour after school. I was still here, so I took the message. Something about bad company. Maybe a bad company? People who spoil things? To tell you the truth, she sounded like somebody upset about nothing. Certainly nothing urgent, so I didn't think you'd want to be bothered at home about it. Was I right?"

I nodded. "But it isn't clear what she wants me to do, given that she's out all day."

"I think she said she'd try to reach you today from wherever she found herself."

Bad companies? What did that have to do with English class, or with her son? Bad company? His friends were the same as ever, and they were an okay bunch, with, sometimes, the exception of Wilson himself, who could get obnoxious. He was cocky about things "working out" for him no matter how little effort he produced. He was constantly winking and telling me—and anyone else who showed emotions—to "chill out" and "go with the flow" and other semiarchaic but still annoying expressions. But that didn't seem to be what was on her mind. Since I had to wait till she reached me, I put the message into my backpack and opted not to worry about it.

So, apparently, did Harriet. "I need to think of something special for my poor baby," she said. "I need to help him get through this crisis."

Erroll had a good thing going, milking Harriet for all she was worth. Of course, I could be wrong, cynical. Taxidermy could be his life's passion, belatedly but sincerely found. His struggles could be heroic, his depressions severe when he failed to meet his standards of excellence.

He might even intend to marry Harriet someday, and shower her with the wealth his preserved turkeys, frogs, and boa constrictors brought them.

And stuffed pigs would fly.

"Sounds perfect," I said, but before I could get away, Maurice Havermeyer's office door opened, and he emerged, looking flustered until he saw me. "Ah, good," he said. "I was about to send for you."

More grief? My shoulders dropped along with my spirits

until I remembered that I was in charge. I was ready to be fired. Nothing he could do to me mattered.

But it could surprise me. "I'd like your input on a situation," he said. "Right outside the door. The student notice board."

We walked out of the office and faced the messy board, which always looked as if it were shedding. "What is the meaning of this?" he asked before I'd said a word.

My first thought was that he'd spotted and disapproved of the peculiar party announcements I'd seen a few days back, and I looked for one of them now, for the headless pumpkin man, the "don't get hung up" message, the added "don't put yourself in this picture."

But those messages were gone or covered up, and being that alert to subtle changes in his environment would have been quite un-Havermeyerish. The board looked its usual self, layers of messages about lost backpacks and textbooks, pleas for articles for the newspaper, or attendance at a basketball game, and all the pages generously peppered with exclamation points. Everything urgent and high-pitched.

Today, again the strident messages were heavy on orange and black, urging EVERYONE!!! TO MAKE SOME MISCHIEF!!! ATTEND THE PARTY!!! it would be SO FUN!!!

I looked back at the headmaster, feeling like a bad student trying to read the teacher's expression as if the right answer might be visible there. His face looked grim, but didn't yield a clue.

"I'm sorry," I said. "I don't understand. What situation?"

His lips pursed and he pointed at a specific orange sheet, already half covered by a plea for information about a lost notebook. "What is this about?" he demanded. "Who is missing—and who is against what? This is not the place for negative statements! Don't students understand there are rules about posting on this board?"

I followed his finger's direction.

My eyes had swept right over it, registering it as another Halloween message, but now I read the words, written in thick black marker:

THE ANTIGONE BRIGADE IS HERE!!!!

I swallowed my immediate response of delighted surprise. Why was he talking about negative statements? This was a clear and positive declarative sentence—a little heavy on the exclamation points. Was that what bothered him? Was I going to be in still more trouble for failure to contain excessive punctuation?

And then I realized what he was seeing as compared to what was there. My bombastic headmaster, the self-declared educator, the pompous, self-important champion of "the canon" as he insisted on calling whatever he deemed a classic, that Maurice Havermeyer was mentally pronouncing her name not as *An-tig-o-nee* but as *Anti Gone*.

How do you inform an employer who is already unhappy with you that he is an ill-educated ignoramus?

Of course, given that this was get-myself-pink-slipped day, saying that would be an easy route out the door, but with larger issues at stake than pronunciation, I didn't want my firing offense to be tactlessness.

"Oh, Dr. Havermeyer," I said. "You're so clever to make puns about the classics! As if you didn't know how to pronounce Sophocles' protagonist!" I chuckled. He didn't have to know what was making me laugh.

His second chin wobbled and his eyebrows danced over a series of small muscle movements that illustrated a range of emotions from stymied to perplexed to worried to belligerent. For those moments, his face seemed a transparent

mask over his brain, and I could almost read the thoughts
circling his skull in letters as bold as the Antigone Brigade's
and with as many !!!'s.

He finally settled on a tenuous expression of superiority.
"Yes, yes," he said in a bluff tone. "Of course. My little
joke, heh-heh." He cleared his throat. "But the serious
question remains: What is this—this—this person—"

He didn't know who she was, or even that she was a she.

"—*about*? What does this mean?"

"This is the first I've seen it. I have no idea."

I didn't know what it was about, though I knew its ori-
gins, and to me, it was about having hope for the future.
The same people who'd frightened me with their secretive
surliness had redeemed themselves.

To me, this primitive scrawl was about freedom of expression, about patriotism, about preserving and caring for
the basic rights of citizens, about knowing right from wrong,
and being willing to stand up for what was right.

And I knew that poster made my heart expand with renewed faith in mankind in general, and in the class that
had so worried me specifically.

None of which was safe to say to Maurice Havermeyer
because he might actually understand that he was the villain of the piece. "I don't know," I said again.

"Why Anti-goners? Is it *goner* as in a dead person? How
can anybody be against dead people?"

I hadn't pronounced her name when making my face-
saving joke and now, once again, I had to save his. "Why
name themselves after"—I looked at the poster, not at him,
as I carefully pronounced the name—"Antigone?"

He frowned as he realized nothing was "gone" or
"against"—nothing he understood, in any case—then retained the frown and looked back at me. "Then I repeat—
what is this about?"

"I don't know. My seniors just read the Oedipus trilogy. They seemed quite moved by the ideas."

"Oedipus," Havermeyer murmured. "The one who married his mother? Why *him*?" I would probably now be charged with teaching incest.

"Her. She was his daughter, you recall."

"Who?"

"Antigone."

After a beat, he said, "Of course." I waited while the idea swam around in his skull, looking for a toehold. It obviously found nothing except resentment that a planned tirade against anything beginning with *anti* had to be shelved.

"But did she—I don't recall—been a while—did she have an army?"

I shook my head. "Acted alone. It got her in a lot of trouble with the king."

The King of Philly Prep worried for a moment. "The classics," he said, back to blustering. "People should not twist the classics to suit their own—are you certain you don't know what this is about? Why doesn't it say what it is? Why doesn't it say what it wants? It says to join—but it doesn't even say how to do that!"

"Kids," I murmured.

He huffed as if building up steam, but he couldn't find purchase. "I will investigate this further on my own," he finally said. "Thank you for your time. Mustn't keep you." He looked at his watch, which hung, along with the fake Phi Beta Kappa key, on a chain across his wide belly. "School day's about to start."

I didn't see why he had to check the time. Surely the noisy onslaught of students pouring through the door not five feet away from us could have convinced him school was about to begin. On fine days, high school students did not spontaneously burst into a schoolhouse before they had to. But as usual, he wasn't overly sensitive to what was going on right around him. Besides, he loved any excuse to use that pocket watch, that gold chain, that fake award.

After he'd walked back to the office, I inspected the Antigone Brigade's announcement to see if I'd missed anything. But even with the lost notebook announcement moved off it, it simply announced its existence and invited others to join, saying nothing about what it stood for or intended to do.

With my new awareness of the adolescent subterranean communication system, I knew that most of the school population would be able to fill in the blanks. Further, they'd know that the faculty, lumbering around outside the loop, would be left in the dark.

I'd forgotten to turn my cell phone off, and it rang. I was glad I answered, because it was Mackenzie, whose voice I am always glad to hear.

"Sodium," he said by way of greeting.

"The same to you," I said.

"Remember, last night, you told me about the girl in the lab and how she thought Reyes said 'Oh, no!' right before being blasted?"

I certainly did. Once Pip was on his sofabed, watching TV with earphones on so the sound wouldn't bother us, I'd filled in the blanks.

"Just remembered a little high school chemistry, and sodium explodes when a rush of water hits it or it's tossed into water. If he turned on the faucet, leaned in to put out his cigarette in the water, and saw what was directly below it—he'd say something. He'd know what was about to happen. Does that make sense?"

It did. And I didn't think I'd told Mackenzie about the missing sodium. "How did you know that?" I asked.

He chuckled. "I figured it had to be something pretty accessible that combines with water, given the sink and the 'oh, no!' and I suddenly remembered high school. Given the glass was all over, and his cuts, it must have been sitting there in a jar or something. We were . . . scientifically curious, but nobody got hurt. Gotta run," he said, "but I wanted to tell you, for whatever it's worth, before I forgot."

I thanked him, hung up, turned off the phone, and walked upstairs to my room.

It made terrible sense. And it meant the note that said the explosion had not been an accident had been written by somebody who knew the truth and was trying to speak it.

Including the prediction that "something worse" was about to happen.

Fourteen

I DIDN'T KNOW WHAT TO DO WITH THIS NEW KNOWLEDGE, except look and listen until I understood what it might mean. And in the meantime, it did not seem wise or kind to spread my anxieties. I didn't know what else would happen or when, and I couldn't protect any of us against it or make any sort of rational accusation.

I'd call the police later, and they would politely sneer. "Something bad," "sodium," "um-hm . . ." And they'd already know about the sodium because I assumed they took samples of the glop on the floor.

It seemed best to stick to today's plan for as long as I could and that, of course, was to foment a revolution.

I didn't have to rouse any eleventh grade rabbles. Cheryl Stevens was their classmate. They knew about her problems and the solution she'd chosen without my saying a word. She'd told enough of them (which may have meant only one), and now they were all enraged.

"It was a good poem," a chubby girl named Ginger said. "It made me feel sad and it made me think."

Of course, that was its crime in Havermeyer's eyes.

All I had to do was give them a forum for their indignation and outrage. I murmured that their sentiments were shared by the seniors, and I mentioned the notice about the Antigone Brigade. But they knew about the brigade already, so my actions hardly constituted authentic agitation.

If they wound up in a kerfuffle, it would pretty much be because they'd arrived in one.

It was fun, moving from class to class, building on the rumors that had crisscrossed the school. Perhaps I had invented a new occupation: inside agitator. Cheryl Stevens became a rallying cry, a promise. All I had to do was prey—or, more politely, build—on their innate disdain for whatever adults had done, to set their adolescent energy free and watch it be ignited by righteous indignation.

No wonder so many of the world's most appalling revolutionaries were practically children. They're ready and eager for almost anything—as long as it doesn't smack of being a part of the established norm, and in this case, the curriculum.

It was almost too easy to get them going, and only now and then did I wonder if all boneheaded rabble-rousers were as convinced of their rightness as I was. I'd seen tragedy defined as the deadly clash of "right and right." I pushed that idea away. How can you think of yourself as radical if you're basing your argument on the Constitution of your country?

At lunch, Louis Applegate made it a point to sit as far from me as possible—not that I minded in the least—and to avoid all eye contact. Fine with me. I tried to psych out the rest of the faculty, to see if I was a demon in their eyes, too, but I couldn't get a feel for it. What I thought I sensed was fear. They knew about Cheryl, and I didn't want to believe they thought the treatment of her "infraction" was correct. But jobs were few and far between, and boat rocking was frightening. Their polite table talk was forced and stilted.

I felt as if weights had been put on my head. Not that our situation here was world shaking, but it was, on a small scale, a good example of how repression takes over. With jobs and security at stake, who speaks up?

The silence also gave me a moment's pause about what I was doing, but turning back didn't feel possible. I didn't know what would happen when the axe actually fell, but having decided to put my neck in position for the executioner, I wasn't about to move it. However, I didn't want to sit and feel the chill any longer than was necessary, so I ate quickly and excused myself to take a short walk. The air would help clear my head.

I didn't make it past the office. Harriet swooped out and grabbed the corner of my sweater, saying, "Look! Here she is!"

"Who?" I asked.

"You! Here you are—I recognized the blue sweater and guess what? Mrs. Wilson's here—she just popped in and wants to see you."

"Now? I was going for a walk." By this point, the solid and intent Mrs. Wilson faced me, nodding.

"Thought I'd have more time today," she said in a rapid clip, "but things piled up. I was on my lunch hour and realized this was it—now or never—so here I am. Let's talk."

No wonder her son was so good at sports. He'd have had to learn to run fast to avoid this human dynamo. Not a syllable asking if this was a good time for me.

I tried again. "I was just going outside for some fresh—"

"Good. We'll walk together. Too many students here anyway and this is sensitive."

I was feeling fairly sensitive myself, but with Harriet rolling her eyes in the background, I meekly accompanied Wilson's mother out the front door. I wasn't sure my blue sweater was warm enough but the woman would not have tolerated indecision, so I walked out, shivering in the brisk air.

"Mrs. Wilson, I'm sorry, but I don't have much time before—"

She held her hand up before I had finished the sentence.

"Serenity." She walked briskly, as if we had to reach a goal before my time ran out.

I thought "Serenity" was a password, a goal, an aspiration, and I didn't know how to respond and wound up stammering. "I—I—Mrs. Wilson, I—"

"Call me Serenity."

How disappointed her parents must have been with their optimistically but wrongly named child.

"First name, no formality," she snapped. "I'm asking a favor." She didn't bother to slow her pace or look my way as she barked out her sentences.

I wondered what constituted a favor for her. She seemed the type to take what she wanted, or beat it into submission. I walked as quickly as I could, and waited for the next move.

"It's Donald."

Again, I missed a mental beat because nobody called him that. A few people called him Donny, but Wilson was the almost-universal name used.

"Donald must be transferred to another English section and I want to know whether that will hurt his grades."

"Wait! What? We don't have that many sections. His entire schedule would be . . . Why?"

"His future is jeopardized."

"By my English class?" It is difficult demonstrating righteous indignation while running to keep up with somebody. I wanted to tap her on the shoulder and make her turn and notice my insulted expression.

"Not your class," she said, still looking and marching straight ahead. "Not your fault. The people in it. He needs to be separated from corrupting influences. This is his senior year. Everything matters. It's too late to change schools. He wouldn't be on the teams. He wouldn't stand a chance. He—"

"Halt!" I shouted.

A woman who'd made her way halfway across the street stopped and turned, then shook her head and trundled on.

"Stop and speak to me directly so I can understand what you're talking about."

Un-Serenity continued walking, but she slowed down and eventually stopped. I flashed back on those driver's-ed films that told you how many yards it took a car going twenty-five miles an hour to stop; how many yards if you were going fifty, and so forth. It took Serenity Wilson half a block. "The people in his class," she said, turning toward me.

"What people?"

She shook her head. "This is about Donald. I am not going to get other students in trouble. Even if I believe they should be. This is about my son."

"Academically? Have his grades noticeably changed? As far as I can see he's performing pretty much as he always—"

She shook her head again, and one foot nervously tapped. "Do you know—you must, right?—that his chemistry teacher is near death?" She waited for formal acknowledgment.

I nodded.

"Do you realize that did not have to happen?"

"What are you saying?" A headache clamped my temples. How did she know about it and would she tell me?

"I thought I made that clear. I want my son placed in classes with other people. Different people. The school is small, but not that small. And a man is judged by the company he keeps."

"His friends—"

"They aren't true friends. Not anymore. And that is my decision to make, in any case. My question is whether relocating will harm his grades."

"I don't even know if it's possible because of what it would do to his other classes, his entire schedule—"

"Why don't we leave that to *me*. I know it might be complicated, but I'll handle it. I'm starting with you because English has never been Donald's strong point academically."

I didn't think Donald had a strong point academically. He had strong legs and great hand-eye coordination and upper body strength, but the thinking muscle wasn't much to write home about.

She cleared her throat.

"I can't answer you," I said. "I teach one other senior section. If he enters that . . ." I shrugged. "They're following the same syllabus, so—"

"It won't make a difference, is that what you're saying?"

"If he moves into that section. But if he moves to another teacher's class—which might be necessary because—"

"—of the rest of his schedule. Yes."

I shouldn't have been as angry as I was, but what should or shouldn't be wasn't mattering much at the moment. I wasted a moment considering telling her off and using that avenue to being fired, but once again, she was peripheral, not the issue, and unworthy of that honor. I wanted to be fired for sowing dissension, for spreading insurrection. I wanted to deal with ideas, not overly protective and obnoxious mothers.

She did make me soften to Wilson, whose aggressive and rough-edged personality I now understood a bit. Another teacher had warned me that his parents had delusions of their son's grandeur and any failings on his part were blamed on the school.

I guess this time it was his classmates who were to blame for whatever it was that was going wrong, but what was? And why his friends? "Can you give me more information about your reasons for this?"

"It's a bad class. There are terrible influences in it and

my son is susceptible. It's a dangerous place to be and . . . and . . ."

I couldn't believe she was faltering, searching for words, unsure of herself.

". . . I'm afraid for him."

That stopped me for a minute. "What do you fear? What's happened? What connection does that class have to Juan Reyes's accident?"

She had lost all her bravado and she looked directly at me and said, with no animation, "I don't know. I only know something's different. Something frightening is going on."

"What gives you that—"

Challenged, un-Serenity returned. "I simply know! They are dangerous and the chemistry—their chemistry—is bad. I want him out."

"Who are these 'they' you keep mentioning?"

"That class. That group."

"His friends."

She shrugged.

"Then you should talk to the headmaster." I tried not to sound as chilly—physically and emotionally—as I felt. "And the counselor. I can't change anybody's schedule."

"And if he switches to your other section, he won't have any additional difficulties." It was a declaration, an instruction, not a question.

"I hope not." And luckily, before she tried to make me promise her humiliating actions wouldn't have any effect on her son's behavior and grades, neither of which were good to begin with, the bell rang, saving us all.

I HEARD THE DIN UPSTAIRS EVEN BEFORE I WAS ON THE first tread. I forced myself to walk the steps at a normal pace, thinking only: Do not let that noise be coming from my room.

But, indeed, my room or the space right outside it was the noise's epicenter. It was some relief to realize that while the students sounded agitated, they did not sound as if a catastrophe had taken place, and in fact, most of the talk was relatively hushed.

Nita and Allie were again in a huddle off to the side, across the hallway from their classmates, and judging by body language, once again disagreeing. This time, few words were exchanged, as if they both knew the other's position and had reached an angry impasse. Nita stood her place, hands folded across her chest, half turned away from her friend, her expression stony.

Allie reverted to shaking her head slowly, then more quickly, then slowly again, as if she could not get beyond the gigantic "No!" roiling inside her.

I am not arrogant—or insane—enough to interfere in the normal fluctuations of the student body's interpersonal relationships. I see histrionic displays on a daily basis, but at this point, this ongoing dispute between the two girls warranted a question or two.

The worst that could happen would be that they'd unite against a common enemy—me—and be as happily close as they'd been the past two years. "What's up?" I asked, keeping the question casual.

"Nothing. Why?" Allie's voice was brittle as an icicle. "We're *talking.*"

I felt a hand on my arm. "Miss Pepper," Susan Blackburn said, "how is Mr. Reyes? Do you know any more about his condition?"

"That's what we were talking about," Allie said.

I didn't bother to look at her or Nita. She was lying, and if Nita didn't correct her, she was lying, too.

Nita said nothing.

I repeated what I'd been told. "He's alive, but critical, and as far as I know, still unconscious. He's had surgery, and if he recovers, he's going to need a great deal of cosmetic surgery because most of the glass hit his face, his lips, and eyes in particular."

All three girls winced, as did everyone within earshot.

"He lost a lot of blood, too. He has, at best, a long haul ahead."

I felt cruel, making the prognosis as painful and slow as it really was going to be. The unvarnished truth felt like a whip with which to punish them.

Which I supposed was my frustrated motive, because even though I couldn't prove it, I believed that they—the sodium-stealing seniors—some or all of them, were involved in Juan Reyes's disaster.

"Thank you." Susan's voice was tiny and defeated.

I turned back to the girls at war, and caught Allie giving Nita a look that chilled me through, it was so clearly a warning.

"Thank you," Nita said to me, and turned and walked into my room, followed by Allie, both of them silent now.

It had been a useless nonconversation except for realizing that Nita was the weak link. All I needed now was an idea of what the chain was, so I'd know what to do with that information.

I entered the room to warning *shhhh!*s, a scramble to get to their chairs, and then, silence.

I thought the easiest road was to behave as if nothing exceptional was going on. Maybe that would make it so. "Today," I said, "we're moving ahead to the unit on critical thinking. You'll be reading, discussing, and then writing on a variety of subjects, most of which are controversial, so there are no right or wrong answers. The point will be to formulate your position and express it in writing."

I gave them a moment for the obligatory expressions of pained boredom, then switched gears. "But before we get to that," I said, "I saw the notice about the Antigone

Brigade. Anybody want to bring me up to speed on what that means?"

Allie's expression changed to one of self-satisfaction. "It means we have values, beliefs, and we know our rights— everybody's rights."

"Great. But what's the *brigade* part about?"

Now there were sideways glances, a silent mass checking in with one another. The decision had been made. Do not tell Pepper.

"We've got ideas—but only in the planning stage," Allie said.

I asked a few more questions and received a few more abstract responses about the Bill of Rights, freedom of speech, and democracy. The brigade was for those things.

"You can't just let things happen," Allie said. "You have to protest, to stand up for your rights—for everybody's rights."

A great sentiment, so why did Nita dart a look of pure anguish at her supposed best friend?

I suddenly felt their silence grow deeper and more significant, and I knew it wasn't anything I was doing. It was the hush that anticipates something, the same something, perhaps, that had caused the preclass buzzing.

Almost in unison, their glances shifted to the doorway, as well they might.

Wilson stood there in his T-shirt, holding a white-and-blue-striped tailored shirt up to his face. Only one slitted and swollen eye was visible as he glanced at me before heading toward his seat.

"Wait—" I said, "you shouldn't—you need—" I couldn't help but think of his mother. Had we been standing outside the school talking about dangerous acquaintances while this was happening to her son? She'd said she was afraid for him. Her fears seemed justified.

The class still looked at the doorway, and I turned again

and saw Seth, with a red-blue bruise covering his cheek and a bloody nose he was trying to stanch with an already saturated tissue.

"My God! Both of you—come here—you need the nurse, or a hospital. Who did this to you?" I admit I was babbling, helping nothing, covering the silence that grew ever more dense and frightening.

The bleeding boys and their classmates behaved as if their entry and appearance were completely normal, as if it was standard operating procedure to enter class leaking valuable bodily fluids.

Nobody had gasped in surprise. No one now whispered or commented. The room remained unnaturally still except for the shuffle of the two boys' steps and the snuffles from Seth's battered nose.

I had to repeat "Come here!" three times until they turned at the same time—they looked choreographed—and moved toward me.

"Who did this to you?" I asked, sure some renegade group of toughs had decided our school was fair game. It was the big city, after all.

Wilson raised one shoulder a millimeter.

"You don't know who they were?"

Three eyes—one of Wilson's was so swollen shut it might as well not have existed—stared blankly at me. I checked the classroom for cues, but the seniors were into meaningful eye contact with one another, not with me.

I looked back at the bruised boys. "Then you were not attacked by invaders from Mars. What is going on? Why would you . . . No matter what disagreements, why . . . You guys play on the same teams, are friends!"

No. Maybe still on the same teams for sports, but no longer close. Seth had seemed separate from them—physically and emotionally—the past few days.

The poisonous glances about the exam. Was that it?

I cleared my throat. "Why would you—?"

"Don't report it, please." Wilson rasped out his words, as if his throat had been hurt as well. "We'll be suspended."

This was a particularly damning time in his life for that. If you needed to punch somebody out, a testosterone-based need I couldn't fathom, best to not let it go until first semester of your senior year, when everything mattered too much.

With a bloody fight fresh on their minds, teachers and counselors writing recommendations were going to have questions and reservations. Plus, you couldn't take exams or quizzes while suspended, and you were graded as if you'd failed whatever you'd missed, so the all-important semester's grades would be lowered.

It surprised me to realize that I'd never had to cope with the aftermath of this kind of fight before. If there'd been a brawl, and surely there had, it had been spotted, and stopped by someone else, and necessary disciplinary action and medical attention had been taken care of before I knew about it. I had never been the first line of defense.

I therefore relied, possibly to my shame, on old movies I'd seen where the benign figure—always male—looks on the combatants sorrowfully, gives a brief moral talk, and then says, as I now did, "It's time to shake hands and apologize." That apparently was the manly thing to do, even while the men dripped blood onto the shaking hands.

Maybe fighting was a necessary male rite of passage. I'd have to ask Mackenzie. I knew he was strong and capable of doing physical harm, but I couldn't envision him willingly doing so. I tried to imagine him young, skinny, hair dark brown with not a strand of gray, beating up a friend. I was glad to be unable to formulate the image.

But maybe I was simply behaving like the skittery womenfolk in those same old movies.

Seth shook his head and Wilson, one beat later, did the

same. "I have nothing to apologize for," Seth said. "I'm not to blame, and I'm not sorry, and I'm still angry." As sore as his face must have felt, he pushed it forward in a classic position of belligerence. His lip was split; each syllable was fuzzed around the edges and must have been painful to utter, but he stood his ground. "I'm. Not. Sorry," he repeated, as if I'd challenged him.

"Well, I'm sure not," Wilson rasped out.

"You need medical attention," I said.

They shook their heads, both wincing as if it hurt to do so. "S'nothing," they said as one.

I walked them out into the hall and looked at them again. A black eye, a bloody nose, a bruised cheek, and who knew what else that I couldn't easily see. Seth's cheek looked raw, as if it had skimmed over cement.

They must have battled behind the school where nobody spotted them except the silent seniors who, I suspected, had watched the whole thing.

"What's going on?" I asked in the lowest possible voice.

"Ask him." Seth sounded sullen, foreign to me. But of late, everything about him was unlike my mental construct of him, so why not his tone as well.

"Wilson?" I asked.

Wilson continued to stare at the ground, shaking his head, as if he hadn't an idea in the world what or why this had happened.

"Some things get broken." Wilson looked at me with his one good eye. "They can't get fixed."

Seth glared.

"Nobody wants to fix them, either," Wilson added.

I looked back into the now softly buzzing classroom, and finally understood that every member of the class except for me knew what had happened. They might even know why.

We weren't a class. My role and relationship wasn't what I'd thought. We had somehow become antagonists.

"A person needs to believe in something," Wilson said, speaking to me more than he had ever chosen to before. "Like right and wrong."

Seth made a choking noise. "How would you know?" His voice was muffled through the cloth held to his nose. "You're the one afraid somebody—"

I caught Wilson's fist in midswing and held on. "You have to—both of you—you have to stop this right now."

When they finally and reluctantly agreed to see the nurse, I returned to the classroom, feeling as shaken and battered as the two combatants must have, and no closer to the truth of this thing that had fallen on the school and injured everything it touched.

Fifteen

It felt next to impossible, but when this most miserable day was over, and much as I wanted to crawl into bed with several layers of covers over my head, I had to switch gears instead and once again don my other virtual hat and pay attention to Berta Polley, the imaginary invalid.

Amanda Pepper, semi-private-eye.

First, still in my teacher and good citizen role, I phoned the police about the possibility the explosive substance was sodium. I did not choose to share the information that bits of that substance had been missing from Juan Reyes's room because I could not remember what he'd said was back in place and what wasn't. "No," I said. "I don't know who placed it there."

The official response was as patronizing and bored as I'd anticipated, but I'd done my civic duty.

I'd give Mrs. Polley two hours. I had *The Long Goodbye* on tape. I thought listening to a real down-these-mean-streets detective's adventures would help pass the time and inspire me, but of course Philip Marlowe was never reduced to staring at a row house, watching nothing, and if he had been, someone would have come along and overturned his car or taken a shot at him. Not that I wished such events upon my own sleuth self, but there had to be a midground somewhere.

At least today, or tonight, was the last of the surveillance. The funds to pay us allowed only so many hours.

I settled in across the street from her house. Two hours of this, then the market, then dinner, then papers to mark, then . . .

I can't say I felt overwhelmed by the prospects, but I definitely felt whelmed.

I called home, but nobody answered. Good. Pip was out exploring the city. I punched in the answering service numbers, and listened to my messages. I did this more readily than in the past, because as soon as I'd said "I do," my mother found herself at a loss for words, and both the number of maternal messages and their annoyance potential had gone into serious decline.

The only message was from Pip. "I'll be late. You were right. The Constitution Center is radical and I met somebody and we're hanging for a while so . . . See you!"

Judging by his vocal buoyancy, the met one was female. You had to admire how quickly he could pick up the pieces of his broken heart and pat them back into perfect shape. Farewell, Bunny Brookings, life was worthwhile again. Of course, I could be completely off base, and Pip might have met a charismatic cult leader.

The weather was changing, with more and more hints that winter was huffing around the corner. My suede-cloth shirt-jacket didn't make enough of a difference over my sweater for the damp, chilly inside of the VW. Rain was imminent, and I yearned to be home and warm.

I thought I was listening to Raymond Chandler's brilliant words, to adventures infinitely more thrilling than mine, but then I realized that the narrator had become white noise while I mentally gnawed at the confusing happenings at the day job. I had not, apparently, done a thorough job of changing hats.

I tried to arrange the series of events, looking for their

cause; I got nowhere. I took out paper and made a list. It added up to nothing. My missing roll book hadn't been part of a greater scheme. Maybe I was working too hard to tie the rest together.

Or not.

I was getting nowhere and was beyond bored watching nothing. At least I could take care of something doable—ask for another conference with Serenity Wilson, and one with Seth's parents as well. I did not want to get the boys in trouble if I could help it, did not want to take my worries to the administration. I didn't know how Havermeyer would react, but I was willing to wager that it would be inappropriately. I didn't want permanent records besmirched unnecessarily at this point, but I did want to understand what was involved. Personalities don't change overnight unless something—life or drugs—is pressing them out of shape.

I was dialing Seth's home number when I heard two toots of a horn. I looked up and realized I'd almost missed the crucial moment I'd been waiting for.

I slammed my cell shut and watched Berta Polley appear at her door in fuchsia sweats, shouting obscenities at the departing delivery truck.

She was not using a walker or a cane as she stepped out onto her cement patio and stared down at the large carton that had been left on her front pavement.

The car's roof suddenly clattered as the rain that had threatened became an actuality. Fat drops fell straight down, as if the rain were fake, a badly engineered special effect from a hose held right above us.

Do not let the rain drive you away before I get your picture, I muttered. Do *not*.

Berta Polley looked up at the sky with the first drops, then down to the pavement and her package, frowning as she watched the water splat it. Then she looked left and right, saw no neighbors, I assumed, and took a deep breath.

Her chest rose and fell, like a bellows being inflated, while I positioned the camera.

I managed five shots of Ms. Polley not only scampering down the three steps without so much as a limp and on her own, but then hoisting the heavy-looking package with no apparent strain and carrying it up the three steps, across the small patio, and into her house.

So much for the disability claim. I blessed digital cameras that showed me I'd gotten precisely what I wanted. I'd cracked a case even though it had involved nothing more than staring and taking snapshots.

These days, I took my triumphs where I found them.

But now, sleuth extraordinaire had to go to the market even though Nora Charles never had to grocery shop.

And once home, again unlike Nora, I had to phone those parents about their children's aberrant behavior. I gazed at the Thin Man poster while I waited for someone to answer at Seth's house. Nora would simply have had another martini at this point—and after the way my conversation went with Seth's mother, she'd have had still one more.

The woman nearly burst into tears at the idea of a school conference. Her husband was out of town on business, she herself was trying to work from home because Seth's younger sister had broken her leg and arm in a horseback-riding fall; the housekeeper was home sick with the flu and—her voice continued to rise—yes, Seth had come home bloody and a mess and *what was going on?*

The bottom line was that she could not come to the school any time in the foreseeable future. There was a doctor's appointment the next morning, probably a long wait at the office . . . and on and on. Poor frazzled woman. I decided that if I was going to add to her woes by being the bearer of bad news, I might as well do it literally, and carry it to where she was.

We made an appointment at her home for that evening.

*   *   *

PIP APPEARED, DRIPPING WET, ABOUT FIVE MINUTES AFTER we'd given up waiting and had dinner on the table. Once again, I understood why nature didn't start parents out with teenagers but instead softened them up with years of cuddly bundles first.

Once Pip had taken a shower to warm up and had put on dry clothes, Mackenzie did the obligatory parental number about being home on time for dinner, which I am sure Pip heard as white noise, but politely so.

While we ate our pork chops, salad, and mashed potatoes, talk moved from my Berta Polley triumph, duly hailed, to guy-talk about the Phillies. C.K. and Pip energetically debated a rookie's potential for next year, but to me, it was a mere time-filler until we could get to the important stuff: Whom had Pip met?

Mackenzie finally broke the ice. "And how was your day, Pip?" I was grateful, because I knew that had I asked, even in precisely the same manner, it would have been interpreted as prying. With C.K., it was gracious southern cordiality.

"Great!" Pip nodded with such animation that I feared his encounter had been with crime. The only other time I'd seen him light up this way was when Mackenzie touched on things forensic. "I know you said the center was good, but I thought . . ."

"You thought it would be—"

"Educational," he said. "You know?"

It made me sad, but . . . I knew.

"But it wasn't." He still sounded surprised. "And I learned a lot of stuff!"

I was proud of keeping still, not asking how "learning stuff" was great while being "educational" was boring. Mackenzie, out of his nephew's sight line, first rolled his beautiful blue eyes, then crossed them.

Pip ate a bite of pork chop. "This is good," he said, "all of it. My mother's mashed potatoes, well . . ."

"Lutie's talents never seemed to lie in the kitchen," Mackenzie said.

It was turning into a good day, as long I didn't count the bad parts. I'd caught out Berta Polley, Pip had dropped his hangdog look, and even Macavity was purring in anticipation of yummy table scraps.

"The show was interesting. The guy called the Constitution an ongoing experiment. Like it keeps growing and changing, like when girls couldn't vote, or black people, or when you had to be twenty-one. I never thought about that. That it still could change."

"Sounds like you picked up a lot," Mackenzie said.

Pip's eyes and mouth opened. He looked from one of us to the other, but said nothing.

"I meant information," Mackenzie said. "But judging by your reaction—do I understand you met somebody?"

Pip focused on his remaining salad for a moment. "Yeah," he said in a lower voice. "I met this girl. She's pretty cool. She was, like, doing research." He sounded surprised by this, too, by, perhaps, the idea of a cool female scholar.

"Is she from around here?"

He shrugged. "I don't know the neighborhoods."

"I meant from Philadelphia, not a tourist," I said.

Mackenzie was watching him quizzically, perhaps even critically.

"Oh. That. Yeah. I got her phone number," Pip said.

Mackenzie nodded approval, and the two of them actually did a high five.

"You know, Bunny . . . well, she'd have hated the place," he said. "She's really, like, small-town. Not that smart or interested in stuff."

Bye-bye, Brookings. You've been supplanted.

"It happens, you know," Mackenzie said to his nephew. "Your eyes open up and the girl looks entirely different, suddenly wrong for you. Then you meet the one someday and that doesn't happen and that's how you know."

"Guy talk," I said. "So enjoy yourselves—and the dishes. I've got to run."

"On the other hand," Mackenzie said, "sometimes you think she's the one and then she leaves you with the dishes to do and . . ."

A joke, I was almost sure.

Sixteen

SETH FREMONT LIVED IN ONE OF THE RARE BROWNSTONES in Philadelphia, a city that favors bricks. The houses on this strip of Spruce Street had been built around the same time as Philly Prep—the late nineteenth century—and I suppose someone had been in a New York kind of mood. It isn't easy living in the oversized shadow of the Big Apple, so someone decided that if Manhattan had brownstones, so would we. But we have only a sampler, to show that we could have them if we really wanted to.

I walked up the marble entry stairs and pressed the bell. The brass door-knocker was otherwise occupied with a dangling wooden scarecrow, and an orange-and-black flag hung between the door and the large front window.

I'd been told the mansard-style roofs and round-headed windows meant these were Second Empire–influenced, but as I was never certain what or where the Second—or for that matter, the First—Empire was, I merely admired the solid and spacious-looking homes for what they were. Had I not been increasingly uncomfortable about this visit and what it could possibly do to help the situation, I'd have been more excited about finally being inside one of these homes.

The shift of relocating our meeting from school, where it would have felt less urgent, to home, from school hours to this evening, shouldn't have meant that much, but it definitely seemed to. I felt like an intruder, and the problem with Seth, now that it was outside its normal schoolhouse confines, appeared larger than I'd have wanted it to. Plus, I knew I was adding to a harried woman's woes when there was no absolute necessity, only vague suspicions.

Laurel Fremont was on the defensive, anxiously and sadly, from the moment she opened the door. "Has he done something wrong?" she asked repeatedly. "Besides getting into a brawl. I know that was wrong, but it happens."

I reassured her that I didn't know of anything he'd done wrong. I was once again balanced on the fine edge of the truth. I didn't know that he'd stolen my exam. I didn't know that he'd set off a false alarm. I didn't know that he had something to do with Juan Reyes's accident, and I didn't know why he was involved in a bloody fight with Wilson. I had my suspicions, my unhappy theories—but I honestly didn't know.

"I thought, since he's home, Seth could be a part of the meeting, but he said he'd rather not. That he didn't have anything to say, and that this was—whatever this was—between you and me and you hadn't invited him," she said.

"But it would be fine if he—"

She shook her head. "I don't know what's going on with that boy. At home, he seems fine, and he's been such a help with Lucy. It's her bedtime soon. I'm letting her watch cartoons, a video. I don't usually allow that, but . . ."

I wanted to hug her, to pat her back, to tell her that things were all right, that she needn't be this worried, or explain herself to me this way. But she had a son whose behavior had changed dramatically, and who'd been close to a series of mishaps, pranks, or actual violations too often, and who'd now come into my class bloodied and defiant. So I murmured about how difficult sick children could be, and how I remembered being allowed to watch soap operas when I was ill, and that seemed to relax her.

She was a pretty woman, currently pale and drawn, but I was sure that was purely situational, as was her smile, which was tentative and fearful. I tried my best to put her at ease as we walked from a spacious entry hall into the living room, its wide-planked floorboards gleaming with generations of waxing. It was a room designed for comfort, with its cushiony furniture, a piano with music open on its stand, interesting art—Haitian, I thought—and something I always notice, good lighting so that people could settle in with one of the many books in the cases on one wall.

You can't judge a child by his parents' décor, and probably shouldn't judge his parents by it either, but the livability of this room and its values made it feel like a place where the right things were given time and space. I wasn't surprised that Seth—at least until-last-week-Seth—had grown up here.

"Please," she said, waving me toward the burgundy sofa. "I'm sorry I don't have a thing to offer—anything an adult would want to eat except a cup of coffee or tea. I haven't been able to get to the store for three days and—"

My turn to say I'd just had dinner and didn't want a thing, and to once again try to convince her that I wasn't there on a punitive mission but rather was trying to understand a situation and, perhaps, to help.

She sat down across from me and leaned forward in her chair. "His *face*," she said. She blinked hard, as if she might cry. "He said he and Wilson had a fight, but he wouldn't say why, but Seth doesn't fight that way—not since he was a kid. And not with Wilson—they've been friends for so long. They aren't like that! What happened?"

"I don't know," I said. "That's why I'm here."

"He's been so different this past week and he wouldn't say why. I know what you're thinking—but he is *not* on drugs." She shook her head while she said it, just in case I hadn't understood. "He's entitled to have moods. He doesn't have to be perfect."

"Of course," I said. "And I didn't really ever think it could be drugs. He's still doing well academically."

"He's just . . . he's a typical moody teenager. But even so, and I understand that, still—how could I not worry? He's been so irritable this week, so . . . different! And my husband's in Asia till tomorrow and Lucy's sick, and it's like watching a stranger sit down and take your kid's place."

I felt great sympathy for her, but I also knew that moody didn't cover split lips and black eyes. Moody didn't explain stolen exams, acid in briefcases, petty pilfering, vandalism, or erudite threats for the science teacher.

"Do you have any idea what's going on?"

She shook her head. "I was initially afraid, ever since—I mean, he did what we thought was right, his father and I. And Seth, of course. We talked it through, but even so, you read about hideous things happening, brutality—but I thought not here. This is Philadelphia! And we were right. Wilson was great. The other boys on the teams were great. A big nonevent, he said. We shouldn't have been so worried. Nobody—it would never happen there, at his school where he has such good friends, and of course his teammates.

"My husband's more cynical. He thinks that if Seth wasn't such a fine athlete, maybe his teammates wouldn't be so accepting. But that's just how my husband thinks."

From upstairs, a wail, and a call, "Mama!"

She stood and went to the bottom of the stairs. "In a minute, Lucy. I'll be right there."

I stood up, too. "This is a bad time," I said. "But I'm confused. Are we talking about this week?"

"No!" She shook her head, had one hand clasped in the other, in position to start wringing. "No. That was two *months* ago—August, and *nothing happened*. Two months ago is ancient history in a teenager's life. That's why none of this makes sense. Why would it take two months to matter? If that's it at all. Besides, Wilson's been his friend, his ally through all of this, and Seth's helped Wilson with his homework for three years now. Why hurt each other this much?"

I thought I knew what she was saying and not saying, and what she assumed I understood, but I needed to be certain.

Another wail, from upstairs.

"So sorry. But the doctor—they were bad breaks and I have to—I thought we'd be able to talk, but—I hate to say this but could you let yourself out?"

"Of course, but please, one last thing. This nonevent two months ago—I'm not sure I know what you mean."

She had half turned, had her foot on the first riser, and she swiveled her torso to look at me. She looked surprised by my words. "Seth came out in August. Told his friends—his close friends—that he was gay. He wasn't going to keep it a secret anymore. You didn't know?"

I shook my head. Not that I needed to know a student's sexual orientation, but it was one more thing I hadn't known in a long list this week.

She walked up another step, then turned around and called out to me as I moved toward the front entry. "But the point is, that didn't create any problems," she said. "So don't mix it up with whatever is going on this week. Do you understand?"

I nodded, though that was far from the truth.

Seventeen

I WAS POSITIVE THAT I'D ALREADY PUT IN MORE THAN FIVE days at school. Surely we were into the weekend. But the calendar said Friday. Mackenzie verified it and even Pip, awake and alert this particular morning, agreed that it was still the same interminable week.

I guess it was T.G.I.F., but I would have been happier with T.G.I. Saturday.

"What awakens you before noon?" I asked Pip as I set out three cereal bowls.

"No fair—I don't sleep that late," he said. "Besides, you're not even here to see. Why'd you say that?"

"Amanda's in a bad mood," Mackenzie said. "She thinks somebody's sneaking extra days into her week."

Pip considered the two of us before opting to answer my question. He ate his cornflakes and banana with much deliberation. He wasn't slick at evasion yet, and it was obvious he was stalling, deciding how to answer me. "I've got some plans to hang out," he finally said.

"Where?" Mackenzie and I asked in unison.

He looked startled. You could almost see him searching for an untrue response. "Maybe here," he said with a painful lack of sincerity. "I like it here. Cool place you've got."

"Got up early to go nowhere?"

"You don't have to worry about me, you know. I'm not

a kid. There's a lot of stuff on that list you gave me, places and stuff to see."

I nodded. "Are you maybe hanging out with the girl you met yesterday?"

"It's a possibility."

"Doesn't she go to school?"

"Speaking of which . . ." Mackenzie nodded in the direction of the big schoolroom clock on the wall. "If you're still planning to walk, which I hope, because I could use the car today."

We were down to one shared car, C.K.'s ancient VW. My beloved burgundy '65 Mustang had wheezed and creaked to impossibly expensive maintenance and replacement costs. The VW was also geriatric, but better for our budget. One car made better sense, but also complicated logistics.

"She kind of goes," Pip said.

I took a minute to remember what I'd asked. "What's that mean? This girl kind of goes to school?" I carried my bowl to the sink, grabbed my jacket and backpack and headed toward the door, and Pip hadn't yet mustered up an answer. I paused to kiss Mackenzie good-bye and whisper, "Find out, okay? Who is this girl? Doesn't sound good," to wish Pip a good day, and to ask for call-ins about his whereabouts, and then I was out of there, all sorts of imagined Pip-responses playing in my head, none of them what I wanted to hear. The girl had dropped out of school precisely as had Pip. The girl was a decade older than Pip and went to school part-time. The girl was the female equivalent of Harriet's Erroll, "kind of" going to school forever. The girl had been on the prowl looking for an innocent bumpkin to snare for God knows what purpose . . .

I walked to school, again, still astounded by the Halloween decorative frenzy I passed. When I arrived, I cut into the alley behind the building and entered through the back door, where I was less likely to bump into early-bird students.

I love school when it's wrapped in anticipatory silence. This is the time of day when anything seems possible, and the aroma of old walls and the generations of children who've inhabited them is bracing, invigorating. This is, in short, the ideal, lacking only the factor that makes things less than ideal—students, who tend not to understand or respect my fantasies of the educational process.

"Good morning!" Harriet sang out so brightly that I knew things were going well with Erroll. "Happy Mischief Day, and be sure to check your mailbox! You've got mail!" She chuckled.

Of late, I'd come to fear messages, but two out of three were innocuous. The good news was that Carol Parillo had recuperated. That was nice for her—and for Mackenzie and me, since we were off the hook now for chaperoning the party.

The bad but not surprising news was a message from Laurel Fremont, who'd phoned the office to thank me for my concern, and to say that Seth wouldn't be in today. She requested that any homework assignment be e-mailed.

I couldn't tell if the note was a polite brush-off, a way of saying stay away because everything's taken care of—or not.

The third note was neutral, meaningless. All the folded paper said in large computer-printed letters was: FRIDAY.

The day of the week. Nothing frightening about that per se, but it nonetheless accelerated my heart rate.

"Shame Seth is sick," Harriet said, "but something is certainly going around."

Something always was "going around" in the gigantic petri dish we call school, but we always reacted with surprise and amazement, as if the newest something was a rare anomaly.

"Even my Erroll," Harriet said. I wanted to grab my hat—if I'd had one—and head for the hills, but I still hadn't a clue where those hills were.

"He's all sniffly, and aren't men the biggest babies when they're sick?"

I knew I was supposed to nod in a show of superior sisterly smugness. I knew from prior experience and from other women that lots of men became peculiar if they sneezed once, but the man with whom I coexisted was neither whiny nor infantile. So, torn between sisterhood and the truth, I resorted to my Harriet *hmmm.*

As usual, she took it as agreement, and smiled. "Also—"

As if to save me from hearing any more about Erroll's nasal disabilities, the door to the headmaster's office opened, and Maurice Havermeyer himself emerged, skin flushed and eyes squinted in a furious scowl. "Are you aware of what is going on?"

Harriet looked so awestruck and fearful, I thought she was about to drop to her knees and bang her head on the floorboards.

But at that moment, he realized she was not alone. "Hah!" he shouted, wheeling and pointing at me. "Are *you* aware of what's going on?"

"I try to be. I read the newspaper and—"

"Outside!" he said. "Right here!"

"What?" I felt the way a puppy must, sure by the master's tone that I'd displeased him, but without a clue as to what I'd done, when I'd done it, or why what I'd done was so bad.

"You said it was a play!"

"Sir?"

"Right at our doorstep!"

I shook my head. "I came in the back door—only a minute or so—"

"The *front* doorstep! The one everyone in the world can see—and certainly will now, won't they?"

I looked around, though I don't know why, unless I thought I'd developed super powers while I stood there, and I could now use my X-ray vision to see to the street and to whatever was driving Maurice Havermeyer to the brink of insanity.

Didn't work, so I looked to the window. This was an equally stupid move because the main office sided on a narrow alleyway between our building and the one next door. The only thing I saw through the blinds was the shadow of what I hoped was a prowling cat.

"How did this happen?" Havermeyer stormed. "Why didn't somebody stop it? Look for yourself!" he shouted, motioning Harriet and me into his office. "And then tell me it's a play. A play!"

"A game?" Harriet whispered.

"No—a *play*. With actors—a drama! Look for yourself." He pointed toward his office. "You'll see this is no *play* no matter how you mean the word."

His sanctum must have had double-paned windows, because the room was muffled in silence even as I gazed onto an amazing sight. What looked like most of our student body was on the pavement, circling in a fairly organized loop and carrying signs. In their midst, Cheryl Stevens addressed them and the world, a microphone to her mouth and her free arm punching the sky.

Several students had bright red tape across their mouths. Others carried signs. Mostly, I saw the sides of the placards, but when students turned to speak to one another, I could catch the words, and I immediately saw ANTIGONE BRIGADE on one.

"Oh," I said. "*That* play."

Another placard wobbled into sight reading, WHAT HAP-PENED TO FREEDOM OF SPEECH? and another had blood

red letters saying, CIVIL DISOBEDIENCE IS SOMETIMES RE-
QUIRED! That one was so large that the diminutive girl
holding it tilted backward.

Any rebellion might have produced Havermeyer's fit, but
he was over-the-top because this insurrection was outside.
In public. With witnesses.

Forget issues; forget meaning. Think *bad publicity.*

The "drop-off and pickup only" zone in front of the
school was occupied by a van with call letters on it. I was
surprised a high school demonstration was newsworthy
until I remembered that Cheryl's father had some sort of
operations job at a local network affiliate.

A familiar TV face pushed a microphone in front of a
succession of students.

"It's her fault," Havermeyer growled. "That girl with
the poem. Her words were a call to violence. Look what
she's done."

"All Erroll has to hear about is kids taking to the streets
in favor of violence," Harriet said. "He'll insist that I quit
and find a safer job."

Right. He'd hate to have his Sugar Mommy be a victim
of violence and stop shelling out his tuition. "This is a
peaceful demonstration," I said. "There's no violence."

"Ring the bell," Havermeyer said. "Harriet, ring the
bell."

"It isn't time yet, Dr.—"

"This is an emergency—ring the bell."

After a few minutes of readjusting settings, she did.
We could see eyes roll toward the school, acknowledging
the sound, but that was all. Their attention returned to the
pavement.

"They heard it!" Havermeyer sputtered. "Why aren't
they listening if they're such peaceful people and this is
such a peaceful event?"

Because the party and the reporters were outside? Maybe, even, because they might believe in what they were doing?

The TV reporter approached a group, her microphone out to catch comments. She seemed of a different species than our students, at a more advanced evolutionary stage. She gleamed and sparkled and had none of the look of morning about her. The students had enthusiasm going for them, but that was about it. Their skin lacked her expensive mother-of-pearl shine. Their lips didn't beam out star-shaped gleams with each movement.

The reporter spoke to Cheryl, her eyes wide. I was impressed by how she could keep a photogenic smile while having a serious conversation about Cheryl's blinded cousin. That was real talent. No wonder she was paid the big bucks.

Cheryl answered with much less panache, but great fervor.

While I was enjoying what felt like a Technicolor silent film, Louis Applegate came "onscreen." He took in the entire scene, his slow boil visible as his face warmed from its normal pallor to pink to the color of decaying meat. He looked around, and then saw Cheryl, whose back had been to him. His mouth curled, and only because students in front of him turned around did I realize that he was speaking or perhaps even shouting. His lips formed the same pattern over and over.

"What's he saying?" Maurice Havermeyer demanded.

I lip-read. He was accusing them of civil disobedience. Over and over, now and then adding that they were a disgrace.

Let Havermeyer learn to lip-read for himself. I wasn't going to help the enemy. "He keeps speaking—I mean saying drivel," I said.

"Drivel?"

I nodded. "Odd, isn't it?"

The reporter was spending a long time with us. Hard to believe that either poetry or freedom of speech had become big news. Odds were better that the reporters had shown up as a courtesy to Cheryl's father, and that the tape would never reach the air.

So the smart thing would be for Havermeyer to do nothing except let this play itself out. But *smart* was not a word used to modify Maurice Havermeyer, and now, as if I'd turned and pointed to him, saying, "Your cue to do something stupid," he said, "It's time I spoke with the reporter and insisted she desist. This is a matter of school policy, and furthermore, these people are interfering with our school day."

He looked at me, waiting for agreeable acknowledgment. I did not agree and I didn't have to pretend to. I was invulnerable by virtue of being ready to be fired. "Actually," I said, "going outside doesn't seem a good idea. It's a peaceful protest, and we shouldn't look as if we object to that. We aren't that newsworthy, and the media will soon lose interest."

And then I realized that the reporter had turned her tidy body away from Cheryl, and had pushed her microphone up to a dazed, gee, I'm on TV!! smile—a smile I had last seen at my breakfast table.

Forget my wise stance of leaving things alone outside. I bolted through the outer office, into the hallway, and out the building, which meant that Pip had more than adequate time for a few sound bites. If only I could have leaped through the window.

"The Constitution of the United States of America guarantees free speech." He spoke with the gravitas of a Supreme Court justice.

"Say what we will!" the marchers chanted. "Say what we will! The Bill of Rights lets us say what we will!"

I liked the cadence and the idea, but I wasn't sure I liked Pip involved in this. Was this what his mother would have hoped for?

Louis Applegate walked over to the reporter and spoke in a determined voice. It worked. She aimed the mike at him. "I teach history," he said, "and until now, I saw no evidence of this great interest in the Constitution. These students would rather make news than study it. How can they be unaware—how can any American be unaware or refuse to understand these are not normal times? I'd suggest more studying before parading around on the—"

His voice was drowned in the general din. Cheryl had climbed on an overturned crate. She held up a sheet of paper, waved it, and the chanting died out, as if that had been a prearranged signal.

The reporter, good at her trade, sensed where the center of the action was, and turned, holding the microphone up to Cheryl, who, as soon as it was sufficiently quiet on the pavement, recited:

> The news tallies casualties and we
> Check the numbers dead and sigh.
> But a wound makes you an also-ran.
> You don't count.

"Disgraceful!" Applegate shouted.

"Be polite!" "Shut up!" people shouted back, and although he looked mildly apoplectic, Louis Applegate kept quiet while she continued to read her poem.

Havermeyer still stood on the front steps, his skin an unphotogenic green. He kept touching the strands of hair he combed over his head, as if he might suddenly rip them out.

A handful of other students had memorized Cheryl's

poem and they joined in and managed to sound more numerous than their actual numbers.

—*Make people understand that*
Being twenty-one and blind forever counts.

It wasn't great, perhaps not even good, poetry, but it felt powerful out there on the street.

She finished and the students cheered and started the chant again. "Say what we will! Say what we . . ."

Applegate considered that permission to resume his complaints. "I don't want to see any of *my* students inciting people to—"

Pip's large sign said: AMENDMENT I: CONGRESS SHALL MAKE NO LAW . . . ABRIDGING THE FREEDOM OF SPEECH, OR OF THE PRESS; OR THE RIGHT OF THE PEOPLE PEACEABLY TO ASSEMBLE, AND TO PETITION THE GOVERNMENT FOR A REDRESS OF GRIEVANCES.

It must have been heavy, and as he was apt to gesticulate when he spoke, it wobbled dangerously. The reporter kept ducking and moving to the side.

"*I'm* not your student!" Pip shouted at Applegate. The reporter pushed the mike under his face. "I'm from Iowa, and I saw the Constitution for the first time yesterday. And I learned a lot about it and"—he seemed older than he had in the loft—"We. Have. The. Right. And. No. School. Can. Take. It. Away. From. Us!!!"

The picketers cheered.

"Iowa?" the anchorwoman said. "What brings you here?"

What brought him here was dropping out of school and lying about his whereabouts and plans this morning. It wasn't going to play that well or help the cause, but how could I interfere without becoming yet another censor of his freedom of speech?

"What brings me here?" Pip repeated rhetorically. "The Constitution of the United States brings me here!" He still wore that goofy grin. He was on TV!

"Who *is* that?" Havermeyer was literally breathing down my neck. I had the sense he was hiding behind me, using me as a shield against real or imagined enemies. "Did he say Iowa? He's an outside agitator!" He wasn't trying to keep his voice down. "The media deserves to know. Reporter! Reporter! Miss! This is important. We've got a professional outside agit—"

"He is anything but professional," I said.

The anchorwoman had lost interest in Pip's dazed expression and unrevolutionary pronouncements. She didn't want to talk about the Constitution. She moved on, glancing once at her watch.

"You belong in class!" Applegate shouted. "And you know it. You're all guilty of desertion."

A little slip of the tongue because the man had been in the military too long. Students close enough to hear him laughed out loud and saluted.

"Aunt Amanda!" Pip shouted, blowing my cover. His smile was genuine.

"Aunt! You're his aunt! You're related!"

I could almost see Havermeyer's brain searching for official language about hereditary big-mouthedness. I controlled the urge to palm Pip off as part of the family Mackenzie. "He's visiting," I said, "and he was quite dazzled by Constitution Hall yesterday. Couldn't stop talking about it."

"Doesn't Iowa have schools?" Havermeyer didn't wait for me to answer. "He shouldn't be here. Look what he's doing!"

"Doing? To whom?"

Havermeyer waved his arms at a vague everything: students, reporters, the news van in the drop-off zone, ran-

dom faculty members. He was truly upset and the proof
was that he wasn't using jargon. I could understand what
he meant. He had no idea how to protest the protest. Pip
waved the First Amendment and the reporter hung on
every inflammatory word she could find, and there was no
dignified, let alone legal, way to halt any of it.

"Outside agitators," Havermeyer muttered. "Insurrection. I won't have this! I want their names. Harriet, get
everybody's names."

He maneuvered his way around me, toward the front
door, and as I stood there, wondering if we were becoming
a mini–police state, I glanced across the street, to the Square,
and, to my surprise, saw Seth.

The note had been accurate. He wasn't in class. But there
he was, shouldering a heavy-looking backpack and watching us through bruised eyes.

Why had his mother told me he wasn't coming to
school? And if he'd changed his mind and was in fact joining us, why was he across the street, watching with laser in-
tensity? I'd have thought he'd be on our side, literally and
metaphorically, not studying his peers as if they were a
problem to be solved.

I wanted to ask him, but I had a more immediate concern. I cornered Pip, now that the reporter was gone. "Why
are you here?" I demanded. "And why didn't you tell your
uncle or me where you'd be? You aren't playing fair with
us. Why run away from your school and show up at mine?"

He appeared flustered. "It's the right thing to do."

"How did you know about this demonstration?"

He shrugged.

Cheryl circled closer, holding her placard. "Good job,"
she told him, smiling. "You were really impressive."

I got it. Tardily, I admit, but there was his interest in the
Constitution in the form of one cute junior.

Cheryl moved on, and I waited until she was out of

earshot before I spoke. "That's who you met yesterday at the Constitution Center, the one who sort of goes to school, correct?"

"It's got to be all right for me to meet people," he said.

"Well, sure, but it's also all right to be forthcoming and honest."

"She was there doing research, and—"

But she was back, close enough on her rounds to speak to me as she again passed. "Not much of a vacation for him, is it?" she said, and I was aware of our having a new relationship. We were both connected to Pip now. She was my demonstration-in-law.

"I mean," she said, "all his experience with nonviolent protests sure helped to plan this—but still, to come this far to get away from all that for a while and to bump right into it again . . . and in Philadelphia. The city of brotherly love." Smiling, she moved on again, her words hanging in the air.

The splots of color on Pip's cheek grew more intense, and it would have been a kindness to let Cheryl's words float off in the ether, but I wasn't feeling a need for that level of compassion. "I had no idea you were—what? A professional demonstrator?—a political radical back there in Iowa. Were the protests also about civil rights or something else?"

His eyes nearly crossed in a panicky roll, then he squeezed them shut, reopened them, and said, "Okay, maybe I exaggerated a little—"

"A little?"

"Okay, maybe a lot. Maybe I made the whole thing up—"

"Maybe?"

"Okay, I made it up, but she was all fired up about, you know, free speech and the right to assemble and the Bill of Rights . . ."

"Besides, she's cute."

"No," he said. "I mean yes. Okay, she really is, but she's also right."

At which point, the bell tolled for all of us again. Havermeyer had made it back to the steps, and was watching the crowd, which had grown, with latecomers and stragglers reluctant to enter the building once they saw what was going on.

Nobody responded to the bell's summons. But I did see Cheryl talking to the group around her, glancing toward the headmaster, apparently debating whether or not to go to school. Cheryl, of course, was student non grata, but a protest policy maker.

From his post, Havermeyer glanced at his watch and glowered. Harriet stood with a tablet on which to write down the protesters' names. It would have been more efficient to pull the entire school roster, and tick off the names of the few who were not on the pavement.

Cheryl nodded in Havermeyer's direction. I moved closer, shamelessly eavesdropping, and heard fragments that suggested they might end the demonstration, but pick it up again at lunchtime.

That meant I had to get ready for class, or homeroom. I wasn't sure how we'd organize this late-starting day. I left the conspirators and walked over to Maurice Havermeyer, whose face was still red enough to make me worry about his blood pressure. "I was wondering how we're going to work the day," I said.

"They're all going to be suspended."

"Everybody? The entire school?"

"What other recourse—look, they still aren't paying attention—I rang the bell again and look at them!"

Louis Applegate stood to the side, his lips pressed together in frustration at being unable to send the lot of them to the brig. His near apoplexy gave me great pleasure.

"Students!" Havermeyer shouted. "Students! This is your final warning, your last chance to avoid—"

Even if people were listening to him, nobody heard because history, which Applegate was still shouting we should study, appeared to be repeating itself in the worst way as the crowd was stunned by—

Déjà—*BANG!*

Eighteen

I WHEELED AROUND, THE CHEMISTRY LAB EXPLOSION RE-playing and echoing in my mind, the danger now expanded to a crowded sidewalk and hundreds of teenagers who screamed, pushed, bumped into each other, and moved back to where they'd been, still screaming.

"I saw it—I saw somebody throw something," a blond girl with braces said.

"Who? From where? What did they—"

Another explosive sound and more screams, including those the girl who'd seen something was now making. I tried to calm her. "What did you see? Where? What's going on?"

"A guy—over there." She pointed across the street. "Somewhere." She burst into tears and had nothing more to offer.

And then the sound of sirens—somebody had called 911—breaking into a scene as close to bedlam as I care to be.

I looked where the girl had pointed, where I'd earlier noticed only one person.

Seth was no longer there.

The police were out and everywhere, students milling. Whimpering came from within the group and a girl emerged, holding her side. "She hurts!" her friend said to the police, who hustled her off to the paramedics.

"What *happened*?" Carol, the math teacher, said. "I was inside and heard the noise and then—what's going on?"

"Bombs," Louis Applegate said. "You stir things up, upset—"

"Which of our kids would bring a bomb to a—"

"Cherry bomb," a voice said with some authority, and I turned and saw a boy I'd taught the year before. He looked both proud of his savvy and slightly ashamed.

"How do you know about bombs?" Louise Applegate demanded.

He shrugged. "I know about *firecrackers*. Most everybody does. That was—they were probably cherry bombs. They're illegal, but you can get the recipe on the Internet. Or else it was some other kind of firecracker."

"They should not allow the Internet to—"

I turned away. It was too tumultuous a time for another debate about free speech.

Cherry bombs were probably not what Applegate had in mind, but it didn't actually matter. The sidewalk was as much in turmoil as if a Molotov cocktail or fertilizer bomb had been detonated in its midst, except that we didn't seem to have many casualties.

As far as I could tell, after a few minutes of watching, in addition to the girl who "hurt," two students' clothing had been partially scorched and a boy had been knocked off the curb and had fallen in the confusion. I still didn't know what had hit us, but at least it hadn't hit us with as much devastation as I'd feared.

And then I spotted Seth on our side of the street, now a part of the general tumult. I managed to get to him and discreetly—I thought—separate him from the herd, though he looked annoyed, his bruised face sullen every time he glanced at my hand on his letter jacket.

"I thought you weren't coming in," I said. "I was sent a note—"

"No point staying home. That wouldn't solve anything."

"Solve what?"

"So when they phoned about this—"

"Who?"

"The chain. Some kid named Billy. I didn't know him. You know, how they call people for a snow day? Whoever had me on their list phoned and said there was going to be this demonstration, and then I had to come."

"But you didn't participate. You stood across the street."

"I realized finally that I wasn't going to join the hypocrites, but I wanted to see who was there."

"Why are they hypocrites?"

"Why is anybody one? They don't mean what they say."

"They don't believe in the Bill of Rights?"

His expression clouded, and I had the sense that he pitied me my ignorance and confusion. "I don't believe in them," he said. "You can't trust anybody," he said in a low, resigned voice. "Not anybody."

There's not much worse as a guide for life than that sentiment, and I wished I knew what had been going on in Seth's life. "Seth," I said, "I know you're going through a hard time."

"They want to get me," he muttered.

"Why? Who?" I hated this conversation and my growing fear that Seth had fallen off his tracks and was in serious trouble.

"Don't worry. I'm smarter than they are. That's partly why they want to get me."

How would a paranoid adolescent elude his perceived enemies? Too many news stories about school murders. Too much evidence of immature brains—normal ones—being unable to think through to the logical consequences.

I should phone his mother again, I thought, mentally wincing at adding to that beleaguered woman's plate. Make him empty his backpack right now, so I could check it. Or tell somebody—but who? And what exactly would I say? I've got this feeling?

"You think I'm crazy, don't you?"

There are times when the truth is not the best option. "Of course not," I said. "But I think—I know—you're profoundly upset, and I can't see how a demonstration about censorship has anything to do with you."

"It doesn't! But it should, it—" He seemed to collapse from within, as if something keeping him going had just dissolved.

"Help me understand," I said. "What's going on? I truly want to help you."

He shook his head. "I can't. You wouldn't . . . Nobody can help me. I have to take care of this myself."

"Look at your face. That's not a good way to take care of things. You can't let people beat you down, exclude you. It doesn't make sense to stay home from school."

He nodded, surprising me. "I know. That's why I didn't. Because if I did, it would mean they won."

"Won? What is this, a contest?"

"It's a war."

I took time out to digest what he'd said, then asked him, "About what? Between whom?"

"Between me and everybody else." His words were laced with sorrow, not anger or antagonism.

I put my hand on his shoulder. "You've got to believe that things can be worked out peacefully. Not by beating each other senseless. You're strong and smart. Don't let yourself be bullied or defeated. It isn't like you to stay home or stay apart or—or hide, in essence. This is your senior year."

"I know. I can't wait until it's over and I'm out of here."

"Don't miss it, though. Don't let them do that to you."

He looked less defeated. "Miss it? You mean tonight's party?"

I'd meant life, not a school dance, but why not? "Sure. Like everything that isn't self-destructive or involves punching each other out. If you want to go—go. Why wouldn't you?"

He looked at me and started to object, then stopped himself. "All right," he said as if he meant it. "You're right, so—all right. I'm not backing down."

At that moment, two things happened. First, I realized I was not going to be fired. Havermeyer was too much of a coward. And I wasn't going to quit. I was going to take my own advice and not miss my life—and a great portion of my life belongs in a classroom. My classroom.

Second, the police reached us, and made it clear they wanted us in the auditorium as soon as possible.

Seth shrugged and did as he was told. I watched him for a long moment. With my newly calmed sense of my future, and with Seth's back to me, his bruises and generally sullen expression not visible, his actions most ordinary, I thought, perhaps, that everything would now be all right.

IT TOOK HOURS, THE BULK OF THE DAY, TO TRY TO UNRAVEL what had happened and where responsibility should be put, and even then nothing was resolved or determined. The police were interested in the firecracker and questioned and searched every student; the paramedics treated the girl's burns, which, luckily, were minor; the burned clothing was replaced; and Havermeyer, goaded on by Louis Applegate, continued to focus on agitators, both in-house and imported. Havermeyer was sure Pip was the guilty party. He was from Iowa, for starters, about as outside an agitator as you could get. Who needed more evidence than that?

Lists of names were drawn up, theories expounded, and at the end of all that time, with nothing explained and no progress aside from treating the superficial injuries, with everyone questioned and baroque arrangements made so that no one could pass guilty material to anyone else, with no one suspended and even Cheryl for all intents and practices back in school, and with the idea that one unknown idiot—in all probability not one of our students—had gone too far and tossed two cherry bombs for the hell of it, we had no conspiracy or agitators.

At approximately forty-seven minutes before the bell would have normally rung, Maurice Havermeyer waved the white flag and declared school ended.

The joy this produced was mostly relief from a day that had begun with a bang and wound up an exercise in excruciating boredom. The truth was, the faculty looked much more delighted about the way things had worked out than the students did. School had been scheduled to end at noon, for this was to have been, in theory, a teacher prep day. For students, it's an afternoon off. For teachers, that translates into an afternoon's agony of useless nattering by Maurice Havermeyer, except for those times when he'd find an "expert" as stultifying as he was to take his place.

Early dismissal would have meant the party planners had time to do their thing. The committee, sitting in a huddle on the gymnasium bleachers, looked glum.

When the bell finally rang, I watched Allie rouse herself and go from silent and sullen to frenzied. "It's all *ruined*!" she said. "We should have been working for two hours now! Why did they have to take so long? Stupid, anyway. None of us threw that firecracker at ourselves. And acting as if it had something to do with Mr. Reyes." She paced and sighed histrionically and waved her arms. "I can't believe it—all that planning—for nothing!"

"There's still time," I said. "The party's hours away."

"That's *nothing*! Sorry. Didn't mean to be so—but we have to construct the scarecrow, and inflate the balloons and put up the photo booth and—I told them we needed a

whole *day,* but they said starting at noon had to be enough—
but now, look, it's three o'clock! And people are standing
around here, so how can we get anything done? We might
as well cancel the party altogether."

"Surely not," I said. "Everybody would understand if
things aren't one hundred percent finished."

"No they wouldn't. They don't understand!" She uttered
a tiny sob. "It was going to be *perfect*!" She shook her
head. "If I'd had any idea that this would happen," she
said, "I would have left civil rights till Monday. Forget
Antigone. Who knew a jerk would toss cherry bombs and
spoil everything!"

"It'll work out," somebody said nearby. "I'll help."

"Our costumes," she wailed. "When is there going to be
time—and look at all the people *still* standing here! Aren't
they going to ever go home? How about their costumes?"

"It was advertised as costume optional," I reminded her.
"Maybe they weren't ever planning to be in disguise."

"I was!" she said too loudly. "I was and my friends were.
It was part of the *fun.*"

"I'll help. Maybe speed things up." That was spoken by
a ninth grader and surely not one who'd have been on
Allie's A list. Her clique was so tight, and her rule so established, that I was intrigued to see if she'd accept help from
peons.

She did, albeit with another sigh and a resigned shake of
her head. "I don't know where to tell you to start, though,"
she said. "If only everybody would *leave.* Can you help
move people out of here?"

"Can I help?" Pip asked. I'd forgotten that he was still
here, and that he didn't belong here in the first place. He'd
become a piece of the scenery.

Allie squinted. "Who are you?" But before he could
answer, she snapped her fingers. "Wait—you're the kid
from . . . Idaho?"

"Iowa."

"Right. The outside agitator." She smiled. "Sure, you can help. Why not?" And then she turned to me. "Did they find him?"

"Who?"

"The cherry bomber. After all this—" She waved vaguely at the room around her, at the afterimage of the police who had spoiled her decorating potential.

"They didn't tell me if they did."

She leaned close, lowered her voice. "Was it Seth? I saw him there, across the street, staring at us, and I don't want to get him in trouble, but did he do it?"

If you really didn't want to get somebody in trouble, did you go out of your way to suggest he'd committed a crime? "Why'd you think that?" I tried to calculate backward through the week, to pin together the hints, suggestions, and glances that had pushed suspicion toward Seth. My stolen test—had that been Allie who glared, or was she one of many faces glowering at Seth when I deposited a new version on her desk? Had it always been Allie making me wonder about Seth?

I didn't think so. Besides, why would she?

I asked her again. "Why would you think Seth did something like that?"

She looked at me intently before rearranging her facial muscles into a bland, pleasing mask and spoke slowly, as if thinking through each sentence before she said it. "No reason in particular. Playing detective, I guess. Trying to be logical. I mean we were on the curb, and the building's on one side of us, so it's not likely somebody inside tossed it out at us. And I'd seen him and he looked peculiar, staring at us that way. So, well, you know. But I guess I'm not a detective!" Her smile was brightly insincere.

Of course, she had other things on her mind, and a to-do list pressing on her. I was an annoyance and further delay.

"There were undoubtedly other people in the Square," I said quietly. "You noticed Seth because you know him, that's all."

If possible, her smile became still less sincere. "That must be it!" she said brightly.

"Good luck," I told her and Pip and the eager ninth grader. "I'll be . . . I'll be . . ." I didn't know how to finish that sentence. Where would I be now that I didn't have to be here tonight? What would I do with a gift of time?

First, I went and sat on the back stairs and phoned Mackenzie and left a message of freedom on his cell. Then I checked my messages and heard a last-minute, casual dinner invitation from Sasha. "Only one other couple, Wesley and Nick, are coming, so don't change, or dress up, and come six-thirty, sevenish, okay?"

We had met Nick and Wesley before, and they were funny and quick and involved in professions that had nothing to do with teaching adolescents. It sounded like a perfect place and way to wind down from this horrific week, so I called Mackenzie again and changed the message. I'd meet him at Sasha's.

It suddenly felt like a true T.G.I.F. except for a residual thrum of anxiety I couldn't shake.

FRIDAY, the note had said. Why?

I went back to the gym and observed Allie directing Liddy Moffat, or trying to. One did not direct the custodian, but she lived to clean, and so seemed quite happy to help, broom and pan in hand. The ninth graders had apparently been given litter detail, and they crawled over the bleachers, picking up notes and doodles and homework that had been hurriedly scribbled in case there had actually been classes today.

I was going to read about Allie one day, I thought. Her aspirations at the moment were in the arts, but she could as easily run a corporation or lead a platoon. I watched her make the rounds of her committee, advising and guiding each one as well as Pip, who looked as if he were willing to move the entire gym elsewhere if that's what she wanted. I was momentarily puzzled by his energetic altruism until it registered that Cheryl, apparently back in the Philly Prep fold at least for the dance, was his work partner.

FRIDAY.

What's wrong with this picture? I thought.

But nothing was.

Even that made me nervous.

Look here, I told myself. Observe this most innocuous, ordinary all-American scene. Students readying the gym for a school dance, believing that with crepe paper and posters they can transform the room into their fantasies. Listen to the happy drone of people working together, planning a party. This could be a saccharine greeting card, it's so ordinary and pleasing, so be pleased.

I took a few more deep breaths, but the mild jitters, the uncomfortable sense that my veins were rushing the blood through persisted.

I saw no sign of Seth or Wilson, though Wilson had been part of the demonstration, wearing his bandages with a swagger. Maybe he'd gone home to get into costume. Or maybe his mother had decided to surgically remove him from the bad influences even before rescheduling could be effected.

I watched another of the recent strange and strained Allie-Nita interchanges. Nita looked overwhelmed, propellering her arms and doing the head-shaking that seemed to be her basic communication with her best friend these past few days.

I felt sorry for both of them. They had worked hard and there really wasn't enough time to get everything done. I thought I might help with triage—pick the most important task and do it—and I walked over to them to say so.

"It'll all be your fault!" Nita was saying. "You could stop it and you aren't!"

"They aren't going to—"

"They're *crazy*!" I could see the tendons in Nita's neck. Her voice wasn't loud, but strained with the emotions it was barely containing.

I doubted that they were talking about the gymnasium décor. Nobody cared that much. But there I was, beside them, so I felt obliged to say something. "Could I help?"

They stared at me blankly.

"I know you're up against the wall with time, and I could take care of something, if you'd like. Maybe putting together that scarecrow you mentioned, Allie?"

They glanced at each other and then at me. "It's all right," Allie said. "It'll get done, but thanks. Thanks a lot!"

It didn't seem the right time to leave. Apparently, even preparty, they needed some kind of chaperone or referee.

When I looked back at them, Nita had huffed off, so I thought things had simmered down. I watched Allie collar Erik, who looked as if he wanted to bolt and run as she gave him instructions—several times. Erik behaved with her the way he too often did with me, blankly staring, then visibly letting his attention wander, his eyes checking out who was left on the bleachers, who else was still around— I nodded politely as he took note of me—and then he checked out what, if anything, might be going on up on the ceiling.

Allie looked up, too, following his glance, then drilled her index finger into his chest. He shrugged and nodded at the same time, said a little more, and moved on out of the gym. Maybe that's what Allie had been requesting—a cleared-out room and space to work.

Such high drama over a possibly less than perfect Mischief Night party. Teens were exhausting.

My blood was percolating again, as it had repeatedly all this week. I couldn't tell if it was due to accumulated events or apprehension about what was still to come.

I still had that note in my backpack saying something worse was going to happen.

When?

What?

Was the Friday note the answer to that?

Taking deep breaths did not help.

I checked the time. Too early to go to Sasha's. She's a photographer and even though she now uses the computer more than the darkroom, she does still work at home a great deal. I did not want to interrupt.

I could go see Juan Reyes. As soon as I had the thought, I felt better. Maybe by now he could have visitors and I could make him feel more a part of the school community. I didn't know if he had any family close by, or whether Tisha Banks had the fortitude or interest to see this through with him.

Even if I couldn't see him, maybe I could at least get more information about his condition, or I could find out something I could do to help out.

At the very least, it would feel like a step in the right direction of paying attention and respect. The illusion of doing something seemed preferable to doing nothing at all or continuing to hang out with teenagers.

He was at HUP—the University of Pennsylvania hospital. I glanced at my watch. The bus would get me there in a matter of minutes.

First, I found Pip. "What are your evening plans?" I asked.

He shrugged. "It's kind of not up to me."

"Then promise you'll stay here and help out for the next hour or so—until I get back. Then you can tell me what has or hasn't worked out and if you're staying, we'll iron out the logistics."

He promised, and I went to catch my bus. The daylight was shrinking and the temperature falling, issuing stern reminders that it would be November in two days and any happy dreams we had of ongoing Indian summer warmth were naïve and irrational. I was lost in my shivers and contemplation of whether my coat, which was just about ready to collect Social Security, could make it through another winter, when I realized that in addition to a tiny Asian woman, a red-cheeked sturdy woman in a thick wool coat, and two dark-eyed, dark-skinned girls who looked like twins trying to not look like twins, Erik Steegmuller, in the ubiquitous thick winter letter jacket, was waiting for the same bus, and not only that, looking at me with concern.

His expression flattened out instantly. "Miss Pepper!" he said. "Going home?"

I smiled and shook my head. "How about you?"

He looked down at his feet. "Not really," he said.

"Not really" is a phrase that drives me to distraction. What does it mean and why can't they simply say "no"? Why do they feel obliged to hedge, to skirt the periphery of possibility? *Not really.* Then what? Yes falsely? In his delirious imagination, he was going home, but not in reality?

"Getting ready for the party, then?" I asked.

He nodded. "Have to find Nita first, though."

"It looks like it'll be fun," I said insincerely. "I'm sorry to miss it. Are you coming in costume?"

"Well, we thought, probably. Everybody is. Unless . . ." He shrugged. "They don't. Then . . ."

He could get a job as living proof that some people were impervious to twelve years of instruction in the mother tongue. You could try to leave no child behind, but some children were determined to stay where they were. "Kind of a cool costume. You'll like it."

"Can't wait. Meanwhile, I'm going up to the hospital," I said.

Erik took a step back from the curb. "You okay? Were you hurt today?"

"No, no. I'm going to try to see Mr. Reyes. Or at least see about him."

He nodded, as if I'd verified a theory he held. "Well, then," he said. "Well, then . . . is he—can he talk now?"

"I don't know."

He looked worried. "I mean, is he awake, you know?" He shrugged and realigned his muscles. He looked as if he had no idea what to do with his hands. If only he had a basketball to dribble. "I heard he was still pretty much unconscious," he mumbled. "Like it's . . . unusual to go see somebody unconscious. I mean, I guess it's nice, but . . ."

"You know, they say people can hear what you're saying while they're unconscious."

"Really? But, like—he can't talk yet, can he?"

The bus approached, and I believe we both heard it with relief. It wasn't until I had boarded that I realized Erik hadn't gotten on.

"Changed my mind," he called out. "Getting late. See you."

"Kids," an exhausted woman next to me said. "They're all idiots."

I WALKED SOFTLY, BUT THE HOSPITAL WASN'T QUIET THE way I always imagined it. Even here, in a semi–intensive care unit, nurses called out to one another, spoke brightly to patients and visitors; families with active—and often noisy—children picnicked in waiting areas; and all of that might have annoyed the truly ill, but for the moment, it was a good thing because when Nita saw me, she shrieked.

In a hushed place, her scream would have cracked the plaster walls, but here, it almost blended into the low-grade din.

"Nita!" I said, clutching the small flowering plant I'd bought in the gift shop. "What is it? Why are you acting afraid of me?" I didn't say I was surprised to see her here, because I wasn't, not after Erik's pitiable attempt at casual conversation. He'd been headed here, looking for her, but turned back when he realized I was going in the same direction, though I couldn't understand what I had to do with his mission. "Nita?" I repeated.

"Nothing," she said. "I'm—surprised."

"Well, so am I. Why are you here?"

"I come every day," she said in a low voice. "I—I needed to know how he is. I mean, really know."

"And how is he?"

She shook her head. "Not good. No visitors. He might . . . He's not getting better. Not enough. It's . . . ." And then her nose turned red and her eyes welled up.

"Nita," I said softly. I braced the plant on my hip and put my hand on her arm, gently, almost to keep her from fracturing and falling apart. "What is it?"

She looked at me with wide, overflowing gray-blue eyes, and shook her head. "This is all so horrible. He could die or be blind or disfigured. Nobody ever, ever meant anything like this to happen."

"What do you mean?" This elicited nothing but silence. "What, instead, *did* somebody mean to happen?"

"Nothing! I said nobody meant anything!" She pulled away from me. "Please," she said, sniffling. "I can't explain. I would, but I can't. Don't ask me to."

"Why do you keep coming here?"

She looked at me as if I were ignorant of the most rudimentary rules of civilization. "Because he could have died!" she said. "And then what?" Her voice rose, became tight and shrill. "Then what?" She was still sniffling and her eyes still teared. "And nobody else comes. Nobody else *cares*. What's wrong with them?"

"He's lucky to have a friend like you," I said. "You must be quite fond of him to keep visiting."

"Not really."

There was that phrase again. Did that mean she was somewhat fond of him, or disliked him?

"Nobody liked him," she whispered. "He didn't like us, either. But even so, nobody meant . . ."

She didn't need to say anything more definite. "I know somebody put sodium in a jar in the sink, meaning it as a prank. Probably just part of the hide-and-seek you were doing with the chemistry supplies. But the person who put it there didn't realize that if the water tap was turned on, it would explode. Is that what you're talking about? This horrible result was an unintended consequence."

"Can there keep on being unintended consequences?" she asked. "Forever? Something happens, then something else, and then because of that, something else—and nobody meant any of it at the beginning?"

I didn't know how to answer. I hated that we were talking in code. "I suppose so," I said. "Maybe we'd call it cause and effect? Action and reaction?"

She said nothing except: "I have to go now."

"First, please, I'm worried that something else is going to happen, that somebody else is going to be hurt."

She'd gotten back control of herself, and she stared at me with deliberate blankness. A slate wiped clean. "Yes?" she said.

"Nita," I said. "I can help you, or at least try, but you need to help me."

"I've been trying to as much as I can."

"Tell me what you know. If nobody meant any harm—"

"That was then."

FRIDAY, the note had said. Was she the one who'd sent me the warnings? Trying as much as she could to tell me something worse was going to happen—today?

"No offense," she said, "but you have no idea what you're talking about, because if you did, you'd know you can't do a thing about it. You think everything's like in your books, but it isn't."

I waited for an explanation, but when none came, I asked for one.

She blinked. "Like Antigone. Like you think you can just decide what's right and be brave and go ahead and do it, but even there—look what happened to her. She died!"

"But—but—today was the perfect example of doing what was right with all of you out on the street, protesting something you thought was wrong."

"Oh, that. That was different. That was something everybody agrees on. I mean, freedom of speech—come on! It's basic."

"So something else is more complicated. That doesn't mean you can't still talk about it, and wind up doing the right thing, does it?"

She said nothing, and in fact, bit at her bottom lip as if to make sure it didn't act independently. "Don't feel bad," she said. "You're a teacher, not Wonder Woman."

"But I want to help."

"Nobody expects you to. Everybody knows it's impossible."

Everybody except me. I was useless, uninformed, misguided, and, worst of all, deluded into believing I could change things or make a difference.

Nita put her hand on my arm, a gesture of consolation. "Don't blame yourself," she said softly. "Some things . . . well . . . they just have to play themselves out. It's fate."

Nineteen

I SPOKE WITH THE NURSE AND REALLY DIDN'T GET ANY more information than I had from Harriet. She did add that although the potted plant was quite lovely, we could all probably hold off on visits and gifts like that for a while.

It didn't take long to hear what in essence boiled down to: not a good situation, but not without hope—now go home.

I phoned Sasha from the hospital. "I've got time on my hands," I said. "Want some help getting ready?"

She again told me how casual it would be and that I didn't have to—but if I really wanted to, she'd like the company. It seemed a plan.

When I reached the bus stop, Nita was there and, undoubtedly to her dismay, we were headed in the same direction, doomed to travel together, and worse, when we got on, there were two empty spots next to each other.

We rode in silence. I tried to use the time to digest the idea that I was "only a teacher" and possibly well-meaning, but unable to do anything worthwhile. I knew that I had failed to turn out a generation with perfect grammar or spelling, or a comprehensive knowledge of the Western canon, so what was left if I'd also failed at helping a few young people out of a distressing situation?

I knew she'd meant no harm and in fact had meant to

console me, but it stung to think that she was more in touch with reality than I was.

The silence grew oppressive. "Erik was looking for you," I said. "When I was waiting for the bus to go to the hospital. I thought he was going to get on as well, but he changed his mind."

She looked straight ahead, not at me, but even from the side I could see the muscles of her forehead tighten. "He knew where I was." She spoke without looking at me.

"He seemed . . . jumpy."

She turned her head toward me at last. "That's how he is," she said, and I had to admit it was at least partially true. He couldn't finish a sentence, and was uncoordinated except on a court.

"And this year's worse, being a senior. His parents are on his case all the time. His parents went to Ivy League schools and he's not . . . he never was, you know what I mean, so why now . . ." She shrugged. "You know. Expectations. It's not like his parents are the only ones or anything, but Erik's fidgety anyway and they don't help." She sighed.

Did they really expect Erik to get into a top college? It was a totally unrealistic expectation unless they had endowed their alma mater so generously that the admissions office couldn't see over the pile of greenbacks.

"Everybody's nervous," Nita said. "Not just Erik. So much is riding on now. Like the whole rest of your life, is all."

Part of me itched to respond to her observation the way it deserved. "What a revelation," I wanted to say. "What was your first clue? Could it have been the past twelve years, starting with kindergarten, of teachers doing everything but standing on their heads—and maybe that, too— trying to develop study habits and an appreciation for learning the material?"

I kept my sarcasm-hatches battened down.

"It's too much pressure," she said. "Too much to worry about."

"But you'll be fine. You've got good grades, lots of extracurricular activities—"

She sighed and shrugged, as if I'd missed the point. Again.

We rode a few more blocks in silence. My expedition had been a waste of time. I didn't know more about Juan Reyes, had certainly not been of any use or comfort to him, and I also knew as little as ever about what was going on with the senior class. The fact that they were worried about college applications wasn't news, nor was the theory I was hammering out. I decided to try it on Nita.

"You—your class—somebody—wanted Mr. Reyes to quit," I said. "That's it, isn't it? He was too strict, wouldn't give a re-exam even though you'd all done poorly. Didn't understand high school, and your GPAs were going to suffer because of him. That's why the pranks, the supplies missing then returned, and the warning about the martyred teacher. You wanted him to give up and move on."

Her lips tightened, and she said nothing.

"It's okay. It's obvious that something went wrong. Everybody would understand that nobody intended to actually hurt Mr. Reyes." I needed to believe that was so.

"I don't know about anything like that. I don't know anything."

I kept the rest of my theory to myself. I knew there was one person—one—in that class who had the most at stake if Juan Reyes was impossible to please. Seth had a good chance of getting into the school he wanted, and he'd worked hard for what he had. His expectations had to be higher and more intense than most of the rest of his class. And he was smart enough to plan the series of frustrat-

ing mishaps that he hoped would drive the man out of the
school.

Also smart enough to know that sodium explodes i
water's poured onto it. But was he cruel enough to plan
that? It didn't fit anything I knew of the young man, but as
Nita had so cordially pointed out, I didn't know a thing.

"Nita, does *Friday*—just that—have any special meaning
for you?"

"It's today." She gave me a how-can-you-possibly-not
know-that look, her brows pulled close and lowered.

"Yes," I said. "I am aware of that, but is something sup
posed to happen today?"

"The school party."

"Help me here—aside from that?"

She shrugged.

"Did you warn me about today? About something that's
going to happen on Friday?"

She turned quickly to look at me, and her expression no
longer suggested that I was speaking nonsense. She looked
frightened. Then she clamped her lips together and removed all expression from her face.

She knew what was going on, but that knowledge did
neither one of us any good because she was not going to
share it with me. Or maybe she had already, and my guess
was right, that she was the author of those cryptic notes.

"Well," I said as the bus approached the cross street for
the school. "Maybe the party will cheer you up."

"I don't think I'm going. I don't feel well."

"But I thought—when I saw Erik—"

She shrugged. "He doesn't need a date. We decided not
to go in couples. It isn't that kind of party." She looked as
if this were an important point. "*Most* people won't have
dates."

"Needing a date isn't the point. You worked so hard to
make it work. You and Allie and your committee—"

Her eyelids lowered, as if I were boring her into a stupor.

"I hope you'll change your mind," I said lamely. "I hope you'll at least come to see the fruits of your labors."

"That's what I'm hoping to avoid," she said. "See you. This is my stop."

I wanted to ask what she meant, but the words died unsaid in the stale vapors of the bus because Nita was on the steps as the doors opened, and then she was gone.

I WAS ABOUT TO CONTINUE ON TO SASHA'S, half a dozen blocks closer to the Delaware, when, with a rush of mortification, I suddenly remembered Pip. I'd made him promise to wait for me, and then I'd nearly forgotten.

Sometimes it takes more than a village—or at least more than a village idiot. I rushed to get out of the bus two stops after Nita had left and walked as quickly as I could to Philly Prep, hoping he was still there.

I nearly bumped into Allie, standing near the gym doors with her hands on her hips, surveying the décor.

"Looks great," I said, deliberately ignoring both her frown of disapproval and the surprisingly bland decorations that had necessitated so many meetings and so much planning: plastic jack-o'-lanterns with bulbs inside, a haystack made of ropes and wires, orange-and-black crepe paper streamers, a scarecrow made of stuffed gym clothing and long socks, and an unsuccessful attempt to tent part of the gym with orange-and-black burlap. The far wall was dominated by the silhouette of a witch, her broom, and her black cat, back arched. And her completely homely baggy dress. Allie had not been able to think outside the broomstick; Gabby Mackenzie's work was not yet done.

"Nothing's the way I thought it would be," Allie muttered. "There's not enough; it's not enough different from normal."

"It's not easy to disguise bleachers," I said. "But wait till it fills up with people, feels like a party. That'll make all the difference."

She was not convinced. She squinted and I could almost see the wheels of her imagination redo the room, turning it into an autumn fantasy.

Allie wanted to be a set designer for Broadway or Hollywood. Her dreams were enormous and compelling, and she had her path to those goals all mapped out. The gym probably wasn't a measure of her talent, since her disappointment seemed to be with herself. A failure of vision.

"Someday," I said, "you'll be able to create precisely what you envision. You'll have the budget and the manpower and the time."

"First I have to get accepted," she said between gritted teeth. "They take one out of forty-seven applicants."

"But I'm sure you—"

"Thanks," she said. "Like they say: from your mouth to God's ears."

There was a miasma surrounding the seniors, but this was not like Allie Deroche. She was, if anything, overly sure of herself, and I'd never thought it was bravado on her part. Of course the world would want her—she had *it*. "What's wrong?" I asked.

She gestured at the room. "This! It's—it's crappy. Ordinary. I told Nita! She just doesn't think *big* enough! This was our chance to make a mark, to do something . . . extraordinary." She exhaled loudly. "And she didn't even help—not one single bit today. Sorry," she said. "I didn't mean to—it's too late to change anything, anyway, so what you see is what we've got." The words were accepting, but she still looked as if she wanted to shoo everyone out the door and start over.

I didn't say that I found it charming and in the grand tradition of sleazily decorated high school gyms. It takes years away from high school to appreciate such a thing, and Allie

ad never been interested in being part of that long second-
ate tradition.

Beautifully decorated or not, the gym was slowly filling
vith students, mostly the younger grades, whose parents
ropped them off before going to their own Friday night
lans, and would pick them up later. The way Mackenzie
nd I would have to remember to do for Pip.

Lots of costumes on the young'uns. For my taste, too
nany based on pop figures, their rubber celebrity masks vi-
rating with their breath. There were also girls as bunnies,
he floppy-eared sort, and girls as action figures I couldn't
dentify, boys as the president of the United States and as
errorists, or so I thought their attire was meant to suggest.
hey'd be unsuccessful terrorists, however, because they so
latantly advertised their professions.

And there were many in ordinary street clothes, includ-
ng Pip, dressed as Boy in Throes of a New Crush.

He sat down beside me on the bleachers. "I'm doing
reat," he said. "Great day." He nodded agreement with
imself. "Great party!"

"It hasn't started yet," I reminded him.

"Yeah, but it's going to be great. I can stay, can't I?"

I tried to keep my smile to myself. "I'm glad it worked
ut. We'll have to make arrangements for later."

"So . . ." he said. "Me and Cheryl—"

"Cheryl and I." I hate to be that way, but I hate "me
nd" even more.

He sighed. "Cheryl *and I* got to talking, and you know,
he didn't know you were into crime-fighting, too. You're
vay too modest!"

"Honestly, Pip, crime-fighting is a little more dramatic
han watching a lady's house."

"She was impressed."

"It is not important to me to impress Cheryl in that
vay." I would have loved to have heard how he described

Mackenzie's and my efforts at Bright Investigations. In
fact, I probably would have loved to be one of the people
he imagined, at least for a while.

"So," he said, "we were talking about what makes people commit horrible crimes, and given your expertise,
Cheryl said I should ask you. So I am!"

"I don't have any special expertise, and where is Cheryl
anyway?"

"Went home to change into some costume," he said.
"Will I look too stupid not having one?"

"Say you're disguised as a kid from Iowa."

"So what's the answer?" he asked. "Why do people do
bad things, commit crimes—like, say, murder. Are they just
crazy?"

"I think anybody who deliberately harms another person is a little crazy. I'm sure the perpetrators think they
have lots of reasons, or motives, but my own theory is
that whoever it is, and however wrong they might be, the
murderer feels as if his own life—or what makes it worth
living—is at risk. He has to get rid of the other person to
stay alive, not necessarily physically, but often emotionally.
If you thought somebody jeopardized the thing that mattered most to you, was destroying your life in essence—
maybe we all have it in us to go berserk and commit an
unspeakable act. That's how murders—and wars—start."

Which of course made me think of Seth, sadly saying he
was involved in a war. What had begun that one? His declaration that he was gay? Or something more? And did
Juan Reyes's explosion somehow fit into that?

I couldn't make it work.

"Anyway," I said to Pip, "your uncle has had a whole lot
more experience with people pushed to the edge, and he's
studying why crime happens, so maybe he has a completely
different theory." I didn't think so. We'd talked about it
many times and we were basically in agreement.

I was enjoying this bit of philosophizing, but Pip sighted the return of Cheryl, dressed as Bo Peep, and we barely had time to talk about picking him up later before he'd lost all interest in my conversation.

In a way, I wished I had been staying. The room was filling up, and a few other teachers had arrived, including Edie Friedman, dressed somewhat unimaginatively as a referee because, she told me, she had a referee's outfit at home and she thought it was slimming. Never knew who might show up at a thing like this. A single parent, picking up a child, for example.

Carol, the math teacher, still red-nosed and carrying a box of tissue, but a good sport, arrived dressed as a bassett hound. "My nose kind of fits the costume, doesn't it?" she said. "Now go! You're free to spend the evening with adults." I thanked her and wished her well and almost made it to the door, but Ma'ayan, dressed completely in pink—shirt, linen slacks, shoes, socks, and bicycle helmet—was bearing down on me, trailed by Ben, looking as awkward and even more lovesick than ever, because he'd made himself up as a sad clown with a big plastic tear on one of his cheeks.

Ma'ayan greeted me effusively, and then she put her hands on her hips. "Do you know what Ben thought I was? *Who* he thought I was?" She rolled her eyes, and if he'd been less blinded by love, he would have shriveled to the size of a raisin by the force of that expression. "He thought I was *Finney*!"

The name didn't register for the moment. "Funny?" I asked.

"*Finney!* From *A Separate Peace*. You know!"

"I only—" Ben began. "It was only a guess. I didn't mean—"

"The pink shirt! He thought that's who I was because I'm wearing a pink shirt!"

Ah, yes. The annual Episode of the Pink Shirt and the dull annoyance of having to go through it every year. The nervous laughter, sotto voce jokes from the back of the room. The suspicion of gayness, of the shirt signaling homosexuality. The raw material for a tenth grade snickerfest, as it had been.

I knew they were sexually unsure of themselves, fearful of not fitting in, of not being precisely like everyone else. Still, I wished that just once it didn't happen. And I couldn't bear to think about Seth—all the Seths—sitting through all those classes in silent agony.

Nothing really changes, although we like to believe we are making progress. We deal with it in class and know it won't make a difference ten minutes later when the jokers are outside the room.

Maybe the progress was that we did try to deal with it in class. It certainly didn't feel like much. "Finney, yes," I said.

"But I'm not Finney!" she said. Ma'ayan would possibly go mute if we removed all exclamation points, both real and theoretical, from her vocabulary. "I'm a piece of bubble gum!"

I had been pining for imagination and individuality and here it was, and it taught me something. Imagination wasn't the be-all and end-all.

And poor Ben! He didn't stand a chance. He'd thought he was being insightful—drawing on their common knowledge and reference, creating an insiders' bond—and instead he'd gone splat on his face with her. How could he—anyone?—have suspected bubble gum?

"You would have stumped me, too, but now, of course, I see it—and you do, too, don't you, Ben?"

He nodded gratefully, and Ma'ayan sighed, but they drifted off more or less together.

I sat there thinking about Seth. I wondered if he would

show up at the party, and even if, as Nita said, his friends or former friends were coming in groups, not dates, how it must feel to know that nobody in the group is yours, or eligible to be yours.

Maybe that was behind the mystifying and meaningless pranks. A private initiation or revenge. Maybe it was akin to Macavity's tail on the TV—placed where it will block the most vision because, as Pip had observed, he could.

I called Sasha again and apologized. "I forgot I was with child," I said, and when she began cheering and exclaiming, I had to backtrack and explain that I'd meant Pip. "I'll be there in a half hour. I'm on foot."

She reminded me to be careful, that it was Mischief Night.

The room had filled still more while I'd been engaged with the bubble gum girl, and now, about 50 percent of the newcomers were in prefab culture-hero costumes. I felt a thousand years old by not even knowing the names of those people whose plastic replicas were popular masks, or what they'd done to achieve this odd sort of immortality.

I saw a stocky Spider-Man, two Batmans—Batmen?— eyeing each other joylessly, one ballerina, two cowboys in homemade getups—how retro and refreshing at this point— an ominous Darth Vader in the far corner, a SpongeBob and two Teletubbies, one green, one purple. It felt almost a relief to see old-fashioned movie icons—a *Wizard of Oz* Tin Man and a Dorothy in sparkly red slippers. And in a dark robe and ghostly white open-mouthed grimace, somebody being either Ghostface from the movie *Scream*, or much less likely, Edvard Munch's *The Scream*.

Lurking near the door, making an appearance while appearing as little as he could manage, was Maurice Havermeyer. I hated the idea of making small talk with him, especially as I was still on his evildoers list, so I stayed where I was a little longer, feeling like one of those elderly women who sat at the side of grand balls and fanned themselves in *Gone with the Wind*. I found myself thinking like one, too, looking for gossip and scandal and coming up with clunkers like: Was Batman talking to Bo Peep? What's going on with that? And a Princess Leia, complete with the bagels-over-the-ear hairdo, was sulking because The Scream was handing a glass of what I hoped was pure punch to a girl with peach and aqua spiked hair and studs punctuating her lips, nose, and both eyebrows. I wasn't sure whether or not she was in costume.

But wait—the screaming mask was also posturing in the other corner. He was obviously a popular item at the costume rental spots because, while I was still amused by the duplication of Screams, a third entered.

All three were tall, half a head at least above most of the rest of the people in the gym.

My stomach twinged. I told it to relax, that it was coincidence, nothing more.

Then three more Screams wandered in. Team Scream. "Kind of a cool costume," Erik had said. "You'll like it."

I didn't like it.

I assured myself it didn't matter how I felt about it. There was nothing necessarily sinister in a group of buddies deciding to dress the same way. They did it all the time as teammates.

I made my way toward the door. Havermeyer was no longer standing there, which was a relief.

I walked briskly down Walnut Street toward Sasha's. The wind had picked up and felt damp, and I shivered in the jacket that had been the right warmth earlier in the day.

Happily, I'd seen no evidence of Mischief Night in action, but it was probably too early. They say it's a dying tradition, and I hope so. It was too frightening to contemplate what *mischief* might mean these days. I hoped Mackenzie had the car in a safe place. Old and seasoned as it was, I didn't want it egged, another harmless-sounding prank that wound up costing thousands of dollars to replace a ruined paint job.

And then I was at Sasha's condo, which was as yet undraped with toilet paper, unsprayed with whipped topping, and looking pretty normal. I went up to her spacious quarters and enjoyed the pleasures of a heated home.

She also looked normal, which is to say, happily bizarre. She wore a body-hugging shrieking orange sheath from the 1950s and amber beads the size of babies' heads. The dress was the color of those cones they put down on the highway as a warning.

"You said casual," I grumbled.

"Anything half a century old is casual. Besides, I blend with the table décor and flowers this way. I have been so pathologically organized," she said, tweaking a yellowed leaf off the coffee table's bouquet of bronze chrysanthemums that her dress in no way matched.

I would have liked to have met the six-foot-tall fifties woman who originally dared to wear that dress. It gave me an entirely new vision of that era.

"Anyway," Sasha said, "there is nothing for you to do but keep me company. I have turned over a new leaf."

"Obviously." I knew as I said it this leaf would be turned back before the night was out. Being organized, planning for more than five minutes ahead, bored Sasha. The good thing was that she never seemed to recall previous identical experiments.

"Everything in this household has been organized—closets, drawers, desk, address book, pantry."

"You're saying you've become insufferable."

"Yes! I was so tired of being inventive and spontaneous and interesting. This is much calmer and actually leaves me lots of free time. Dull time, but free."

"And what will you do with it?"

She waved toward the dining area where I'd already noticed the table. It was difficult to avoid it, draped to the floor as it was in satin that was almost the same orange as her dress. That was in turn covered with pale yellow tulle. A pumpkin carved into a puzzled expression sat in the center, filled with yellow mums and black ribbon bows.

"I'm thinking there's room in this country for another household goddess," she said. "Somebody with maybe a less . . . generic sensibility."

"I wouldn't give up your day job just yet," I said, nodding as she opened a bottle of Sauvignon Blanc and held up a glass. "I envy your obsessively tidy week. My week has been anything but organized. It's included minor league annoyances and major disasters, an explosion that left a teacher in a coma, and my thinking I'd be fired. But there was also a student demonstration—a good one, for a good cause—that distracted all of us from things like firing me and also included two more explosions."

"Wow," she said. "Teaching's a lot more interesting than I thought." She was silent for a moment, sipping wine. Then she smiled. "Hey—we could be partners in my new business. Co-domestic goddesses."

"Does it bother you that I don't have any of the necessary skills?"

"What skills do goddesses need?"

I was sitting with my backpack on my lap, and I started to put it down on the floor, out of sight, and then, spurred on by Sasha's newfound organizational expertise, I thought I'd do some light housekeeping while we waited for the rest of the party. "I've become a packrat," I said. "That is not goddesslike. I've been saving evidence that means nothing. It has either amused or annoyed Mackenzie all week and now it's annoying me. It's over, whatever it wasn't, and I might as well toss it all."

"Do not try to explain what you just said. I'm happy not knowing," Sasha said.

I pulled out my actual work, the poetry text the eleventh graders had used, and a few late papers and one makeup exam I'd been toting around for too long. Those went into the save pile. There were other papers to keep as well, though I was tempted to chuck the entire lot and rethink my decision to stay in my classroom.

Ethics prevailed, though feebly, and I put that stack to one side and kept removing papers. Havermeyer bulletins I'd failed to toss immediately, a few notices about the party tonight, and random detritus, notes I'd intercepted, more notes, and the anonymous doggerel that I'd thought was an extra poem in the eleventh grade collection. Nobody had claimed it and I certainly didn't want it, so too bad—out it goes.

But first, I would share it with Sasha:

Mischief Night and are we scared
For big trouble we're prepared
But what's a prank and what's a crime
And is the only difference time?
Friday till midnight is all right
That's the meaning of that night.
But if it's done another day,
Then somebody's gonna pay
Ghosts and goblins say they will
When they have some time to kill.

"Ghosts and goblins say they will what?" she asked, quite reasonably.

"They will pay?" I suggested.

"They'll pay for doing something bad when it wasn't Mischief Night? They'll pay when they have the chance? It still doesn't make sense."

"It also doesn't scan well and it's got nothing going for it. I can't decide if it was an honest effort or a deliberate spoof because I asked them all to give poetry a try." But I couldn't help but register that the poet hadn't said "when he had time." He'd said when they had "time to kill."

My cell rang, and I listened to Mackenzie's softly slurry voice telling me he was on his way. "Got caught up in the research and forgot the time." He sounded out of breath, as if he was running while talking. "Car's parked halfway across town, too."

"Don't worry. The others won't be here for a while. It's okay," I said.

"Good to hear you soundin' so relaxed," he said. "How glad are you this week's over? All those goblins and ghosties gone."

Unfortunate choice of words, or at least, unfortunate timing. I must have been quiet a beat or two too long.

"You are over it, aren't you?" he asked. "Don' mean over what happened to the teacher—not at all, but over your . . . well, you know."

I did know. Over hallucinations and grabbing at signs and portents that were anything but. Half a passed note. A stupid poem. A look. Two girls fighting every day.

"I'm trying to be," I answered him.

His turn to be silent a beat too long and then to say, "Good. I'll see you soon as I can get there."

Like so many women before me, when confounded as to what to do, I returned to housekeeping, making order where there was none. If only I could reach into my mind with a duster and tidy that up, too.

"Here's a gossipy note about precisely how much Kiley loves Brett, and half of one about what Daley's wearing tomorrow night—that would be tonight, actually, and here's . . ." I stopped, for some reason seeing the page I'd picked up in a new light.

I'd considered it mawkish gibberish when Liddy Moffatt
first handed it to me. A pathetic, sweaty attempt to be poetic and nothing more.

But now I saw that there was more.

Dim candles burn
Incense on the air
Evening has come
Far in the mist
Against all fear
Greatness arose
Limited nowhere
Intent fulfilled
Armor and Shield
Resist the night

"What do you think of this?" I asked Sasha, passing the
sheet to her.

"More bad poetry? Thanks a lot. How about we talk instead?"

"Please read it."

She frowned as she did, then she looked up at me. "No
offense, teach, but I think it means you have not inspired
them to greatness."

"Read it again."

"Really, Manda, it's refrigerator poetry. Like they had a
bunch of words somebody thought were poetic—incense,
mist, resist—and they strung them together."

"Please?"

"Okay." Sighing for my benefit, she again read the lines,
then looked up at me. "Was I supposed to see the glimmer
of genius this time? You know I don't know anything
about poetry in the first place but . . . I still say it stinks."

"Yes, of course, but the first letters of each line," I said
softly.

"Diefa—oh," she said slowly. "But that must be a coincidence because what would be the point? *You* got the poem, right?"

"It was on the floor, under a desk. The cleaning woman is a fanatic about saving things. If for no other reason, she'd think we could write on the back of the page, use the paper."

"So that means you don't know when it fell on the floor, which class, if anybody besides the wretched poet saw it, or if it has anything whatsoever to do with your students or real life." She tossed the paper onto the coffee table and yawned.

"It does," I said softly. "I'm sure it does."

"Manda, you're really overreacting. You look stressed out, you've had a rotten week—give it up. This is trash. Bad poetry and not worth a second glance."

"It's Mischief Night."

"And what else is new?"

"Time to kill. That other poem about Mischief Night, about crime?"

"It was nonsense, too. What are you doing?"

"Maybe they were left on purpose, but not for me—for a victim. For somebody they were tormenting."

"I really wish you'd—"

"I have to go. I'll be back—you'll see. I'll be back before you all finish your cocktails—but I have to go."

She stood up, all six feet of screaming sheath. "You just got here, and here is where you're supposed to be—we're having a dinner party—and what on earth is wrong with you?"

"I'll sound crazy but—"

"You already do."

"I've been getting signals—"

"Please don't say from little green men with antennae?"

"From kids. From poems like this. From random remarks. I think from kids who were too terrified to speak directly. A kid." Nita. I was sure she'd sent the messages, including the concise one that simply said FRIDAY. But why did she have to remain anonymous, afraid to speak to me even this afternoon? "I caught the signals, but I misread them."

I was up by now, grabbing my jacket and nearing the door. "And today I made it worse. I think a kid's going to wind up being humiliated or hurt tonight because I meant well. He told me he was in a war, and I didn't think it through. I think I sent him into an ambush. And if that's so—or if he anticipates it—I don't know what he'll do in return."

"Call the cops if you think something dangerous is going to happen!"

"I wouldn't know what to tell them, and I don't mean that level of danger. It's at school, after all. Lots of people, but I've felt something was coming to a head. It's so amorphous—look how I can't convince you, so how could I convince cops?" I shook my head in frustration at the vagueness even I could hear. "I don't know what I'd say." It wouldn't bring out the forces if I said futures were about to be destroyed.

"There are adults there, right?"

I nodded.

She smiled, playing coy. The dress helped the act. "What could happen that's worth missing dinner with great people?"

I could easily envision a brawl. Property damage. Havermeyer going ballistic. An arrest record. Futures upended and curdled.

I thought of Nita saying she was probably staying home tonight because she didn't want to see the fruit of her labors. Whatever was scheduled to happen had been planned. The quarrels made sense if she'd refused to be a part of what was going on, or had once been a part, but then broke with the others as the war escalated.

I'd spent too much of the week looking for the villain of the piece, becoming convinced it was Seth, but I'd been duped. Juan Reyes had been duped.

Nothing rankled more than the idea that one—or several—of my students had set me up, except the idea that it had worked.

"Wait till Mackenzie gets here. You can go there to gether, later. Meanwhile, eat something. Have another glass of wine, and then you can go. Maybe it'd be best if you let the kids work it out together. Whatever it is, in the end, they've got to handle it themselves."

She stood there like a stone wall, a blind alley. I sighed and nodded, and she looked relieved.

"I'll get us more wine," she said and retreated into the kitchen. Luckily, the condo she'd inherited as a by-product of one of her parents' many marriages and divorces was rambling and large, so that she was out of sight—and then so was I.

We'd work it out later.

I had to do this. The worst scenario would be that I was completely wrong and I'd be humiliated. I'd already been there, so that prospect didn't even rankle. But I had created a situation that I was now sure would be bad and I couldn't shrug and ignore it, sit back and allow Seth's, and possibly his antagonist's future, turn dark.

There were indeed other teachers there, but poor sniffly Carol had no inkling of what had been going on, and neither did Havermeyer—if he actually stayed in hearing distance—and Edie Friedman would be guarding her gym or looking for a parent to date. The hapless parents who were chaperoning would be oblivious as well. And even if I could send a warning, what would I say? I didn't know what would happen, only that something would.

I walked double-triple time in the damp dark chill, wishing as always that Benjamin Franklin, who'd first thought of the good idea of daylight savings time, had thought it was good enough to be in effect all year long. Wasn't winter dark enough without making it worse with the clock change? Wasn't daylight always worth saving? I grumbled my way toward school which, luckily, was only a matter of a few blocks' walk. It was so much easier to be angry with Franklin and the daylight wasting lobby, whoever they were, than with the mess at school. Still, it would help, would always help if everything had to be done in broad daylight. For starters, there would be no Mischief Night.

I passed one knocked-over city trash can, one soaped-up dry cleaner's window, and what looked to be a new splat of red paint on the side of a corner deli, but I didn't see any mischief makers. Still, I upped my pace even more, wished for better streetlights, and was relieved to turn the corner toward the school.

The Square was dark across from me, and silent, though I could see the ghostly outline of a tree that had been toilet-papered.

I also could hear music from the school. The sound system worked and the party was apparently in full swing. I was only steps away. I took a deep breath, squared my shoulders against what, I didn't know—and heard footsteps, loud and fast, and garbled words, "It's her!" from behind me.

I whirled around, expecting to see kids running from toilet-papering another tree, but the masks were the first clue I was wrong. Unless they were headed for the school dance dressed as burglars, there was no reason for the black Zorro masks the trio of lummoxes wore. Halloween was tomorrow.

Before I could do or say anything, they grabbed me, each

arm held in a vise grip, one of the attackers behind my back, hands on my shoulders.

I screamed as loudly as I could.

A hand was clapped over my mouth. "Chill!" a gravelly voice said from behind me. "We're friends of Mitty's!"

His words were slurred and he sounded drunk. I didn't chill, and I couldn't speak with that huge hand over my mouth, couldn't say I didn't know Mitty, wasn't Mitty, didn't care about Mitty—and what kind of friends grab women in the street?

They laughed—all three. Different laughs, drunken but vastly amused laughs.

I struck out with my only free appendage—my leg— trying to kick sideways at one of them. Sideways kicks are rather pitiable.

"Whoa, whoa," another equally drunk-sounding voice said, and then he laughed. "Fierce, isn't she?"

"C'mon, calm down. It's Mischief Night and we're the Mitt's buds!"

Whoever they were, they were strong. I tried to move my lips, to get some distance from the hammy paw over my mouth to bite it, but I couldn't, and nibbling his fingers wouldn't help much.

"You don't want him to think he's in love with a bitch, do you?" one said as I struck out with my other leg which, alas, also didn't have much room to move. "He never stops talkin' about you, Madeleine—thinks the world of you! We know you're still seein' Drake, but you're making a big mistake and we're here to prove it."

" 'Cause it's Mischief Night—and we're makin' mischief— the good kind."

They found that observation hysterical. If they weren't still clamped on to me, they'd have doubled up and rolled around on the ground from the sound of it. As it was, I could feel their bodies shaking with laughter. I thought I might get drunk myself on the alcoholic fumes their laughter produced.

"Hey! Mitty and Maddy! It even sounds good together!"

I shook my head as much as I could. I wasn't Madeleine. I didn't know a Mitty, was not dating Drake, and Ham Hand had to get his paw off my face.

"Don't be scared—come on. You'll see, it'll be fun. Mitty's home—you're our Mischief Night surprise."

I realized that they were stupid and drunk but probably not malicious. Still—who cared what their intent was? They'd terrified me and they were keeping me against my will.

Where were other pranksters or passersby or homeless people when I needed them? Nobody was on the street. Nobody would hear me even if I could free myself and scream. Nobody would save me. I had to save myself.

I moved and squirmed as much as I could, pulling sideways and rolling my head, shaking it in a futile *no-no-no!* and rolling my eyes up toward the skyline with a momentary fantasy that Superman had relocated from Metropolis to Philadelphia and if I screamed *Help! Help!* he'd rescue me.

If I could scream, of course.

Surely they could look at me and realize I was not the girl they had in mind. If they had minds.

They weren't vicious. They didn't react by increasing pressure. They were stupid. They laughed more. I didn't know that was much better.

Then my eyes and head rolled back and up toward the rooftop, and I had one of those times when what the eye sees and the brain is willing to receive don't mesh. What I saw was impossible. Therefore, I took too long to see it.

Superman wasn't on the roof, but six Screams were.

Robes darker than the sky against which they were silhouetted, bone-white distorted skull heads with frozen screaming mouths gleamed in the light of a sliver of moon. If I hadn't had a hand across my mouth, I would have joined in their screams, been the voice for all of them.

The rooftop. What was there? The art studio. The music room. The tennis court.

But those were enclosed, and these figures were outside, on the off-limits part of the roof where, in the warm months, a small garden was planted, and botany experiments attempted. The spindly tree struggling to grow in a large pot up there was also silhouetted.

Why there? And was that another figure, one in street clothes? Without the costume, the grotesque mask, he looked so much less substantial than they did.

This was it: the worse thing that was going to happen. The Friday thing.

I'd thought they had humiliation, at worst a fistfight in mind. What was more useful than using the crowd downstairs to thoroughly embarrass someone? Leaving the audience behind made no sense.

In their black robes, they looked like the nightmare jury of six that they in fact were, a jury of his peers who had found him guilty a long time ago. This, I feared, was the sentencing.

The group shifted, but whatever they were doing—debating, accusing, taunting—they weren't touching him.

All this probably took up no more time than an eyeblink, but it felt centuries, geological epochs, and it meant I had to get up on that roof before time ran out altogether, drunken louts or not.

The trio was well beyond sensitivity or nuance. Time was running out. I had to resort to primitive means.

I went limp and thought about Cupcake, the dog I'd had in elementary school, the sweetest dog ever, who'd broken away from me while I walked her, and had been run over by a truck. And as always, the guilt and loss and the sweet memories of that dog filled my eyes with tears.

The ham-handed one pulled his paw off my mouth. "She's crying!" he said. "Don't cry, don't cry! We thought it was funny and Mitty—"

"I'm not Madeleine!" I sobbed.

"What?" One of them came close and blinked as he looked at me. "Sure you are."

"No. You could check my ID, but there's no time."

"But this is where he said you—"

"And he was almost right. I know where she is. She's here on this street. Follow me—"

They weren't ready to spring to action. "You're not the right girl?" one of them said. "You sure?"

"She's at that party up there—see? Quick—before she goes off with"—What was his name?—"Drake!"

They listened. In their stupid dazed way, they half understood and nodded and followed me as I ran them around to the back entry. I did not want to be detained by Havermeyer at this moment. Then up the stairs, up and up until we were on the third floor, inside the school.

"Is she gone then? I don't see her!" the third stooge said, looking around.

"Nobody's here. You lied!" his comrade brilliantly observed.

"You're probably Madeleine!"

"They're outside. Remember—you saw her from down on the street because she was outside."

"Oh, yeah. Right."

I led my band of jokers to the door that led outside. "Shhh," I said. "Let's surprise her."

"Wait," one of them said. He sounded as if he might be sobering up. "Wait. This isn't such a good idea." His features scrunched together as he looked out the glass pane. "I don't see her, anyway."

"She's probably in disguise," I said. "She is, in fact. She's disguised as a famous painting."

"A painting? That's nuts. Is she in a frame, is she—"

"Shhh! Don't scare her." I hoped that the entry of three large and unfamiliar males and one teacher who could name names would at least stop events for a while.

"Shhh," I said again as I quietly opened the door, which had a narrow wedge keeping it from locking. I wondered when in the week the seniors had taken care of that. "Shhh. Don't say anything till I give the sign, okay? I'll point to where she is."

They nodded, but the one who was sobering up looked as if he was trying to think of an objection. Happily for me, his thought processes were not yet, if ever, swift. Before he could think it through, we were outside, creeping onto the dark terrace, the rough shadows of dead and dried-up flower beds next to us. "Now?" one whispered, but I shook my head. We crouched at the back near the wall in dark shadow.

"Jump!" a female voice said. I hadn't noticed her from below, but Allie stood to the side, arms folded across her chest. The sight of her in that position made me shudder. She was orchestrating it—whatever it was. Disguised as her or not, she was Lady Macbeth. "Just *jump* and end everybody's misery. It's either you or all of us, so guess which it's going to be?"

"Her?" the nearly sober one said. "She's not Madeleine. She's a blonde and Madeleine's—"

"Shhh—I told you, she's in disguise. One of those people in the cape and mask," I whispered.

Seth was encircled, but nobody was touching him. He'd backed right to the edge and was pressed against the wall, which was low, too low. All it would take was minimal hoisting . . .

"No—don't jump," a low voice said. His back was to

me, but I thought it was Wilson. His voice was strained, his tone urgent. "Don't. Come on, man. Just agree to keep your mouth shut. Don't tell. You tell and we're all screwed for the rest of our lives, starting with not getting into college. Nobody'd believe you, anyway. They think you did it. All of it."

"Because you framed me," Seth said. "You were my friends and you—"

"How can you be friends with somebody you don't even know? Who will never give in or compromise? Who doesn't care about anybody else? Who thinks he's the best person on earth—maybe the only one?" Allie's voice was low, flat, and cold.

"You didn't make it easy, man." Whoever said that sounded sad about it. "We asked you not to, just to stay cool, but you had to push. You started it all."

"The party could have been *perfect* if you hadn't insisted on your so-called Rights." Allie's voice sounded like a snarl.

Seth was quiet. I had missed the beginning of this, but even coming into it now, I could feel we were in a lull, a held breath, after which things could go either way, and one of the ways was too frightening and insane to contemplate.

"Go!" I said to my trio. "She's one of them." And then I used my only attack weapon, The Teacher Voice. "Stop right now!" I shouted in the ultra classroom decibel. "You! Wilson! Erik! Jimmy!!!"

The various Screams froze in place, making it even easier for Curly, Moe, and Larry to reach them, and though the drunks were outnumbered, they had the element of surprise, bulk, and alcoholic bravado on their side.

"What are you—"

One of my would-be kidnappers was working on pulling off a mask. "My head!" a male voice shouted, pulling off the mask himself. It was Wilson, his bruises from the fist-fight still visible.

"You aren't Madeleine!" the drunk said. "Hell—you're not a girl!" He turned to me. "What's going on?" He turned back. "Madeleine? Where are you? Which one are you?"

By then, I'd reached them. "How could you do this? Are you crazy? On drugs? Drunk? What on earth—you wanted him to *die*? I can't believe you're *murderers*! I—I—" I ran out of words, of ideas, of anything that could encompass what had been going on.

"It was up to him," Allie said in that new frozen voice. "He threatened *us*."

I'd heard them ask him to promise not to tell, and they surely didn't mean about tonight's fracas.

"He threatened all of you by saying he'd tell about what happened to Mr. Reyes," I said as if I knew it to be true. "About the jar of sodium."

"Nobody meant that to happen," Erik said. "Honestly, Miss Pepper. *Nobody.* Just for him to find it there and get mad again, like with the other things. We left other things in the sink, too, 'cause you couldn't see them there at first, so it was a bigger surprise. We didn't mean . . ."

"We only wanted him to leave—to quit! To stop giving us such bad marks and ruining everything for us. He kept acting like he was going to—threatening us. We thought we'd speed it up, give us a chance."

"So what's the point of Seth telling what happened? The cops think it was an accident—and it was!"

They looked at me, their masks in their hands or dropped on the roof, their anonymity gone, their expressions bewildered, as if I'd startled them awake, and in fact, I thought I had.

They looked pitiable. Barely grown young men, vulnerable and human without their disguises.

Bad company, indeed. "This started because you wanted better grades for college," I said, punching out every word. "Better grades! And look where it took you—to trying to murder someone! What happened to all of you? How did you get from there to here?"

The red-haired drunk poked his finger into my shoulder and spoke with the air of revelation. "Madeleine's not here."

"Sorry," I said. "My mistake."

"This is boring," the heavyset one said. "These are kids. High schoolers." And the three of them turned and walked back into the school. I didn't try to stop them, though I knew I should—they didn't belong in the building. I hoped they'd find their way out, that Havermeyer wouldn't find them first, that if he did, he wouldn't find out how they'd gotten into the building in the first place, and that en route they would do no damage.

They were now in the hands of fate. I had my hands and attention sufficiently full up here.

Allie looked like a broken toy. Her hands hung at her sides and her eyes focused somewhere internally.

"How *could* you?" I asked her, and the question wasn't rhetorical. "To try to goad somebody into—" I had to stop. I was controlling the urge to cry because it hurt too much to believe this could be true. I cleared my throat. "This morning you were crusading for civil rights, marching and talking to the TV reporter and now, now you wanted a friend to *die*. Why Seth? Why pick on him? Is it because you don't approve of his emotions? Of his right to be who he is?"

She snapped into attention and defensiveness. "That's not it! I'm not a bigot—none of us are. Nobody . . . we were all cool with it when he came out. But that was *enough*, and then he pushed it too far. He was bringing a guy to the party, and that was too much. It made everybody uncomfortable, and we tried to reason with him. Nothing would have happened if he'd just . . . given in."

"You have rules for Seth that don't apply to you? Does he vet your dates? Were special exclusions for some people what you were marching for today?"

"That's not the same! We would have all looked . . . Nobody ever did that at a Philly Prep party before, why did he have to say he was going to do it at ours?" She shook her head and sounded as if she was running out of steam, and when she continued, her voice was lower, less sure of itself. "We all said we wouldn't go with dates, but he—it was this *thing* with him. He needed a lesson—that was all—that's all we wanted—just for him to stop being so . . . stop thinking he was better than everybody. That's why we—we were already doing things to Mr. Reyes, but that's why we made it look like . . . like he was doing those things. Two birds with one stone." She looked surprised by her own words.

"Your friend Nita—"

"Not my friend anymore. I hate people who don't finish what they start. You can't count on her. She thought it was a good idea and then—did she tell you? Is that how come you're here? Those stupid poems? Her stupid hints?"

I didn't blame Nita for being afraid of Allie. Allie scared me, too.

"Nobody was supposed to—nobody ever meant—"

I didn't bother to look over and see which boy had spoken.

"We aren't like you think," another boy said softly.

"But you were—" I had to take deep breaths before I could finish. "You were forcing your friend, your teammate off the roof, goading him to *suicide*—do you realize you nearly *murdered* him?" More deep breaths.

One of the robed figures ran toward the edge of the roof and doubled over, sick.

"What—what happens now?" Allie wailed. "What happens to us now?"

I didn't have an answer. What I hoped happened was that they began to grow up, but along with that, I thought the worst had already happened. They were all casualties now. Seth would face the least official punishment, but of them all, he was perhaps the most wounded. It is anything but easy to recover from betrayal by those you thought your friends. I suspect it takes close to a lifetime.

The bass below at the party throbbed into the night like a subterranean heartbeat.

"Think about what nearly happened, about what you nearly did, and what you nearly became," I said, though it hurt to speak. "Think about what you already have done to others and to yourselves while you walk downstairs in an orderly fashion. Do you hear that music? Good, because what happens now is: You're going to face it."

"WHAT HAPPENS" COVERS A WHOLE LOT OF TIME. Forever, perhaps. Where do cause and effect end? A butterfly changes course in Guatemala and there's a tsunami in Asia.

A group of arrogant teens decide to force a teacher to quit because he's grading them too harshly and then, because he's crossed an imaginary line they set, because he's bringing the date of his choice to a party, they decide to frame a friend for their pranks. Two birds with one stone, as Allie said.

And the waves that bird or stone set off continue to stir the air and a prank backfires horribly, maiming and nearly killing a teacher.

And the scapegoat catches on and is horrified and furious and lets them know he's going to report the fact that the chemistry lab explosion was not an accident. Unintended, but the conditions for it had been set up deliberately.

And mass hysteria, the madness of crowds—something—propels them onto the roof to persuade him to remain silent. Or to jump.

So what happened *next* was beyond my ability to know. What happened *immediately* was that all six of them admitted planning to set the sodium in the lab. Wilson ran it in, but he was no more than their courier.

They only wanted to further infuriate Juan Reyes and never thought he'd turn water onto the sodium block. They should have included Seth in their plans. He was a good student. He might have thought ahead, considered the possibilities.

They did not.

As for me, I don't know when, if ever, I'll erase that scene on the roof and what it meant. I look back now on my anxiety and worries about the seniors this week and my imagination seems so limited and innocent. I'd raced there fearing a scene of humiliation for Seth or, at worst, another fistfight.

It sounds so *Leave It to Beaver* now to me, but I wish I could rewind back to that point, those ideas.

The current and future medical bills and lost income Juan Reyes suffered—because he was now on the road to a difficult but real recovery—became the responsibility of the students involved in the series of pranks including the sodium planting, and of their parents.

And somewhere in the bedlam, I had a chance to ask, "Why me? Why the stolen exam?"

"It wasn't stolen," Allie said sullenly. "Never was."

"But why me? Did you want me to quit, too?"

She shook her head. "We wanted somebody to pay attention and at least get Seth in trouble and Mr. Reyes wouldn't. We knew you would and maybe then he would." Her voice lowered to the mumble again. "It made sense back then."

Back then, four days ago, when we were all so much younger.

She looked directly at me. "And in a way, it worked. You paid attention."

Seth told me two things later in the evening, after all the parents who could be summoned had gathered and questions of guilt and innocence had been answered as best as they could be. The first was that he did not want to press charges. "I don't know what they'd be," he said. "And I don't want anything from them anymore. All I want is to finish this year and get on with my life."

And later, outside on the sidewalk, when Mackenzie had come along with the entire cast of the dinner party to retrieve me—we were all, plus Pip, going to an all-night diner to find food for me—Seth pulled away from his parents and said, "Excuse me. There's something I want to say." He looked around, and I was afraid whatever he had in mind would be censored or silenced by the presence of strangers, or perhaps simply by the sight of Sasha, still nothing short of incredible in her orange get-up and a black fur stole.

But I should have realized Seth was not that easily daunted. "Thank you," he said. "I'm ashamed to say it, and now it seems crazy, but right then, I felt as if—I felt so— They'd been my friends, my best friends, and then, for a minute, it seemed easier to just let go—of them, of everything." He cleared his throat and nodded. "I think you saved my life," he added softly.

"Thank you," I said. "I understand, but you saved yourself, and I'm beyond glad that you didn't give in to that feeling, that moment. You'll find better friends. True friends."

He smiled, nodded, stood up straight, and walked off with his parents.

"*Kew*-ell," Pip said later at the diner. "It's just like you said—anybody could kill if they thought it would save their lives."

"Didn't think Amanda would provide a laboratory demo for the theory, though, did you?" Mackenzie said.

"I knew being a detective was more exciting than you pretended it was," Pip said.

"Maybe being a teacher is more exciting than you think."

Pip was too polite to say what he thought of that idea.

"All right, then," Sasha said, "if you saved a life, I will forgive you for missing dinner."

"Pip," I said, "you're going to make a great detective someday yourself. You called this one. When I described all those confusing things going on, you were the one who realized they might not have anything to do with the real problem, which, you said, could be a feud. And you were close to the mark."

He grinned. "As soon as I get my diploma."

Mackenzie whispered, "Cheryl told him she wouldn't date a dropout. He says he's coming back next summer to woo her more, but meanwhile, he's goin' home Sunday."

Which is to say that some things do work out on their own—even when the participants are teenagers. My view of adolescents was balanced and brightened. My view of the future also looked a bit less congested and complicated. I hadn't been fired, and I hadn't compromised myself, either. I was going to hang on doing just that as long as I could.

I plowed through the diner's gargantuan servings of meat loaf, mashed potatoes, and ice cream. I enjoyed the conversation that whirled around me, but I barely participated, happy with my soft, amenable foods. Soon I'd be as comfortable as an oversized sofa and about the same width.

"Tell me," Mackenzie said when I'd finished. "How did you know what was goin' on up on that roof? All week you showed me things that meant nothin'. Not a piece of those bad poems and meaningless scraps would hold up in court, so what was it really about?"

How to answer? Three drunken lugs grabbing me and my accidentally looking up?

Or realizing the poems were trash, but not meaningless trash.

Or knowing that Nita and Allie should not have been at each other all week long.

Or that Seth was not himself.

Or listening to fragments—that some people weren't welcome at the party, or filling in the blanks on the note that told somebody to not panic.

Or using pure and simple common sense.

Or . . .

Mackenzie looked grim. "So Freud—who has been discredited, you know—had this theory that men marry their mothers."

"Oedipus did."

"We're talkin' here in metaphors. Psychologically. So did I?"

"I dress much more conservatively than your mother. And I don't intend to have eight children. And you need not blind yourself."

He nodded. "But how did you know to rush out of Sasha's—she told me—to get to those kids up on the roof? Only thing I can figure is you're one, too. Are you?"

"What?"

He raised one eyebrow and looked at me.

"A witch?"

"What else?"

I considered the idea. It had worked like a charm for Gabby Mackenzie and it saved lots of explaining about the three lugs and the rest. About anything you didn't feel like explaining, in fact. "You think her wedding gift to me was sharing her secrets?"

"Was it?"

I smiled. "Do you think I'd witch and tell?" I tapped my watch. "It's after midnight. Happy Halloween, the new major holiday. And this year, we've got a lot to celebrate."

"Yeah," Pip said. "You broke the Case of the Fake Disability and saved a kid's life."

The group of us clicked our glasses of soda, iced tea, and beer respectively and toasted Halloween and sleuthing.

It felt almost like Nick and Nora's life, if they'd found themselves in a diner eating meat loaf on Halloween.

It felt close enough.

Read on for an exciting preview of
Amanda Pepper's final adventure!

ALL'S WELL THAT ENDS

Available now from Ballantine Books

"She was the best of mothers, she was the worst of mothers. She had wisdom, she had foolishness. . . ."

Dennis's words made me want to snatch the silver martini pitcher from his hand and smash him with it, even though that would make my behavior as inappropriate as his was. We were paying our last respects, except for Dennis, who was paying his final disrespects.

Inappropriate didn't begin to describe posthumously clobbering the Dickens out of your own mother. I don't care how literary Dennis thought he was—not that familiarity with the opening lines of *A Tale of Two Cities* qualifies as anything special.

"It is a far, far worse thing you do than ever you have done before," I muttered to Sasha. Unfortunately, that probably wasn't accurate. To put it as charitably as I could: Dennis Allenby was a jerk.

He'd been a jerk in tenth grade when his mother was married to Sasha's father. Twenty years later, age had not withered nor custom staled his infinite jerkiness. He had a reputation as a specialist in the nearly-illegal scheme, the loophole-finding arrangement, the deal that shamelessly preyed on the gullible.

His mother had been Sasha's favorite stepmother. Despite the divorce, Sasha managed to maintain the relationship through three more of Phoebe's marriages, and two of her own, until Phoebe's untimely death two weeks ago.

Sad, or ironic that having pledged five separate times to be with a man till death did them part, Phoebe wound up alone, dead by her own hand, with only Dennis as a sorry by-product.

I blocked out his drone, forced his voice to dissolve into the bright December morning, to be no more than the crunch of twigs underfoot, the occasional birdcall, or the murmur of the stream; although in truth, the water was silent. It was so chilly, it was probably icing up. So was I.

My chattering teeth helped drown him out. I looked around and could see that my irritation was shared. Maybe we could rush Dennis, push him into the creek along with the urn's contents.

Sasha, dressed intensely in black, from the oversized broad-brimmed hat that wobbled and shivered with each wintry gust to her high boots, looked flamboyantly in mourning. But her face was set with anger, not grief. She opened her eyes wide, the better to glare at Dennis. "You see?" she hissed. "You see?"

She wanted me to see a murderer, but I saw only a middle-aged jerk.

I once again let my eyes travel around the group. On this bright winter day, about twenty people had gathered by the river to remember and honor Phoebe Ennis. The group included her cousin Peter who hadn't seen Phoebe in fifteen years, but had memories so vivid, that he'd made the trip from his home in West Virginia; four women who'd identified themselves in such a rush that I never got them straight; a woman who looked in her eighties and who'd identified herself only as "a former neighbor," though of which time period and/or house she didn't say, and near her, Phoebe's flame-haired business partner, Merilee Wilkins, standing so rigidly she looked planted in the spot. I'd met her a while back when I went to Top Cat and Tails, the shop she and Phoebe owned. I was amused by the idea of a pet boutique, which probably shows what a shallow, uncaring cat-owner I am. But the admittedly funny sight of sale items such as a Halloween costume for a dachshund that made the pup into a hot-dog on a bun did nothing to make me take the place more seriously.

I went for entertainment value, not to buy, and apparently, so did too many others, because the business was about to fold. Merilee's husband was withdrawing his financial support, and not coincidentally, withdrawing from the marriage as well. Somehow, Merilee blamed Phoebe for the weak revenues that she believed had led to her husband's defection, and in her agitated state she'd accused Phoebe of larceny.

Judging by Merilee's grim expression today, the bad blood between the women had stayed bad, which made me feel a twinge of sympathy for the otherwise annoying woman. There couldn't be many things much worse than having a friend die in mid-quarrel. Surely both women hoped, if not expected, that they'd find a way through their anger, that they'd resolve their issues and restore the friendship. Now it was impossible.

Looking less profoundly upset, two men in their forties who had identified themselves in unison as "the Daves—we're just her friends" stood at the back of the small group. Only one of Phoebe's ex-husbands had attended, Max Delahunt, the fourth of "the Alphabet boys." Phoebe's love life had been frenetic, but her marriage partners turned out to be as systematic as if they'd been chosen by a file clerk. She'd wed, in order: Harvey Allenby, Charlie Berg, Bert Carnero, Max Delahunt, and Nelson Ennis. Among the wedding gifts for Phoebe and Nelson had been a set of towels that had the entire alphabet embroidered along the hem. "Pre-emptive monograms," the gift giver called it. Nelson Ennis should have seen the writing on the towel and known he was a short-timer, and indeed, he didn't make it to the getting-divorced stage. He was done in by an out-of-control motorcycle, barely a year into his marriage.

Phoebe probably would have found herself Mr. "F," too, except that she ended the progression by killing herself.

Max's son, Lionel "Lion" Delahunt, a slender, balding man, stood close to his father, looking pensive, representing along with Sasha Phoebe's many temporary stepchildren. He was next to a man I didn't know, but the teenager by that man's side was a Philly Prep student, Mitchell "Jonesy" Farmer.

At lunch, before this ceremony began, Jonesy had told me he was here because it was his weekend with his father, and his father said it was the right thing to do. His father had known Phoebe, Jonesy had said grudgingly, and I assumed that meant the senior Farmer had dated her. I wondered if he'd been optioning for a position as next husband. Alphabetically, at least, he was appropriate.

There were a few other mourners I didn't recognize. At least one, I suspected, was someone who'd been out for a walk, bundled in his sweats and parka, and had spotted something out of the ordinary and opted to join in for the novelty factor.

We stood in a glorious sylvan setting of trees and water, even if the stream wasn't burbling and the trees were bare under the December sky, and we did our best to ignore the human traffic nearby. This part of the park was called Forbidden Drive, which sounds more exciting than it is. Cars are forbidden, but pretty much everything else is allowed, except, I suspect, what we were about to do. In any case, the bucolic silence, if you ignored Dennis, which I was trying my best to do, made Philadelphia's stone and brick feel galaxies away. You don't realize until you're away from it how nonstop noisy a city is, a perpetual motorized grumble, air being pushed aside by crowds of people, gears churning.

But at this point, the idea of a city's enclosed heated spaces trumped the beauty of our setting. I shivered, and my teeth chattered uncontrollably. I stomped from foot to foot and watched my breath frost and puff in the air, envying the joggers on the path behind us for the body heat they'd created. Sasha bent toward me, nearly blinding me with the brim of her hat. "I can't believe he's doing this," she whispered. "It's so openly hostile!" Earlier, she'd said a few heartfelt words about what Phoebe had meant to her, as had almost everyone else who'd gathered here, including the Daves and even Ex-Husband "D."

Not the man in the parka, not Jonesy or his father, not I, not Merilee.

Dennis had taken control of this event, although Sasha had planned and organized it. "I am the only blood relative," he'd snapped. He was in a perpetual fury because his mother had included Sasha in her will. Not that Phoebe had much beyond a modest house, but however much it was, Dennis wanted it all, and his mother had said he could have only half.

He'd been in a sulk ever since he'd flown into Philadelphia. When he bullied his way into running the memorial service despite years of ignoring his mother, Sasha capitulated.

The fact that he'd saved himself and this performance for last was all the more offensive.

"You have got to find out where he was the night she died," she whispered. "Maybe he hired somebody. Maybe somebody else flew using his name and he was here before then. Maybe . . ."

She'd wanted me here for reasons of friendship, but also because after I finished my days teaching, I was training to be a private investigator. I had a long apprenticeship to go before I could get my license, and I meanwhile co-moonlit with my husband, C. K. Mackenzie, who was licensed because he'd been a homicide detective before opting for grad school. I did mostly clerical chores. You don't get points toward your license for teaching high school English.

That didn't matter to Sasha. She refused to accept the

idea that Phoebe had committed suicide, no matter what the police said, and no matter that she had nothing beyond a gut conviction to support her theory.

So with her talent for ignoring the obvious, she'd begged me to observe—as if this were all a grade-B movie, and I was the obligatory cop lounging at the back of the funeral home. I didn't even know why they were there in movies, let alone in real life. What did they expect to see? A killer suddenly throwing himself on the coffin and confessing? Villains twirling moustaches and chortling over their evil accomplishments? Meaningful glances among conspirators?

Why would a murderer attend his victim's funeral?

But since Sasha's current craziness was a by-product of her sadness, I honored it and stood here, wishing I knew what I was supposed to notice beyond a clump of shivering red-nosed people.

Instead, I thought about the one attendee I couldn't see, the one in the martini shaker. When I was in junior high, and Phoebe was Sasha's stepmother, the things that initially made Sasha cringe with embarrassment amused me. I could afford to feel that way—Phoebe wasn't part of my household, so her delusions of grandeur, her fantastic stories of her family's past glories, her regal sweep of arm, her lorgnette (a family treasure, she insisted), her irrational aspirations for us: "Why not the stage? Why not become supermodels, movie stars or roller-derby gals?" seemed colorful and exciting. I made my mother know that her drab pronouncements about how to live: study, do your homework, clean your room, were pitiable "bourgeois middle-class values," a term I'd learned from Phoebe, of course.

The fact that my parents didn't put me up for adoption during that phase is testimony to their saintly goodness.

Phoebe was bigger than life and her dreams were still larger. She dwelt in the waiting room of an alternate universe populated by the glitterati because, she would remind us with a conspiratorial wink, she was of "royal blood."

When we'd barge in after school, as often as not Phoebe would be working on her never-finished family tree. Her grandmother had told her that *her* grandmother was the descendant of a king. Or sometimes, instead, of a "world-famous man." The story had been handled so often, had tumbled through the generations like a long game of whispering down the lane, and as surely as it did in the game, it had acquired polish and spin with each retelling. For all any of us knew, the original message was that she was the descendant of the man who cleaned the king's boots. Or simply, a very nice man who once caught a glimpse of a king. Add to it that grandma had been a tad senile, and fuzzy as to what principality or how far back that royal bloodline began.

Most people would laugh gently at their grandmothers' romantic visions of themselves, and that would be that. Not Phoebe. She searched in vain for that missing golden link. I remember coming to Sasha's house one afternoon and seeing notebook pages taped together covering the dining-room table. Each sheet had webs of lines, circles, and question marks. "A genealogical chart," Phoebe had said. "Mine." I couldn't make head nor tails of it.

Phoebe's pretensions drove Sasha berserk for about a year before the two of them reached détente. After that, they developed a lasting fondness for each other's quirky, loveable selves, and that lasted long after Sasha's father decided that this marriage, like all his others, had been a mistake.

I wondered if he remembered the good parts of his marriages, the attraction and the initial wedded bliss, and if he would have attended this memorial were he not in Spain, honeymooning with whatever number wife or fiancée this one was.

"Phoebe was never mean-spirited," Sasha whispered.

True. She was silly. She was pretentious and possibly delusional. She was probably not the world's best wife. She was a cluttered, distracted housekeeper, though an elegant, extravagant cook and hostess when she put her mind to it, and it now appeared she'd not been much of a business-woman, either.

But not mean. Not ever.

"If he does not shut up immediately," she said, "I'm going to speak ill of the living. Loudly."

Perhaps he felt the heat rising from his former stepsister. In any case, Dennis wound down, grudgingly admitting that his mother had been fun and had always been there in a pinch. "And," he said, "she made a mean martini, so here's to you, Mom." With a smirk, Dennis lifted the silver martini shaker he'd been clutching.

"Hear, hear," the group said with little enthusiasm. Nobody looked directly at him, nobody gave the almost-obligatory encouraging smile that would normally be ex-pected.

The cocktail shaker had been Phoebe's requested resting place till her remains were emptied into the Wissahickon. All of this had been written out years earlier, along with the request that anyone mourning her should "carouse" on the banks. She'd wanted us to drink champagne from the crys-tal goblets she'd collected over the years, to toast her here, on Forbidden Drive, the spot where, apparently, she'd en-joyed a few romantic dalliances in her time.

She apparently forgot that Philadelphia has four seasons, and she envisioned us in sheer summer dresses, barefoot and dancing on the grass. She also hadn't considered the park's rules that forbid alcohol, let alone carousing. And while the official rules kept mum about our particular situa-tion, I doubted that dumping charred human remains into the clear creek was permitted. Launching Phoebe into a dif-ferent existence therefore had a hurried, surreptitious air. Raising bubbling crystal glasses while walkers and runners witnessed it would have been too flagrant. Raising empty glasses felt terribly wrong. Dennis had forged a compromise by using innocuous white Styrofoam cups and hiding the champagne in a duffel bag.

He now extracted a bottle and opened it, and then a second, pouring a small amount in each cup. I hadn't heard of screw-top champagne until then.

"A toast to Phoebe," Sasha said, but she said it too softly for the passing jogger to make note of it in the unlikely event that he had his MP3 player turned off and could hear.

"Safe journey, Phoebe," people said.

The fizzing liquid Dennis was trying to pass off as champagne managed to be both too sweet and too tart, and after one sip, I tipped my cup over and hoped it was good for the dormant grass.

Dennis popped off the top of the martini shaker and leaned over the creek. I watched Sasha frown as she watched him. Ever since the terrible night she'd found Phoebe dead, she'd been blaming herself. I'd heard the refrain, and I could almost see it circle her skull like a roll on a player piano, the same tune over and over. She'd been away in England for too long while anything might have been troubling Phoebe. She'd been a poor correspondent. She hadn't visited enough since she'd been back. She could have, should have, saved Phoebe.

Sasha's self-flagellation was without grounds. She had indeed visited Phoebe as soon as she'd returned to Philadelphia, three months ago, and several times after.

Demonstrating how upset and confused she was, not only did Sasha accept responsibility for Phoebe's suicidal depression, but she simultaneously insisted that Phoebe had not been depressed in the first place.

"She laughed a lot" was part of the loop going around and around in Sasha's head. "She was *sad* about Nelson, but not depressed. I'm not sure that marriage was destined to last much longer even if he'd lived. She said he was a whiner. She said lots of things, but then—*wham*—he was gone. Sad, you see. Not suicidal! And look, she was dating again, she was optimistic, not depressed."

Part of what bonded the two women was the irrational belief that the next man would be better, despite their own histories, which proved that the next ones were seldom as good as the ones before.

Sasha had even used her professional skills to help the hunt for number six by taking photos of Phoebe for an online matchmaking service. She'd needed new ones because all her portraits were in wedding attire.

She never got to see the photos. Sasha was delivering them the night she found Phoebe dead.

"Is ordering photos the behavior of a clinically depressed woman about to end her life?" Sasha had demanded. "Posing, preening, worrying about the lighting and how it would make her look?"

People are unpredictable. Maybe the need for updated photos and an online dating service would make you realize all you'd lost, and drive you into depression. I didn't know Phoebe well enough to know if she'd been putting up a façade for Sasha's sake, or if she was subject to rapid mood changes.

But my private opinion was that this was all about Sasha, who, being human, couldn't deal with the painful irrationality of the situation.

Eventually, Sasha noticed the disconnect between what she'd observed and the guilt she felt over what had happened, and had found a way to reconcile them. Phoebe had not been depressed and Phoebe had not taken her life. If someone else had ended Phoebe's life, then Sasha could feel pain, but not guilt.

Dennis uncapped Phoebe as, with perfect mistiming, the wind changed course and her airborne ashes caught a thermal and landed on Dennis's expensive dark overcoat. All over it.

Retribution for that eulogy, I was sure.

Dennis scowled and brushed, which smeared but didn't remove the gray blots, and he looked as if he was about to shout at his mother one last time. Instead, he took a deep breath, leaned low and shook out her remaining remains, turned away from the stream, left the silver mixer on the ground, and wiped his leather gloves clean before facing Sasha.

Because of Dennis's flight schedule, there had been a lunch before the memorial service, rather than the more traditional gathering afterward. Now Dennis pushed up his smeared coat sleeve, checked his watch, and came over to Sasha. "Keep me in the loop about the house," he said.

She nodded. He'd talked her into finding a realtor and disposing of Phoebe's "treasures," since he lived in Chicago while Sasha lived nearby and was sharing in the profits. To me that meant they should also share the work, but Dennis was Phoebe's executor, and life was complicated enough without getting into this particular battle.

Sasha put her hand on Dennis's sleeve. Her forehead had a long, vertical wrinkle down its middle. "Before you go," she said, "I've been wanting to ask . . . do you . . . did you wonder . . . when you heard . . ." She took another deep breath and cleared her throat. "I don't believe Phoebe would take her life that way."

"She wouldn't use pills and booze? Why not?"

He'd spoken too loudly, so that people nearby turned to watch. "I mean she wouldn't commit suicide," Sasha said. "It doesn't fit her. She was upbeat, looking forward—"

"Wait a minute! What are you suggesting?" Dennis's face darkened as if his blood had been rerouted and was pounding its way toward the skin.

"I'm not comfortable with the official version. Why would she—"

"Damn it, Sasha!" he said, his voice loud enough to scare the Daves, who'd approached to express condolences.

"*You're* not comfortable? This is not about you. For once in your life can you not be histrionic? You're just like her—everything's dramatic and oversized. You want headlines, investigations, your fifteen minutes of fame? Find it somewhere else. She killed herself."

"And it's just like you to want to believe your own mother killed herself. Why would she? She didn't even leave a note." At six feet, Sasha was as tall as Dennis, and with the high-heeled boots and enormous hat, taller still, so she held her ground. The hostility radiating off him would have floored a smaller woman.

"She wasn't one for writing," he snapped. "Or for thinking things through. This was probably an impulse like so many others. That's how she was, an emotional infant!"

Sasha was silent for a moment, very unlike her normal behavior. Then she said quietly, "Don't you even want to know why I think that?"

"I've got a plane to catch." Once again he checked his watch.

Sasha lowered her voice still more. "Are you at all sorry that your mother died?"

"Let me know what's happening about the house." He turned and walked away from us.